9/16x

DISCARD

GIRL

AGAINST THE

Universe

GIRL
AGAINST THE
Universe

PAULA STOKES

HARPER TEEN

An Imprint of HarperCollinsPublishers

HarperTeen is an imprint of HarperCollins Publishers.

Girl Against the Universe

Copyright © 2016 by Paula Stokes

www.epicreads.com

Library of Congress Control Number: 2015961051
ISBN 978-0-06-237996-2

Typography by Aurora Parlagreco
16 17 18 19 20   PC/RRDH   10 9 8 7 6 5 4 3 2

First Edition

To you, the reader
May your Universe be filled with friendship and love.

GIRL

AGAINST THE
Universe

AUGUST

CHAPTER 1
Session #1

There's a thing that sometimes happens in your brain when you're the only survivor of a horrific accident. Part of you is happy because you're alive, but the rest of you is devastated. Then the sad part beats up the happy part until nothing is left, until all you feel is terrible sorrow for the people who didn't make it. And guilt. Guilt because you wonder if the Universe made a mistake. Guilt because you know you're not any better than those who died.

This is what my therapist says, anyway. Since I don't feel like talking, he's talking for both of us. I hate people like that, people who think they know what you need to hear, people who think they can read your mind, anticipate your responses. "We're not all the same," I want to shout. But I don't, because if I talk, then he wins. And I have lost enough already.

"Tell me about the car accident." Dr. Leed leans toward me.

I glance down at my lap. He doesn't need me to tell him about that. He spent almost an hour "just chatting" with my mom. I'm sure she filled him in on the gory details.

It happened almost five years ago, when I was eleven. My dad, Uncle Kieran, my brother Connor, and I were heading home from a day of rock climbing at a park outside of San Luis Obispo, where I grew up.

Connor and I were fighting about this boy who lived down the street when I saw the giant truck veer dangerously into our lane. The driver must have lost control of his rig as he navigated the twisting mountain road.

Dad tried to swerve onto the shoulder at the last second, but we were driving along the side of a hill and there was just a few feet of concrete and a flimsy guardrail. The back of the truck clipped us, sending both vehicles straight through the guardrail and down the incline. Our car flipped end over end and landed in a rocky ravine. Dad, Uncle Kieran, and Connor were dead before the paramedics could get to us.

I didn't even get hurt.

I was still in the ER when the newspaper people found me. They called me the miracle kid. I'll never forget how they buzzed around, asking prying questions about what I remembered and why I thought I got spared. I had just lost three members of my family, and these people wanted to talk about the luck of the Irish.

My mom tried to shield me from the reporters, but eventually she gave up and posed with me for a few pictures so they would go away. She said focusing on how I was alive would help everyone cope with losing my dad and uncle, two of the town's most decorated firefighters. It didn't help *me* cope; all I could think was that I should have been nicer to Connor. He was just teasing me. How can something feel so crucial in the moment and then seem completely trivial after the fact?

"Maguire?" Dr. Leed manages to sound both authoritative and concerned.

I shake my head. Reaching up, I pull the ponytail holder from around my bun. I gather my thick curly hair in my hands and twist it tighter and tighter until my eyes start to water. I coil it around in a circle and secure it again.

Dr. Leed taps a couple of sentences into his tablet computer. I'm not close enough to read what they say. "What about the roller coaster?" he asks.

Right. The next year, when I was twelve, a roller coaster car I was riding in careened off the tracks and crashed to the ground at a nearby amusement park. That accident wasn't quite as serious—we were at the bottom of a hill when it happened, and at least no one died—but every single passenger in our car had serious injuries, except for me. My best friend at the time broke both legs, and another friend ended up needing plastic surgery because she landed on her face. I walked away with a couple of scratches that didn't even require stitches. No one called me a miracle kid that time, but the crazy lady who begs for change at the gas station called me a witch.

We moved after that.

And then a few weeks ago, I left a candle burning on my windowsill and went for a run. When I came back an hour later the next door neighbors' house was completely engulfed in flames. You wouldn't think a brick house could go up like a box of matches from one teensy dollar store votive, but it did.

And so we moved again. This time just to the other side of San Diego, but far enough away to put me in a different school district. Mom said it was because our house had smoke damage, but I'm pretty sure it was because she didn't want to be the mom with the crazy kid who all the other moms whispered about.

That's what landed me back in therapy. Not the moving part—the fire. Because apparently I snapped and ran toward the burning building. Then, as one of the firefighters carried me away from the danger, kicking and screaming, I kept telling him how the whole thing was my fault and how he had to save everybody because I couldn't have any more deaths on my conscience. I don't even remember saying that, but I remember the resulting trip to the hospital and the way the staff all hurried in and out of my room like I was a lit fuse. I remember the psychiatrist asking me if I wanted to hurt myself, the police asking me if I wanted to hurt other people, and my mother sitting next to me in a chair, not asking me anything, her fingers curled protectively around mine the entire time.

"I don't want to talk about that either." I raise my head just long enough to meet Dr. Leed's eyes. They're a warm brown, obscured partially by the navy blue glasses he wears. He runs one of his pinkies along his bottom lip. His nail beds look a little gray, like maybe he sported some black nail polish recently. I swear everybody in Southern California has a secret second life. Housewives are aspiring actresses. Busboys are screenwriters. Shrinks are rock stars. Nobody is okay with only being one person. I get tired just thinking about it.

I lean back in my chair and try to envision Dr. Leed as a punk rocker. It's not too much of a stretch. He's got dark brown hair that's a little long for a medical professional, and I can see the outlines of forearm tattoos through the thin fabric of his long-sleeved shirt.

"What *do* you want to talk about?" he asks.

"Nothing." I scrape the toes of my sandals back and forth across the patterned carpet. It's black with overlapping white circles, but if you squint a little, the circles almost look like skulls.

"Okay," he says. "I can't make you talk." He taps some more notes into his computer.

I watch the movement of his fingers, trying to guess what he's writing, but he's too fast. "What are you saying about me?"

"What makes you think I'm saying anything about you?" He gives me a half smile. "Maybe I'm just emailing my girl-friend."

I return his half smile with a quarter smile, more than a lot of people get. I decide I don't completely hate him after all.

The waiting area is empty except for a boy who looks as if he's been professionally assembled—distressed jeans you can only buy for about two hundred bucks a pop, messy brownish-blond hair you can only get with a fair amount of product and patience, ridiculous tan without any obvious signs of peeling. He's not hot, exactly—his nose is a little crooked and he's a bit lanky, like a baby giraffe still growing into his limbs—but he sure knows how to work with what he's got.

The boy looks up from a sports magazine as I shut the door to the inner office behind me. Cocking his head, he studies me with a harmless sort of curiosity for a moment before dropping his eyes back to his article. He pulls his long legs in close to the seat as I pass by so I don't trip over them. It's the kind of low-key, friendly gesture I appreciate.

"Thanks," I say.

"You're welcome," the boy says, which strikes me as odd. Who says that? You're welcome. It's so strangely formal.

Dr. Leed's receptionist slides open a frosted glass partition and motions to the boy. "He's ready for you," she mouths.

She's got a black phone pinned between her shoulder and ear while she looks up something on the computer. The boy tosses the magazine onto the chair next to him. He stands, stretching his arms over his head. "Wish me luck." He flashes me a conspiratorial grin. Even his smile looks engineered—warm, friendly, just the right amount of lips and teeth. But it aligns all the rest of his features in a way that makes me second-guess my earlier judgment about his hotness.

"Good luck," I mumble.

Little does he know I'm the last person he should be asking for luck.

CHAPTER 2
Session #2

Dr. Leed is listening to wailing guitar music on his phone and eating an In-N-Out burger when I arrive for this week's session. He quickly tidies his desk and slips his phone into his top drawer.

"Sorry," he says, rotating his chair around so he's facing me. "I usually grab dinner before your appointment, but I got a bit behind schedule today."

I shrug. "It's fine."

"What about you? Are you fine?"

"Yep." I fidget with a strand of black hair that's escaped from my bun, twisting and untwisting it around my finger.

Dr. Leed tries the same exact series of questions this week about the accidents and the fire and gets the same (lack of) response from me.

Halfway through the session he gives up and grabs a magazine from a small table.

I glance over casually when I think he's not looking.

"*Science*, huh?" I say. "I had you figured as more of a music magazine guy."

"You think you got me all figured out, do you?" He smiles slightly. "What about you? What do you read?"

"Novels. A lot of action/adventure stuff. Oh, and nonfiction survival guides." When you've got luck like mine, you can never be too prepared for impending disaster.

Dr. Leed and I chat about books for a few minutes, and just when I'm thinking I might like him—a little—he glances at the clock. "We're running out of time. You want to talk about why you're really here?"

And just like that, something inside of me slams shut. "I'm here because my mom says I have to be."

Dr. Leed drums his fingertips on the edge of his chair. "Well, if you're going to be stuck here every week for a while, why not talk about things? I can help you if you let me, Maguire."

I shake my head. "No one can help."

"Why's that?"

"Because the Universe hates me."

My head hurts all over. I tug the ponytail holder out of my hair as I hit the waiting room. Dark curls spill across my pale shoulders. I rub my scalp with my fingertips and then reach down to tuck my mystic knot amulet back under the neckline of my shirt. The mystic knot is a Buddhist symbol of luck that I bought online after the roller coaster accident.

It's supposed to bring positive energy to every aspect of your life. I wear it 24-7—when I'm sleeping, when I'm showering, even in gym class.

Especially in gym class. High school gym can be dangerous.

I cringe at the thought. I can't believe how fast the summer flew by. It's almost time for school to start.

As I cross the waiting room, the receptionist waves and Perfectly Assembled Boy glances up. He gives me a longer look this time—so long that I start to feel a little awkward. I peek back at him as I open the door to the hallway.

"Your hair," he says finally. "It's so . . . big."

I get this sort of thing occasionally, normally from friends of my mom. I've got one of those manes that everyone likes to ooh and ahh over but no one really wants for their own. Thick black hair that hangs past my shoulders in corkscrew curls and sticks out a few inches from my head if I don't tame it down and tie it back. Kind of like that old-school guitarist Slash, only I'm a lot smaller than he is, so my hair looks even bigger. I almost always wear it in a bun.

I freeze with my hand on the doorknob, unsure of exactly how to respond, or if I should even bother. "Yeah, okay," I say finally.

"It's like it has its own life force," the boy continues. "Very stellar."

"Thanks . . . I think."

He hops up from his chair. "Can I touch it?"

"No," I say, a bit sharper than I intended.

He holds his hands up in mock surrender. "Sorry. Stupid question. But if you ask me, you should wear it down all the time."

"No one asked you," I say. But I give this boy a quarter smile too.

CHAPTER 3
Session #3

Dr. Leed has that same screeching guitar music playing this week as I shuffle into the office. I wonder if it's him, and he's reviewing his performance from last night's band practice.

His brown eyes follow me from behind his glasses, like he's analyzing everything—my clothes, my posture, the way I walk. I slide into the chair and affix a neutral expression to my face.

"Let's talk about something you said last time," Dr. Leed starts. "You said the Universe hates you. What did you mean?"

"I mean I'm unlucky. Bad stuff happens around me." I fold my hands in my lap. "You're risking your life just by being in this room with me."

"Maguire, you're not responsible for the car accident or the roller coaster malfunction. Remember what I said about survivor's guilt the first session."

I wasn't paying much attention during the first session, but I think he said it was a form of PTSD. "Yeah, but you weren't there," I say. "You don't get it."

"I understand why you feel the way you do, but there's a difference between correlation and causation. Do you know what that means?"

"It means just because I was present at an accident doesn't mean I caused it. But going rock climbing was my idea. The amusement park was my idea. Everyone else got hurt or *died*." My voice rises in pitch. "And those aren't the only instances. And all the events have only one thing in common: me. What other explanation is there besides that it's my fault, that I'm . . . cursed or something?"

"Maybe you would've gotten hurt too, but you actually have really good luck?"

"Nope. I tested my positive luck." I pull a midsize spiral notebook out of my purse. The words "Luck Notebook" are scrawled in black ink across the cover. "The front part is all the bad things that have happened over the past few years, and the next section is where I entered a hundred contests trying to see if maybe I was lucky and had just been spared. And after that is where I spent an entire summer trying every 'de-curse yourself' spell and product I could find on the internet."

Dr. Leed takes the notebook from me and skims through it, pausing briefly in the middle. He shakes his head. "Look at all these websites. Who knew de-cursing was such a boom-ing business? Tomato juice bath? Isn't that just for if you get sprayed by a skunk?"

"There's a lady in Alabama who swears by it."

He flips back to the beginning of the notebook. "So before the fire there was the car accident, the roller coaster, and then a bit later an issue at a birthday party?"

I nod. "I went to my friend's sleepover party and every-one but me got sick. And then for a while nothing major happened, but there were smaller things, like the time some Rollerbladers fell down while I was running past them."

"Okay, but maybe these events were just an unfortunate set of circumstances? You were in the wrong place at the wrong time?"

"Well, if so, people should probably not be in the same place as me. That's like being hit by lightning five or six times." Only it's not. It's worse. It's like being with your friends and family and watching *them* get hit by lightning while you just stand there, unscathed, wishing you'd never suggested leaving the house in the first place.

"So you really believe that you're . . . cursed?"

"I know it sounds crazy."

"'Crazy' is a word that has been overused to the point of becoming meaningless," Dr. Leed says. "It sounds like a lot for any one person to deal with."

"All I know is my being around other people puts them at risk."

"So then how do you handle that?" he asks.

"I keep to myself," I mutter.

Once I accepted the fact that I was bad luck, I shied away from group activities. And groups. And activities. I started spending a lot of time in my room, tucked under my covers reading books. There's only so much damage a book can do, and I wasn't worried about hurting myself. Accidentally hurting yourself is way better than hurting other people.

Sure, I got lonely for a while. But getting invited to slumber parties just wasn't worth the stress of wondering if I might accidentally burn down the house with my flat iron or be the only survivor of a freak sleepover massacre. And loneliness is just like everything else—if you endure it long enough, you get used to it.

Perfectly Assembled Boy is in the waiting room again, this time looking a little less perfectly assembled. He's wearing shiny basketball shorts and a hoodie. His wet hair is slicked back behind his ears, making his blond streaks look painted on.

He looks up from his magazine and catches me staring. "You can take a picture if you want," he says, his voice perfectly level.

"I'll pass," I snap as I hurry for the door. What an ass. It's not like he wasn't checking *me* out last week, talking all that crap about my hair.

I switch my phone off silent as I head for the stairs. There's a text from my mom. I swear under my breath as I read it. I dropped her car off for routine maintenance at the shop across the street before my appointment, but it turns out they found a bigger problem and are going to keep it until tomorrow. My stepdad is working late, and Mom won't be able to pick me up for an hour and a half. If I were normal, I would just take a bus or a taxi home.

I am not normal.

I text her back and let her know it's no problem, that I'll just find a place to read and she can text me when she gets here.

I find a comfy chair in a deserted corner of the lobby and drop my purse on the small wooden table next to it. As I settle into the chair, I do what I call a five-second check. I scan the furniture, the floor, the ceiling, and everywhere in between. There are people going in and out of the bathrooms, but no obvious hazards. No lurking strangers. When you're a disaster magnet like me, it makes sense to constantly be assessing your environment for danger. I'm not too worried about anything bad happening inside Dr. Leed's inner office because it's just the two of us, but any time I'm stuck in public I try to do a quick check of my surroundings every few minutes.

I knock three times on the wooden table and then pull the book I'm reading out of my purse. I open to the page where I left off and set my special Irish-penny good luck bookmark on the table. Seven chapters and seven five-second checks later, I'm just about to get to a really good part when a shadow falls over my page.

"You're still here."

I look up. Perfectly Assembled Boy has materialized in front of me. For being about six foot five, he's shockingly light on his feet.

"Um . . . yes." I turn to the next page of my book with a meaningful flourish and start reading, but my eyes trace the same sentence over and over because the boy isn't leaving.

He sits down in the chair next to me, crossing his long legs at the ankles. "You don't know who I am, do you?"

I peer over at him. "Should I?" Maybe his comment about taking a picture was serious. I try to reconcile his image with everyone I've seen on TV recently. Nope, no matches.

"No." He grins. Perfect smile 2.0. I have the sudden urge to buy toothpaste. "I was hoping you didn't. Do you want to go somewhere?"

I snicker and then realize he's serious. "Like, with you?"

"No. All alone. I want this corner for myself." He rolls his eyes. "Yes, with me."

I think for a second about what life must be like for this boy, someone who can sit down next to a total stranger and ask her to go somewhere like she's a friend. How does he know I won't tell him to get lost? How does he know I won't accidentally get him run over by a bus? "Sorry. No can do. Waiting for a ride."

The boy runs a hand through his hair. It's mostly dry now and it sticks up in awkward sandy peaks. "Call your ride and tell them I'll drive you home."

"My mom's not going to go for me taking off with some strange guy." Not to mention I would never go for that. Since the accident, I've only been in a car by myself or with my mom. And the only reason I can bear it with Mom driving is because for a while I had no choice. I couldn't exactly drive myself around when I was eleven. Still, my pediatrician had to give me sedatives for several months just to get me near a car without having a major panic attack.

"Okay." The boy points across the lobby. "There's an ice-cream shop over there. Come there with me instead. Plenty of people around to keep you safe from this *strange guy*."

I flinch. I walked past that shop on my way into the building. It was packed. Way too many opportunities for people to get hurt. "I can't. I'm sorry."

My eyes skim past the boy for another five-second check. Furniture fine. Floor fine. Ceiling fine. A lady and her toddler are making their way down the hallway. The little girl's sparkly shoes are moving too slow for the rest of her body. Just when I'm positive she's going to trip, her mom bends down and scoops her up in her arms. They disappear into the ladies' restroom.

The boy is talking. Apparently he's been talking, but I haven't been paying attention. I generally tune people out when I'm doing my checks.

"Am I hideous to you or something?" he asks.

Some girls might find him less appealing today, without his hair product and two-hundred-dollar jeans, but I sort of like his dressed-down look. And that smile is growing on me. Definitely not hideous. "No . . . I just don't know you."

The boy hits his forehead with his palm. "That's why we're going to get ice cream."

"I can't. It's nothing personal. I don't really hang out with people."

He tilts his head to the side. "What do you hang out with?"

"Books, mostly."

"Okay. Well, I know when to give up." He gestures at my novel. "I'll leave you two alone together. Same time next week?" He holds his hand up for a fist bump.

Gingerly, I press my pale knuckles to his overly tanned ones. "Same time next week."

He turns and strides across the marble floor of the lobby toward the ice-cream shop, his hair flopping with each step. For some reason, I miss him a little after he's gone.

But before I can even finish another chapter, he's back, a cup of ice cream in each hand. "I got you vanilla," he says. "You seem like a girl who plays it safe." He sits down in the chair next to me again.

"You got that right," I say. "And playing it safe does not involve being accosted by random strangers."

"I'm not random. I'm the guy after you at Daniel's office."

I arch an eyebrow. "You call Dr. Leed Daniel?"

He mimics my eyebrow and scornful tone. "You call Daniel Dr. Leed?"

"I don't really call him anything. I try not to talk much," I admit.

"Oh, so you're one of those. Perfect. You don't have to talk much to me either." He thrusts the ice cream in my direction. "Here. Take this in exchange for putting up with me for a few minutes."

"What is your deal?" I take the paper cup he's offering. The ice cream is starting to melt. "I thought you knew when to quit."

His cheeks go pink—I've touched a nerve. "Sorry. It's just, you seem normal, and I need to hang out with someone who doesn't know who I am."

"Why?"

"For my homework." He pauses. "You know—the shrink homework." Without waiting for me to respond he says, "Are your sessions different? Do you not get homework?"

"None so far." Is this what I have to look forward to? Shrink homework? On top of the school homework I'll have soon?

The boy taps one foot against the tile floor. "Mine go like this: Small talk. Then I discuss how I'm doing with my goals. Then I think up more homework assignments while Daniel flips through the latest issue of *Guitar Player*. Basically he makes me do all the shrink work and the client work.

Pretty clever on his part."

"*Guitar Player*—I knew it!" I say. "What is he? Full-time psychologist, part-time rock star?"

"No idea," the boy says. "But I'm supposed to find someone who doesn't know me and hang out with them, and since most people know me, I had to seize this opportunity."

"Who *are* you?" I take a small bite of ice cream, doing another five-second check as it melts on my tongue.

He shakes his head. "Nope. That'll wreck things."

"This is really good." I take another bite. "Are you, like, famous . . . or infamous?"

The boy grins. "I would say neither, but certain people would disagree."

"Boy band singer?" I ask. "Reality TV show contestant?"

He shakes his head.

"Failed child actor? College basketball star?"

"Ha. You're getting warmer."

"I give up. You're not even going to tell me your name?"

"I'd prefer not to."

I shrug. "Works for me."

And so the two of us sit there for a few minutes, eating our ice cream and making vague noises of approval. The boy slides my book out of my hand. He flips it over and makes a face. "A book about a boy with mad cow disease? Sounds uplifting."

"You'd be surprised." I peek over at his cup. "You got yourself vanilla too?"

He nods. "I'm more of a mint chip guy, but it's good to do something different now and then."

I think about that for a second. "Yeah, I guess it is."

The boy gives me another smile and the temperature in the room goes up a couple of degrees. "Do you want to see where I was going to take you?" he asks. "You totally missed out."

"Oh yeah?" I finish the ice cream and set my empty cup on the table between us.

He pulls out his phone and swipes at the screen. A folder of images pops up. "Yeah. My friend showed me this place up the coast that you can only get to when the tide is low, this little rock island. Dolphins hang out there a lot." He hands the phone over to me.

The pictures look like they belong on postcards—the blue of the Pacific spraying up onto jagged gray rocks, the sun setting in the distance painting the clouds a rainbow of red and orange, a cluster of seven or eight dolphin fins jutting out from beneath the crystal surface of the water. I would like it; pretty sure I'd love it, but for some reason I feel like messing with this boy. I toss the phone back to him. "Just because I'm a girl means I like dolphins?"

"More like because you're a human. Everyone likes dolphins." He sets his empty ice-cream cup next to mine.

"Well. Probably not *everyone*."

He shakes his head. "Pretty sure everyone. 'Oh, ugh, not dolphins. I *hate* them.' That doesn't even sound right." He pokes me in the arm.

I twitch. I can't remember the last time I was touched by someone who wasn't related to me.

The boy keeps talking, oblivious. "They've got those smiley faces and big brains, and it's so annoying the way they're always learning complex languages in captivity and saving drowning fishermen in the wild."

"Okay, probably most people," I say. My phone buzzes in my purse. I pull it out. There's a text from my mom saying she's parked in front. "I've got to run, Dolphin Boy. Thanks for the ice cream." I hop up from the chair and sling my purse over my shoulder. "We'll have to finish this discussion another time."

The boy points at the floor. "Is that your bookmark?"

Sure enough, when I grabbed my purse I must have knocked my lucky bookmark to the ground. I start to bend, but he quickly reaches down, picks it up, and hands it to me. "See you next week, Dolphin Hater."

I can't help but grin as I head for the door.

But then my smile fades.

Maybe this boy is right. Maybe I am missing out.

CHAPTER 4
Session #4

I'm not just missing out on dolphins.

I'm getting ready to leave for my appointment when my mom looks up from the kitchen table, the pages of a handwritten letter spread in front of her. I recognize the looping script immediately.

"How would you like to see your grandma Siobhan again?" Mom asks.

Siobhan is my dad's mom, a vivacious gray-haired lady who runs a horse farm in Ireland. I met her only twice: once when I was seven, when she traveled to the United States for Christmas, and then again at the funerals. She's actually the one who gave me my lucky penny bookmark. She used to write Mom and me letters when I was little. She'd send pictures of the new foal each time there was a birth. After the accident we slowly lost touch. I figure it's because thinking of Mom and me makes her think of Dad and Kieran. She lost both of her sons in one day.

"Grandma Siobhan wants to come here?" I ask hopefully. "That would be amazing." I scan the kitchen, searching for Mom's car keys, but my eyes are drawn back to the pages of my grandmother's letter.

My mom exhales slowly. "Actually she invited us to Ireland. She's having a special gathering to honor your dad, uncle, and brother. Since this December will be—"

"Five years," I whisper.

Mom nods. "Apparently everyone is going to come. Relatives I didn't even know we had. You could see where your dad grew up, his house, his town . . ."

My eyes start to water. "You know I can't get on a plane, Mom. I can't even ride in a car with other people."

"I told her that's what you would say, but I wanted to run it by you . . . just in case."

"Just in case what? I turned into someone else while you were having other kids?" My mom recoils, and I immediately regret my words. I have a half sister, Erin, who is two and a half, and a new baby half brother named Jacob. They are both adorable, and I love them to pieces. "I'm sorry. I didn't mean that the way it came out."

My mom nods again, but I can see that my words hurt her. "I just thought . . . in case Dr. Leed might be able to help you."

"I don't think he's a magician," I say. "But I guess it can't hurt to ask."

★ ★ ★

But after the receptionist waves me into the office, it takes a few minutes to work up the nerve to mention my grandmother's invitation. "Hey, Dr. Leed," I say as I settle into my usual chair. No music today. He's drinking a coffee from the shop next door.

"Hi, Maguire. You seem . . . different."

"Who's the guy that comes after me?" I ask.

Dr. Leed shakes his head. "You know I can't tell you that."

I tap my flip-flop against the black and white carpet. "Then just tell me what he does. Is he famous?"

Dr. Leed's eyes brighten behind his glasses. A smile plays at his lips. "Why the sudden interest in him?"

I clear my throat. "No, it's not like that. He just made a point of asking me if I knew him, and I was wondering why he thought I would."

"Ah. Unfortunately, I can't talk about my other clients." Dr. Leed sips his coffee.

I cross my arms. "You are not very helpful."

He sets the coffee cup on the desk behind him. "I could be, if you let me."

Grandma Siobhan's letter flashes in my head, followed by my mom's hopeful look. I take a deep breath. "Yeah. About that. I heard you give people homework."

"You heard wrong. I help people create challenges for themselves."

"So like, you think these challenges can fix me?"

Dr. Leed leans back in his chair. "You're not a toaster, Maguire. You're not here to be fixed." He makes air quotes around the word "fixed." "The first thing you need to realize is that mental health is fluid. It's not like you have an infection and a doctor gives you antibiotics and then you're cured. No matter what the two of us accomplish together, you're still going to have good days and bad days. Make sense?"

"I guess," I mumble. "Though I think I might rather be a toaster."

"You and me both." Dr. Leed smiles. "What I try to do is get my clients to tell me where they are and where they want to be. And then we figure out together how to get you there."

"And this has actually worked for you?"

He laughs under his breath. "Once or twice." For a second we both just sit there, looking at each other. Then he says, "What's changed? A few weeks ago you didn't want to talk at all. Why are you suddenly interested in therapy challenges?"

"I want to go to Ireland," I blurt out. I tell him about Grandma Siobhan and her horse farm, about the memorial service, about the look on my mom's face when she brought it up. "I wish there was a way I could do this for her."

"It helps if your goal is something you want to do for yourself," Dr. Leed says kindly.

I take in a deep breath, let it out slowly. "I want to do it for me too. I want to see where my dad grew up, see my grandma again, meet all my relatives."

"So what's the problem?"

"I can't get on a plane! I can't even ride a bus or be in the car when my stepdad is driving."

"So you're afraid of public transportation?"

I shake my head. "I wish it were that simple. It's like I told you last week. I'm afraid of hurting people."

Dr. Leed's cell phone vibrates on the desk behind him, startling both of us. He reaches over to grab it, peeks at the screen, and then tucks it into his pocket. "Sorry about that. Hurting people. But you mean indirectly, because you might be . . . cursed."

"Yes—like I showed you in my notebook. Bad things happen to other people when I'm around."

"Well, I don't know if any challenge is going to convince you that you're not cursed, but the type of therapy I do is meant to help you face your fears and also to restructure your thought processes. That way, even if the same things happen, you'll think about them differently, in a more helpful manner." He pauses. "I understand why you've been isolating yourself, but we can both agree that it isn't healthy, right?"

"I guess," I mutter.

"So basically you need to do things around other people and have nothing terrible happen. And then if that works okay, maybe we can get you on public transportation of some sort, and ideally help you see that you and everyone else can survive a plane ride to Ireland."

"Yeah, that's it exactly." I sigh. Saying it aloud makes it feel like an impossible task. "Sure you're up for the challenge?"

"You're the one who's going to be doing all the work," Dr. Leed says. "I generally have clients come up with a list of ten things and have them try to complete one challenge each week."

"Ten? That feels like a lot. What about five?"

Dr. Leed raises an eyebrow. "What about seven?"

"Lucky seven." I nod. "I guess it could work. But where do I even start?"

"We don't have to come up with the whole list at once, but I recommend things like sitting in a public area, talking to a stranger, riding in a car with someone besides your mom."

I think of Perfectly Assembled Boy. "I talked to a stranger last week," I say proudly. "And can I count school for sitting in a public area?"

Dr. Leed taps a few notes into his computer. "If you think being around people is dangerous to them, how do you manage to go to class and sit in a room with thirty other students?"

"I tried to get my mom to homeschool me after the birthday party incident, but she said no way. So I do these safety checks." I tell him about my five-second checks, how I look for fraying electrical cords or tripping hazards or classmates who look like they could get violent, etc. "I also knock on wood a lot, throw salt over my shoulder, wear a lucky amulet—you know, basic good luck stuff." I shrug. "Can't hurt, right?"

"So your mom forced you into an uncomfortable situation, and you came up with a way to help yourself cope?"

I chew on my bottom lip. "I never thought about it like that. Yeah. I guess I did."

"How much time do you spend on these things?" Dr. Leed asks.

"Not too much," I say. "I have a series of good luck rituals I do each morning when I wake up. And then maybe a few times an hour for the checks."

Dr. Leed enters more notes. "And how much time do you spend each day worrying about bad things that might happen?"

"I don't know. Why?"

"Developing obsessive-compulsive disorder secondary to PTSD would be unusual, but it wouldn't be unheard of."

"Great," I say. "The ER docs said I had anxiety, and you said I have PTSD, and now I have OCD too? Isn't that where people wash their hands like forty times a day?"

"OCD is characterized by irrational or excessive worrying and repetitive behaviors that are done because of those worries, but like anything else, there's wide variance when it comes to the actual symptoms and their severity."

"Oh." I guess I can see where my checks and rituals might qualify. I chew on my lower lip some more.

"What are your grades like?" Dr. Leed asks.

"I get all *A*s. Maybe a *B* in gym."

"And how are things at home?"

"You mean like do I get along with my parents and brother and sister? Yeah, we're good."

"Okay." He types more notes into his computer. "If you're spending less than an hour a day on your coping mechanisms and it's not affecting your daily functioning, then you probably don't fit the diagnostic criteria for OCD. But either way, secondary diagnoses are often transient."

"Meaning you can fix me?"

"Meaning if we address the underlying cause, then the symptoms might resolve on their own," he says. "So back to the primary problem. You don't think you can survive a plane ride by doing your checks and rituals?"

"No way." My heart thuds audibly in my chest as I imagine my mom dragging me screaming and crying onto a plane, concerned passengers recording me with their cell phones, flight attendants calling for airport security.

"Why not?"

"Because I know what to expect in a classroom. I know what to look for. I don't on a plane, and even if I saw something, there might be no way to fix it, you know? I wouldn't have any control."

"I see," Dr. Leed says. "So we need to start with something where you don't know exactly what to expect. Something slightly tougher than sitting in class. What about joining a club, or even better, trying out for a sports team?

Exercise tends to reduce anxiety and improve mood."

The only sport I've done recently is running. I started jogging a couple of years ago as a way to stay in shape. "Would cross-country count?"

Dr. Leed adjusts his glasses. "I'd prefer to see you attempt something with a little more interaction. How about track and field?"

"That's a spring sport, I think."

"Are there any other fall sports that interest you?"

I start to tell him that other sports are too dangerous, but then I stop. I used to play tennis a lot when I was little. Tennis was Mom's thing the way rock climbing was Dad and Uncle Kieran's. Dad, Mom, Connor, and I would play doubles at the park by our house. Connor and I even took lessons for a while. I haven't played in years, but maybe if I got out on a court, the technique would come back to me. And when it comes to safe sports, tennis is probably the next best thing to running cross-country.

"How about tennis? Is that interactive enough for you?"

Dr. Leed nods. "Do you think you could survive trying out for the tennis team if you did your good luck rituals and your five-second checks?"

Most points in tennis are only a couple of minutes long. I could get away with doing quick scans in between them to make sure no one was in danger of tripping over an untied shoelace or a runaway tennis ball. "Probably. But what if I can't? What if I freak out or something?"

"Do you have a certain way you calm yourself down if you start to feel anxious?"

I nod. "My old therapist taught me a bunch of different techniques—square breathing, visualization, relaxing all of my muscles."

"I find coping statements can be helpful too," Dr. Leed says. "Just something simple to remind yourself that the situation isn't as dire as it might feel. Maybe something like 'I can't control the Universe' or 'No one is going to die.'"

"Okay, but what if I go out for the team and don't make it? Or I do make it, and I hate it?"

"Then you quit?"

"And that's okay with you?"

"Anything is okay with me, Maguire. You have to do this at your own pace, but if you want to go from where you are now to getting on an international flight in December, you're going to have to push yourself a bit."

My hands shake a little at the thought of tennis tryouts, at the combination of worrying about other people and being stared at and judged. I guess as the new girl at school I'll be stared at anyway. And as long as I do my five-second checks, a tennis court isn't a whole lot more dangerous than a classroom.

Maybe.

I see Mom's face again, her expression a mix of hope and resignation. This trip to Ireland means a lot to her. It would mean a lot to me too. I was still in shock when my family was buried. I could use a second chance to say good-bye.

I nod. "Okay, I'll try. So that's challenge number one then? Try out for the tennis team? I'll do it. For my mom, and for Ireland."

"And for yourself," Dr. Leed reminds me.

"And for myself," I repeat.

"You're smiling," Perfectly Assembled Boy says. Today he's back in his fancy jeans and button-up shirt, his hair impeccably messy.

"No I'm not."

"Yes you are." He glances down at his phone and rolls his eyes at the screen before tucking it into his pocket. "Did you tell him you talked to me?"

"I tried to get him to tell me your secret identity," I admit. "But he wouldn't tell me who you are."

"Good." The boy looks away for a second. "He doesn't know anyway—not really. I'm not even sure if I know anymore."

SEPTEMBER

CHALLENGES

1. Make the tennis team.
2. Ride in a car with someone besides Mom.
3.
4.
5.
6.
7.

GOAL

Plane ride to Ireland for memorial service.

CHAPTER 5

"Maguire, don't forget you have tennis tryouts after school," my mom says with entirely too much enthusiasm. She's at the counter slicing fruit, the baby monitor propped up against the side of a mango.

"Got it." I stifle a yawn. As if I could forget. My mom was thrilled to hear I was going out for the tennis team. She's always telling me I need to get out of the house more and meet people. Is it me, or is my mom the only mom in the history of ever who told her kid to spend less time reading and more time being social? Doesn't she know the chances of me getting drunk, pregnant, and/or arrested are much lower if I never leave my room?

I spoon some oatmeal into my favorite bowl with the painted white elephants around the rim and take my usual seat across from my half sister, Erin. When my mom isn't looking, I toss a little salt over my left shoulder. Erin catches me and giggles. "Maguire," she says in her high-pitched voice, mangling my name just slightly so it sounds like Mack Wire.

"Shh." I raise a finger to my lips. Her bright blue eyes sparkle. She's just a little kid. She'll play along.

Casually, I let my hand drop to my chair, where I knock three times. My stepdad, Tom, looks up from his newspaper. He's an engineer of some sort. Chemical? Mechanical? Honestly, I don't know, but then I've never made much of an effort to ask. Don't get me wrong; he's not a wicked stepfather or anything. He's basically cool. It's just even after three years, it still feels like I'd be betraying my real dad if I got too close to him.

"I hope the new racquet works out for you." Tom tugs at the knot in his tie.

"I'm sure it'll be great." I force a smile.

He and my mom bought me this top-of-the-line graphite–titanium–moon rock bulletproof two-hundred-dollar racquet. I appreciate the gesture, but unless it's going to play *for* me, there's no guarantee I'll make the team. And unless it's magical, there's no guarantee something bad won't happen.

The oatmeal begins to congeal in my stomach when I start brainstorming about accidents that could occur during something as seemingly benign as tennis tryouts.

"Knock 'em dead, champ," Tom says. Grabbing his keys, he gives my mom a kiss on the cheek and then heads off to work.

I slide my chair back from the table and mumble

something about finishing getting ready. "Dead" is not a word I want associated with today.

The school day proceeds in an orderly fashion, thanks to a predictable routine and my five-second checks. I survive first-hour gym and then sit through European literature and trig. I eat lunch by myself outside, on the front steps of the school.

While I'm nibbling on a PBJ, I flip through my luck notebook. I used to keep it at home, but my mom found it once when she was putting away my laundry. I told her it was a statistics project I was doing for math class, but ever since then I've carried it with me most of the time. It would be really hard to explain all of the documentation I've been keeping.

I flip to the very back page and write the word "CHAL-LENGES." Then I number from one to seven down the left margin. Next to #1 I write, "Make the tennis team." Next to #2 I write, "Ride in a car with someone besides Mom." That's as far as Dr. Leed and I got, but it feels like plenty to work on.

After lunch, it's time for physics. My teacher, Mr. Ginger, messes up my name for the second day in a row.

"Kelly?" he calls. "Kelly Maguire?"

I'm used to people reversing my first and last names, since Maguire is a pretty weird first name. I love it, though. It's Irish, like my dad. When I was younger, people tried to call me stuff like Mac and Mags for short, but fortunately nothing ever stuck.

"It's Maguire," I say.

He rubs at the bridge of his nose as he jots something down on his seating chart. He'll probably spend all semester thinking I'm some jock or ROTC wannabe who likes being called by her last name. I don't mind.

Once Mr. Ginger finishes taking attendance, he gives us the rest of the hour to read the first chapter in our textbook and answer the discussion questions at the end. I finish them early and then fish a novel about a girl spy out of my backpack. I love adventure stories. Reading about people in mortal peril is much more fun than actual danger.

When the bell rings, I shuffle off to yet another boring lecture. Juniors can choose from several electives and it'd be fun to take home ec or maybe even theater. But hot stoves? Precariously placed set pieces? That'd be asking for a catastrophe. I only take gym because it's required every semester. Some school incentive to keep teens active and healthy. What a crock. I'm surprised we're not all dropping dead from high cholesterol due to the buffalo chicken sandwiches half the school eats for lunch.

I knock on my desk three times. I try not to even think about stuff like mass cholesterol casualties.

My last class of the day is psychology, something I signed up for because it sounded more interesting than any of the other social studies classes. Maybe I can learn something that will help with my therapy challenges. Today my teacher, Ms. Haynes, is talking about boring historical stuff, different schools of thought that led to various types of psychotherapy. Dr. Leed said what he does is called cognitive behavioral therapy. Hopefully we'll talk about that eventually.

When sixth period finally ends, I head for the locker room. With my back to everyone else, I wriggle out of my jeans and T-shirt and into a pair of shorts and an embroidered polo shirt that my mom insisted would make me look like a serious contender. *If you say so, Mom.* I toss all of my clothes into my locker, slam it shut, and give my combination lock a spin.

I slink out of the locker room and head for the back door of the school. "Wish me luck," I mutter to no one in particular.

The afternoon sun blasts me in the face as I step outside onto the blacktop basketball court. The ocean breeze blowing in from the west threatens to make my curly hair even curlier.

Beyond the blacktop is the football field, surrounded by our blue and gray track. We're supposed to meet in the football bleachers for an informational briefing session. There are twelve girls lined up when I arrive—three orderly rows of four. I've never seen so many pleated tennis skirts with color-coordinated socks, shoes, and headbands. I suddenly feel like a ball boy in my shorts and polo.

I tromp up to the back and make a fourth row. The two

girls right in front of me are still in their street clothes—one in jeans and flip-flops and the other in a pastel blue sundress and fur-lined Ugg boots. They turn half around to give me a curious look, but neither one bothers to say anything. Both of them were in my psychology class. Sundress Girl sat in the front row and asked a lot of questions about the lecture. Her name is Kami or Kimberly or something.

Coach Hoffman appears from behind the bleachers, a baseball cap pulled low over his pronounced brow and a clipboard balanced on one of his meaty forearms. He paces back and forth on the asphalt track, his neon yellow Nikes treading a repeated path across the stocky body of our mascot, the Pacific Point Porpoise.

A tall Asian girl wearing patterned kneesocks and a black tennis dress emblazoned with purple geometric shapes makes her way up the bleachers, scanning the rows like she's looking for someone. She was also in my sixth-hour class. She sat in the back with me and redid her nail polish behind her book for most of the period.

"Bloody hell," she says to no one in particular, in what I think is a British accent. "I cannot believe I'm going to spend all semester with you turnips." She passes everyone up and comes to sit by me. "You're the new girl, yeah?" she asks. "Maguire?"

"Yeah." I scoot a little bit away as she drops her tennis bag on the ground. It's more of a plain duffel strategically cut and sewn to convert it to a racquet bag. Tiny patches with slogans like "I think, therefore I am (better than you)" and "Death to pop music" cover the front of it.

"Right then," she says. "I'm Jade." She dusts off the bleachers with one hand before sitting down. She's got fresh black and silver polish on every nail except for her thumb, which is adorned with a sunflower decal.

"Jade." I scoot back toward her. "Nice to meet you." Okay, so it's totally dumb to like someone for her name, but jade is lucky in several different cultures. I'm counting this as a good omen.

"Welcome to tennis tryouts." Coach Hoffman clears his throat. "As most of you know, we lost five seniors last year, so this is going to be a rebuilding season."

A murmur moves through the crowd. Sundress Girl smoothes her already smooth ponytail and then raises her hand.

Coach gestures to her. "Yes, Kimber?"

"Given all the people that we lost and the relatively small number here today . . ." She pauses to take a look around at the bleachers, not bothering to look back at Jade and me. "I'm thinking that instead of having last year's squad members go through tryouts again, we might be more useful to you if we spent the next few days trying to recruit some new members."

"Thank you for the offer," Coach says. "But it's always been my policy that every member of the team tries out every single year. For one, this keeps you girls from getting complacent. And two, it helps me decide who will play which positions. We may have lost first, second, and fourth singles, but that does not necessarily guarantee you the top spot."

Kimber's back and neck muscles go tense as she sits up even straighter and another murmur moves through the group, this one accompanied by a few giggles. "Of course not," she says sharply, fiddling with the strap of her sundress. "I was just thinking we might need more than we have here to make a solid team."

Coach does another lap back and forth across the face of our porpoise mascot. "Oh, I don't know. I count fourteen girls. We only need ten and a couple of alternates."

"I see." Kimber's shoulders rotate up and back as she inhales deeply, but she doesn't say anything else.

Jade and I exchange an amused glance.

"Here's how today will go," Coach continues. "First we'll warm up with some calisthenics. Then we'll break up into groups of two and just hit around for a while so that I can get a first look at some of the new faces and see which of my veterans have stayed in shape over the summer. Once everybody is loosened up, we'll go from there. Any questions?"

A girl in the second row raises her hand. She looks nervously around the bleachers before speaking. "Will anyone be getting cut today?"

"Good question. No one will be getting cut until next week, so no pressure. Just have fun and don't try to force it," Coach says.

Kimber raises her hand again. "Isn't Jordy going to be helping you out again this season?"

"Right," Coach says. "I almost forgot. Once again, we're all going to be lucky enough to have Jordy Wheeler at some of our practices and matches, serving as sort of my manager-slash-assistant."

"You call that lucky?" a blonde girl in the front row pipes up. She tosses a sun-kissed braid back over one shoulder. Some of the girls giggle.

"For everyone but you," Coach says. "All right. Anyone who needs to change clothes can go do so. We'll meet back here in ten minutes to get started."

I make a big point of slowly gathering my things, allowing the rest of the girls to descend the bleachers before I start so I can't accidentally trip down the stairs and crush anyone. Even with something as simple as walking, I'm constantly on the lookout for potential hazards. I turn to Jade. "Who's Jordy Wheeler?"

"Shite. You *are* new, aren't you? He's Pacific Point's claim to fame—some big-deal junior tennis star."

"Cool," I say. "Does he play on the boys' team?" I fling my tennis bag over my shoulder and make my way to the steps, my court shoes clunking down each of them like I'm a rhinoceros who's had a few too many drinks.

44

Behind me, Jade's footsteps are quiet enough to make a ninja jealous. "No. He goes to some online athlete school, but I believe he has to participate in at least one activity as part of his graduation requirements. He can't play for the boys' team because he competes in pro tournaments already, so that's why he's going to help coach us."

"Wow. Lucky us."

"I suppose. Half the school has a crush on him." She scoffs. "A bit dodgy, if you ask me."

"Why?"

"Allegedly his parents don't let him date, or even hang out with friends much. He eats, sleeps, and breathes tennis."

"Sounds boring." Really I'm thinking that it sounds kind of predictable and safe. "But not exactly *dodgy*."

"Well, from what I hear, Jordy still manages to get plenty of action, if you know what I mean."

I do. There were guys like that at my old school too, ones who were always single and yet seemed to have hooked up with everyone. Or so people said, anyway. I wasn't exactly dialed into the social scene.

Jade and I hop down from the bleachers and cross through a gap in the fence to the track, where the other girls are either standing around chatting or engaged in various degrees of stretching. "So what about you?" I ask. "Are you from England or something?"

Jade exhales deeply. "Bloody hell, I thought you'd never ask." She loses her British accent completely. "Nah. I moved here last year from Seattle. I'm in theater class. I just like to try out accents with people who don't know me and see if I can fool them." She turns the accent back on. "So I had you going then? For a bit?"

"For a bit," I mimic her.

She laughs. "Brilliant." She rubs her hands together like a mad scientist.

We drop our stuff on the track and do a couple of halfhearted stretches while we wait for everyone to finish changing. Kimber and the girl who was sitting next to her reappear in matching gray skirts and blue tops. Coach Hoffman and a tall boy stroll out of the school a couple of minutes later. The boy has a huge duffel bag slung over his shoulder and a hopper of tennis balls in the opposite hand. It takes me a second to recognize him.

"Dolphin Boy?" I murmur. It's the guy from Dr. Leed's office.

CHAPTER 6

So he's a tennis star. Interesting. He and Coach are deep in discussion, poring over Coach's clipboard as they head toward us. I can't hear what they're saying, but I can see Jordy's animated gestures. One of his shoes hits a crack in the pavement and he stumbles. He flails his free arm in an attempt to regain his balance and nearly drops both his bag and the ball hopper. I imagine the metal basket hitting the concrete, all of us spending the next twenty minutes collecting runaway tennis balls.

Just as I'm trying to decide if my bad luck is to blame, Coach Hoffman reaches out and grabs Jordy's elbow to steady him. Crisis averted. Jordy laughs, and I smother a smile. As he hits the edge of the track, he scans the group, sizing us up. His eyes linger on me for a second and I look down, feigning a sudden need to tighten my shoelaces.

"All right, everyone take a lap," Coach tells us.

He and Jordy stand at the edge of the track chatting while

all the girls take off running. Jade and I quickly move to the front of the pack. I run side by side with her, careful not to veer in front of her or accidentally hip-check her as we turn the first corner. My mystic knot pendant bounces against my breastbone. I reach up and tuck it under my collar, but it flops back out almost immediately. Giving up, I lengthen my stride, sucking in a huge breath of air as we pass the football goalposts. I do a quick five-second check. The girls are spread out behind us. There's nothing dangerous as far as I can tell.

"You're fast," Jade says.

I slow my pace a little. "I run a lot," I tell her.

The sun ducks in and out of the clouds and the wind hits my skin with just enough force to keep me from getting sweaty. Maybe my mom was right. Maybe joining an activity is just what I need. I mean, it can't hurt, right?

Without warning, Kimber cuts in front of me, her leg muscles flexing and contracting beneath her dark skin with each stride. I jerk to the left to avoid crashing into her. My feet get tangled up and I trip, landing on my hands and knees. The rough track bites through the top layers of my skin and into the bloody part beneath.

Okay, so it can hurt.

Jade pulls up short beside me. "Are you all right?"

"Fine." Hopping to my feet, I dust the major dirt particles from my scraped knees and keep running. Everyone else passed us when I fell, and now they're all over a quarter of a lap ahead of us.

"You should probably go clean yourself up," Jade says. "God only knows what sort of germs are living on the bottom of everyone's shoes."

It's a good point, but I don't feel like making a spectacle of myself on the first day of tryouts by freaking out over some skinned knees. My bad luck never hurts me directly, so it's not like I picked up some flesh-eating bacteria or anything.

"Girls!" Coach Hoffman yells. "Come on. More running, less chatter."

Jade rolls her eyes at me but picks up her pace again. We sprint the last quarter of the lap but still come in last. Coach makes a point of looking down at his stopwatch as we finish. "Go on. Catch up with the others."

Everyone else has made two lines across the middle of the football field. Jordy motions to Kimber and the girl who was sitting next to her, and they obediently leave their places in line and trot over to him.

"If you didn't know, this is Kimber and Colleen," he says. "Singles and doubles captains. They're going to lead the warm-up."

"What do you want us to do?" Colleen shifts her weight from one foot to the other. The wind blows her honey-colored hair back from her face.

He shrugs. "Whatever."

"I got this." Kimber steps forward. "Everyone listen up," she barks, like she's preparing to lead a platoon of soldiers through their morning workout. "Fifty jumping jacks. Now."

Jordy and Coach do their stand-around-and-talk thing again while Kimber takes us through a series of exercises I'm pretty sure are designed to make us too tired to actually stand, let alone play tennis afterward. One of them is a squat–push-up–jump thing called a burpee, and Jade mutters something about refusing to do it on principle because the name is stupid. I start giggling in the middle of a push-up and almost face-plant onto the grass.

When we're finally finished, Coach makes some notes on his clipboard, and I wonder if half of us will be cut from the team for crappy push-up form. Jordy picks up the hopper of tennis balls, and we all head down a grassy incline beyond the edge of the track to the tennis courts.

"Everyone take a couple of balls and just get loosened up," he says. "No playing for points yet."

"Do you want to rally with me?" Jade asks breathlessly. Her silky black hair is starting to pull loose from her ponytail. She removes a little sweat towel from the pocket of her tennis dress and mops at her forehead.

"Sure." I try not to even think about what I look like after all of those exercises. I blot my face with the back of my hand while Coach unlocks the gate and all the girls in front of us enter the courts one by one. Jade and I are last.

Jordy looks us over as Jade grabs a couple of balls from the hopper. "Dolphin Hater. I guess now you know my secret." He looks down at my skinned knees. "What happened?"

"I'm kind of . . . accident-prone," I mumble.

"Me too," he says. "Did you see me almost fall on my face earlier?"

"Must have missed it," I lie. I don't know if I'm doing it to spare him the embarrassment or because I don't want him to know I was looking at him. Probably a little of both.

"I'm sure you'll get a repeat performance at some point." He shakes his perfectly messy hair back from his face.

"Wait. You hate dolphins?" Jade asks. "That's unnatural."

"That's what I told her." Jordy plucks a stray bit of fuzz off a bright green Penn #6. He tosses the ball to me, followed by a second one.

Jade glances back and forth from Jordy to me, a puzzled look on her face. "So you two know each other?"

"I've seen him around, but I didn't know his name," I say.

"We go to the same shrink," Jordy explains.

My jaw drops a little. "Hey! You're not supposed to blab people's private medical business."

"No bigs," Jade says. "Practically everyone at PP has a shrink, or wishes they did. My mom makes me go to this old lady once a week so I can talk about the stress of being a teenage girl or whatever." She motions for me to follow her. "I can hold one of your balls," she says, plucking it out of my fingers. "But you should really get some tennis clothes to go with that fancy racquet."

My running shorts only have one tiny pocket, made for

51

keys. Mom and Tom probably would have bought me tennis apparel if they knew everyone else would have it. "We'll see if I make the team first," I say.

She nods knowingly. "My mom will probably call up Coach Hoffman and scream at him if I get cut. She's always on my case." She shakes her index finger at me and makes her voice sound like an old lady's. "You need those extracurriculars if you want to get into a good college."

My mom has starting asking me about college, but I can't think that far in advance. If I do I lose focus on the moment, and that's when someone gets hurt. I figure I'll enroll in an online program, at least for the first couple of years—something safe I can do from the privacy of my bedroom.

I follow Jade down to the far end of the tennis courts, where two other girls are already hitting around on Court Six. "Mind if we share with you?" she asks.

The girls smile and move over so that Jade and I have half of the court. My heart revs up a little at the thought of actually playing against strangers. I scan my surroundings for any possible hazards and then tell myself to relax. It's not like I can kill anyone with a tennis ball.

Actually, there is one tennis-related death on record. (I Googled it. Research is part of being prepared.) It was at Wimbledon; an umpire got hit by a ball going more than a hundred miles per hour, and then he fell and hit his head on the court. I'm pretty sure I don't hit anywhere near that hard.

I reach up and touch my mystic knot. Then I bounce the

ball three times and lob it over the net. Jade turns her body sideways and sends it back at me, her racquet slicing downward so the ball bounces low and I have to lunge to get to it. I return it and then retreat to the baseline. The ball sails back and forth between us as we fall into an easy rhythm. I do a five-second check of the surroundings between each rally, stopping once to warn a girl on the next court about her untied shoelace.

After fifteen minutes, Coach tells us to change partners. Each player shifts one court or section to the right so we're all rallying with someone different. I end up opposite a girl named Mae who hits hard and flat, just like I do. We both cover the court well, and our rallies go twenty or thirty hits before someone messes up.

Coach Hoffman strokes his goatee as he watches us, the beginnings of a smile on his sun-darkened face. "Faster feet, Maguire," he instructs. "Don't forget to get back to ready position so you're prepared for anything."

I do my best to follow his instructions, running back to the baseline center and squaring my body with the net after each shot. Coach nods with satisfaction. He strolls from court to court, occasionally asking people to switch things up.

About an hour later, I find myself down on Court Two opposite Jordy. I didn't even realize he was hitting around with us until this moment. I can't believe I have to rally with some guy who plays in pro tournaments. Maybe I should fake like I need to use the restroom.

"Dolphin Hater. You look scared." Jordy strides up to the net and motions for me to meet him there.

Trying to look calm, I jog up to where he's bouncing a ball off the face of his racquet repeatedly.

"What's your name?" he asks.

"Maguire."

"Like the baseball player?" He holds out his right hand while his left hand continues to bounce the ball off the strings.

I switch my racquet into my left hand and give my fingers a quick wipe on my shorts before shaking his hand. "No. It's an Irish name," I explain. "My dad's Irish. Well, he was. He died." *Oh my God, Maguire, stop talking.*

Jordy's eyes soften. "I'm sorry to hear that."

"It's okay. It was a long time ago," I say. "My mom's remarried and everything." I cough. "I don't know why I'm giving you my whole life story."

He winks. "Girls say I'm easy to talk to."

Next to us, Kimber races forward, lunging for a well-placed drop shot. She hits it wide and heads back to the baseline with a scowl. "Are you going to play, Jordy, or just stand there and flirt with the new girl?"

"You always think I'm flirting with everyone," he says.

Kimber smirks. "Probably because you *are* always flirting with everyone."

"Ignore her," Jordy tells me. "She doesn't understand the concept of being friendly." He gets in position to start a rally, and I quickly back up to the baseline. He bounces the ball and sends it over the net, so deep in the court I almost have to play it off my shoelaces.

I scoop it up and fire it back at him. He draws me into the net with a short ball and then hits a forehand right at me. I punch the ball back at him, and he lunges for it, setting me up with another easy volley.

"Good," he says when I angle the ball out of his reach.

"But you set me up," I protest. "Anyone could have won that point."

"Not anyone," he says. "A lot of high school tennis players will do just about anything to avoid playing net. At least you're not afraid." He points at the baseline. "Now get back there."

I hurry back to my spot as Jordy fires another ball at me. Some of our rallies go as long as mine did with Mae, and I'm surprised at my own abilities. I feel like a legit tennis player, even though I can see Jordy running me from side to side, tiring me out, while he barely has to move to return all my shots.

"You're fast," he says. "But you're just reflecting back my power. What happens if you really put your weight into it?"

I concentrate on putting my whole body into each stroke, and sure enough my shots fly low and hard over the net. And then I mistime one and hit it off my back foot. The tennis ball sails all the way over the fence and up the hill, bouncing off the track before rolling to a stop somewhere on the football field.

I swear under my breath. "I'll go get it." I set my racquet down on the court and jog behind Court One, where Kimber and Coach are engaged in a heated ground-stroke battle. I round the corner and head for the gate. Jordy is right behind me, his racquet still clutched in his hand.

"What are you doing?" I ask.

He twirls his racquet on his index finger. "I figured I'd come with you. Sometimes the balls are hard to spot in the grass."

"Um . . . okay."

Jordy walks beside me as we head up the hill toward the track. "Sorry about the shrink thing. I should have known some people might want to keep that a secret."

"Not you, I guess."

"Nah. Sometimes I feel like it's one of the most real things about me." He pauses. "So Irish, eh? I thought Irish people had red hair and freckles."

"I think that might be a stereotype perpetuated by cereal boxes." Other than my pale skin, it's true that I don't look Irish at all. My dark curly hair is from my mom's side of the family. Some of her ancestors were Greek. But it's not like my dad had red hair and freckles either.

"Are you trying to tell me you're not magically delicious?" Jordy flashes me his perfect grin.

I can feel the blush make its way into my cheeks. I have no idea how to respond to that. Is he . . . flirting with me? Instead of answering, I turn away from him, toward the goalposts, squinting into the sun.

He clears his throat. "Sorry. I try not to sexually harass girls until I at least know their last names."

"It's Kelly," I say. "Not that you should . . . I mean I'm sure you weren't . . . I'm just not used to . . ." *Stop talking, Maguire.* "Look!" I almost shriek, pointing at the twenty-yard line. "It's my ball."

I head toward it, but Jordy beats me to the spot. He reaches down with his racquet, pins the ball against the side of his foot, and flips it up into the air. I reach out and catch it. "Seriously. I hope I didn't offend you," he says. "I'm not really a slick asshole. I just pretend to be one sometimes, for the media people. Occasionally, I forget to turn it off." He's still got half a smile on his face, but there's a heaviness to his words.

"Why not just be the real you?"

"The real me doesn't sell tennis racquets," Jordy says. "Or grip tape or sports sunglasses. Apparently I need a brand to be successful. And sadly, everyone seems to like Slick Ass-hole Jordy better."

I crack a smile. "Not everyone."

"Yeah, well, you don't really know me, do you?"

"True."

"Yet," he says as we make our way back down the grassy hill.

Something about that one innocent word makes me nervous.

We duck back into the tennis courts a couple of moments later, and Coach gives Jordy a long look. "I thought maybe you two weren't coming back. Did she hit that ball into the next county?"

"She's got quite an arm," Jordy says.

We resume hitting on Court Two, where Jordy runs me from side to side and I return his power with a little added extra of my own. Each shot I make is harder than the one before. Vaguely, in my peripheral vision, I see the girls on the nearby courts pausing their games to watch us. Jordy hits a shallow ball, and my momentum brings me up to the net. He tries to lob over me but comes up short. I'm in perfect position for an overhead slam. I bring my racquet back and wait for the ball to fall, squinting hard to keep from losing it in the bright sunlight. *Wait for it . . . wait for it . . .*

Jordy has to guess which way I'm going. I see him lean to my left, so I aim right. I swing hard, transferring my weight forward as I make contact, but my aim is slightly off and the ball flies through the air right at Jordy's body. He tries to get out of the way, but it's coming at him too fast.

Oh no. He's going to get hit, I think. *Bad Luck Maguire strikes again.*

But it's even worse than I imagine. My overhead nails Jordy right between the legs.

CHAPTER 7

Watching Jordy get hit is like watching a bad slow-motion sequence in a movie. His skin goes pale. He flails backward a couple of steps. Freezes. Doubles over. His knees hit the ground first, and then the rest of him. He twists onto one side, his feet and legs inside the court, his upper body beyond the baseline. His face turns red.

"Oh my God. I am so sorry." I stand awkwardly at the net, my racquet dangling from my hand as Coach Hoffman runs to Jordy's side. Kimber is right behind him.

She kneels beside Jordy and looks back at me with undisguised loathing. "Did you just hit him in the . . . ? What is the *matter* with you?" Her dark eyes bore holes in my skin.

"I—I didn't mean to," I say.

Jordy groans. He pulls his knees up to his chest and curls into the fetal position. "That's good to know," he chokes out. "Like I said, Coach. She's got quite an arm."

The girls down on Court Five and Court Six are still

playing, but everyone else has stopped to check out the commotion. A small crowd gathers around Jordy. Titters become giggles become full-blown laughter. One of the girls has her phone out recording the entire thing. This is totally the most humiliating moment of my life.

"Kimber. Go get Reyes," Coach Hoffman says. He turns to Jordy. "Can you sit up?"

Jordy takes Coach's hand and pulls himself into a seated position as Kimber stalks off to get the athletic trainer. His face starts to return to normal color. "Not Reyes," he protests. "What is he going to do? Put an ice pack on my balls?"

Another wave of laughter moves through the rest of the girls. A couple turn in my direction. I look down at my racquet, adjusting one of my bright green strings so it's evenly spaced with the one next to it. Maybe there's a school activity even lower-impact than tennis. Knitting? Too many sharp needles. Yearbook club, maybe?

"Nice one," Jade whispers from behind me. "Way to make yourself known on the first day of tryouts."

"First and last day," I hiss. "I'm never coming back."

"Don't be dramatic." Her eyes dance with amusement. "He probably deserved it."

Looking past her, I see the back door of the school swing open as Kimber disappears inside. I should have volunteered to go get the trainer. Then I could have sneaked out of the school, walked home, and begged my mom to homeschool me for the next two years.

I pick at another one of my racquet strings. Jordy coughs. I look up. He slowly gets to his feet.

"Go on, show's over." He makes shooing motions with his hands, and the girls clustered around him start to shuffle back to their own courts.

"Maybe go easy on him for the rest of practice," Jade murmurs. "More for your own sake than his." She waggles her painted fingernails at me and then turns back to her own court.

Jordy bounces up and down on the balls of his feet a couple of times. He gestures to me to head back to the baseline.

"We don't have to keep playing," I protest. "You should . . . take a break or something."

"I'm fine," Jordy says. "Let's see your serve."

Oh no. Just when I think things can't possibly get any worse.

After Dr. Leed and I agreed that I should try out for tennis, my mom took me to the local neighborhood park to practice, but I didn't have much luck serving. She didn't either, so we ended up just rallying and not playing for points. My ground strokes came back quickly, but I have a feeling my serve is going to be a disaster.

And I'm right.

I slam four balls straight into the net before Jordy crosses his hands in a time-out signal. He runs up the center of the court and vaults over the net. "Forgot how to serve?"

"Something like that."

"Your toss is kind of low and wide. Try throwing the ball up higher."

I follow his advice and manage to land a serve in the box, but it's painfully weak. A decent opponent would have cranked a winner right past me. "Crap," I say.

"Better toss, though," Jordy says. "Keep practicing."

I try a few more serves and only manage to get one of them over. Then Coach comes down to watch me and I revert to my lower toss, the one where I can at least put some power behind my serves.

Too bad none of them go over the net.

Coach Hoffman looks back and forth from Jordy to me. "Your ground strokes are impressive, but they're not much good if you can't put a ball in play."

I drop my eyes to the court. "I'll work on it," I mutter. Unfortunately, teaching yourself to serve is a lot harder than teaching yourself to hit forehands and backhands.

Coach nods, makes a note on his clipboard, and then shuffles back down to the far courts. I swallow back the lump that's forming in my throat, bite my lip so no one will see it shaking.

"Hey." Jordy looks hard at me. "What's wrong?"

"My serve sucks." I blink hard and then look down at the court again, my eyes tracing a minuscule crack in the even green surface. "I'm totally going to get cut."

"Are you kidding me? You hit like a rocket launcher.

You just have to tweak your form so you can get some serves over the net."

"Easier said than done."

"Don't stress. I can help you."

I lift my eyes. "Why would you do that?"

"Because it's why I'm here." He shakes his hair back from his face. "The rest of your game is on point, and Hoffman needs good players. Plus you helped me with my shrink homework. I owe you one."

"Not like you gave me much choice," I say, thinking back to the ice-cream ambush.

"Yeah, like I said, I can be kind of an overbearing ass. For what it's worth, though, you really did help." Jordy claps me on the shoulder, the veins in his lean, muscular forearm standing out like highways on a map. "I have to take off, because I've got a meeting with my coach, but tomorrow I'm yours, if you want me."

"Okay." I give him a tentative smile. "Thanks. And sorry about . . . hitting you."

He laughs. "I've endured worse injuries on the court." Turning toward the school, he squints off into the distance. "Yikes. Here come Kimber and Reyes. Time to bail."

He ducks through the gate and lopes off toward the school, cutting around the side of the track to avoid our athletic trainer. I watch him until he disappears, taking note of his long legs and hair that flops just slightly with each stride. At least he seems fully recovered; no permanent damage done.

Kimber and Reyes duck through the gate and out onto Court One. Coach Hoffman pulls Reyes a few feet away to tell him what happened. Both men start to laugh. I go back to arranging my racquet strings again.

"Check yourself, New Girl," Kimber says.

I lift my head. "What?"

"I said check yourself." Her jaw goes tight. "I saw the way you talked to him. The way you watched him run all the way to the building. Best to stop before you even start. Jordy is off-limits. To everyone. He is . . . singularly focused." She shifts her body so that one foot is sideways in front of the other, almost like a ballet pose. "His whole life is tennis and studying."

I decide not to point out that's two things, not one. "I'm not—I mean, I wasn't—" My words get all tangled up as Kimber crosses her arms and stares at me. "He just offered to help with my serve. I don't even know him."

"That's right. You don't," she says. "Remember that."

After practice, Jade catches up with me on the way to the locker room. "Okay. So first you rack the golden boy and then you talk back to Queen Kimber." She pulls her phone out of the zippered compartment of her racquet bag. "You need to give me your number, because I think I might love you."

I blush a little at the attention. "I wouldn't say I talked back to her. I was trying to figure out what her deal is. She yelled at me just for *looking at* Jordy."

"Yeah. Those two are tight."

I realize she's still waiting for my phone number. I rattle off my digits. "You said he doesn't date. So they just hook up casually or something?"

"I don't know. Apparently, they've known each other since elementary school. All I know is, she freaks out when he talks to other girls."

I yank open the door to the locker room, my eyes roving across the furniture, floor, ceiling, and everywhere in between as Jade and I head down the main aisle. I stoop down to pick up a stray tennis ball that's lying in front of the sinks. "Well, she needs to calm down because he just offered to help me with my game—that's it."

"Right." Jade picks at her nail polish. "She's probably a little threatened by you."

I glance around, hoping no one heard her. Two girls from the softball team are standing at the mirror messing with their hair. They don't seem to register our presence. Everyone else is either in the showers or already gone.

I lower my voice. "Why would anyone be threatened by me?"

"Because you showed up out of nowhere and you're good." Jade and I turn down the same row of lockers. "How'd you learn to hit like that?"

"Like what?" I drop my racquet bag on the ground and spin the combination for my lock.

"Like a homerun slugger?" She tugs the ponytail holder out of her hair, and it falls around her shoulders like a sheet of volcanic glass. Shiny. Smooth. Perfect.

I can't imagine what it would be like to have hair like that after three hours of exercising. I can't imagine what it would be like to have hair like that *ever*. "I don't know. I played when I was little, but I don't remember hitting that hard. Maybe I have a lot of repressed anger."

"Well, whatever you have, it's working for you. I bet Coach has you playing one of the top spots."

"Doubtful. My serve is terrible. That's why I was talking to Jordy. He said he'd work with me one-on-one." I toss the tennis ball into my locker, grab my street clothes, and tuck them into my backpack. Almost without thinking, I knock three times on the wooden bench. "I think I'm going to shower at home."

Jade tugs her dress over her shoulders and tosses it in her duffel bag. She smirks. "Did you just knock on wood? You nailed our resident tennis god in the junk and his response was to offer you private lessons. I don't think you need any more luck. You are going to be the envy of half the school." She blots the sweat from her arms and stomach with her towel.

"I don't see what's so great about him." I slam the locker shut, trying not to stare at Jade's half-naked body. She's the exact opposite of me, long and lean. I can see the outline of her abs through her skin. I'm not fat, but I've got my mom's curves. Even with regular jogging, the only muscles of mine that are remotely visible are my leg muscles. "Sure, he's nice, and he's cute in a manufactured kind of way, but he seems like just another guy, you know?"

"For most of the girls, I think it's the fame thing. He gets interviewed in national magazines and invited to amazing parties. I heard he got to go to Serena Williams's charity barbecue last month."

"So everyone at this school is shallow, or what?"

"Not everyone. Just seventy percent or so." Jade snickers. She wraps a towel around her body, grabs a caddy with soap and shampoo, and heads for the showers.

"Good to know." I scoff. Then I call after her, "Hey, thanks for pairing up. I'm not very good at getting to know people."

Jade turns back for a second, her dark eyes gleaming. "Something tells me you're better than you think."

CHAPTER 8

The next day, I go from being invisible to being that girl who everyone whispers about and sneaks glances at when they think she's not looking.

I first notice it at lunch. I'm outside again, with my PBJ and my spy girl novel, in the same spot that was completely deserted yesterday. Today it seems like everyone needs to pop out of school and go for a short stroll, just far enough to pass me and then double back to the front doors. I tell myself I'm being paranoid—it happens—but after the third or fourth burst of unexplained giggles I pull my phone out of my purse. I check my hair, my teeth, and my outfit. There's no obvious reason that people should be spontaneously exploding with laughter at the mere sight of me. It has to be because of what happened at tennis tryouts.

As I slip my phone back into my purse, my eyes fall on my luck notebook. I realize I forgot to write down what happened with Jordy. I turn to the section where I record all of the unlucky happenings and their outcomes and jot down a basic description.

Sept 9th. Tennis courts. While playing a practice point, I hit Jordy Wheeler with a tennis ball.

No need to be overly descriptive. It's not like I'll ever forget that moment.

"Hey," a familiar voice says.

I look up to find Jordy standing over me. He's wearing track pants and a T-shirt and his hair is damp like he just got out of the shower. Quickly, I shut the notebook.

"Luck notebook," he reads from the cover.

I silently curse at my twelve-year-old self for being so literal. Did I really have to write that on the outside?

"Did I see my name in that?" His lips twitch.

"No."

He kicks at the toe of my flip-flop with one of his giant feet. He's wearing the latest Nike court shoes. They probably cost more than my racquet. "I think I did."

"Well, you think wrong. It's a project for math class." I slip the notebook back into my purse. "Question. Are random people laughing at you today?"

"I don't know. I just got here." Jordy sits down next to me. "I do school online. I only have to come to get my tests and quizzes proctored. Otherwise they think I'll cheat."

"Would you?"

He chuckles. "Possibly. I'm not really big on school."

I watch a group of three girls exit the lobby and turn the

opposite direction from me. "I'm probably just being paranoid."

"Well, someone from the team uploaded a video of my awkward moment," Jordy says. "They caught you standing at the net looking all cute and apologetic. It might be that."

"Wonderful." I barely register the fact he called me cute. "I thought all of those girls were your friends."

"They are, but everyone loves embarrassing video footage, don't they?" He looks down at his phone. "I'd better get going. See you later."

I sit through the rest of my classes doing my best not to call attention to myself or make eye contact with anyone. If I don't *see* them laughing at me then it's not really happening, right? Except, of course, it is, and I can totally *hear* them.

Psych class is the worst. I'm one of the first people to arrive, as usual. I pull out my textbook and open to the section on Solomon Asch's conformity experiments. It's pretty interesting stuff, really—Asch and his team got people to give clearly wrong answers to basic matching puzzles by setting them up in a group of other people who worked for the experimenters and gave the wrong answer on purpose. The results bothered Asch—evidence of humanity's willingness to go against what we believe is right in order not to look foolish.

But as more and more people saunter into the room and I hear whispers and giggles, I sort of understand how Asch's participants must have felt. Confused. Embarrassed. Ganged up on. I sink farther and farther down in my chair.

Jade takes the seat next to me, seemingly oblivious. "How are things?"

"Crappy as usual," I mumble.

Kimber and Colleen stride up the row between us. Kimber stops to give me a long look. I resist the urge to slide even closer to the ground.

"Coming back to tryouts?" She smoothes invisible wrinkles from a reddish-orange T-shirt dress that looks amazing on her lean frame and dark skin.

I try not to stare. I would look like a tomato if I wore that outfit. Next to her, Colleen is dressed more like me— jeans and a T-shirt. She shifts her book from one arm to the other as she waits for Kimber, who is still waiting for me to respond.

I keep my voice level. "Why wouldn't I?"

From the other side of me Jade adds, "Yeah. Why wouldn't she?"

Kimber's eyes flick to Jade and then back to me. "Just asking," she says. "Things are only going to get harder, and it looked like you were struggling with some of the warm-up exercises."

I decide not to point out that *everyone* was struggling with her insane Navy SEAL calisthenics. "I can handle it," I say coolly.

"That's good to know." She flips a couple pieces of

colored paper onto my desk. "Here's some free passes to my gym, in case you ever want to do a little extra conditioning."

Before I can even form a response, the bell rings and the girls hurry toward their desks at the front of the class. The cotton fabric of Kimber's dress snags on the edge of an empty chair. With a sharp ripping sound, a hole opens next to the seam, exposing part of her muscular thigh.

"Son of a . . ." Kimber mutters, gathering the torn fabric around her.

There's a chorus of sympathetic cooing from the girls by her. One girl fumbles in her purse for a safety pin and hands it across the aisle.

"Please tell me you did that with your mind," Jade whispers with a grin.

I force a weak smile in return, but all I can do is wonder. Coincidence or bad luck?

Today at practice it's Colleen's turn to lead the calisthenics. As we go through a series of one-legged squats and side-to-side sprints, yesterday's overworked muscles start to scream in protest.

Next to me, Jade groans. "I feel as stiff as a board."

"Me too," I say as we drop to the grass for some stretching. "I thought those squats were going to kill me."

"Good thing you got those free gym passes so you can enjoy more of this torture outside of school." Jade rolls her eyes. "Some people are so rude."

Someone taps me on the shoulder from behind. I glance back.

"Hey," Jordy says, his brownish-blond hair blowing forward into his eyes. "Ready to tune up your serve?"

"Sure," I say. "Hope you like a challenge."

We all head down to the courts. Colleen and her doubles partner, a girl named Luisa, pass us on either side. Both of them seem to be smothering giggles.

I grit my teeth. "I am so tired of people laughing at me."

"Everyone's calling you the Ballbuster," Jade pipes up. "You slayed the dragon. You're famous." She cackles. "Or infamous, depending on who you ask."

From my other side, Jordy coughs. "Dragon seems appropriate, but I wouldn't say *slayed*."

My face goes hot. "I keep thinking things can't get any worse, and then they do." I exhale a deep breath of air and concentrate on the ground in front of me.

Jordy nudges me in the ribs. "What are you so upset about? I'm the one whose public castration has six thousand hits on YouTube. You're the girl known for her wicked pinpoint accuracy."

I lift my eyes. He's smiling like the whole thing is just a big joke.

"Don't sell yourself *short*, Jordy," Jade says, a slow grin spreading across her face. "I'm sure it's bigger than a pinpoint."

He laughs. He reaches across me toward Jade like he's

going to grab her. "You wish you knew."

She dances out of his way. "No I don't." She flips back into her fake British accent. "I've no interest in becoming one of your conquests."

Jordy snorts. "Conquests? I think you're giving me too much credit."

"Perhaps." Jade cocks her head to the side. "Perhaps not."

One of the girls on Court Three hollers at her. She ducks through the gate and breaks into a slow jog, leaving Jordy and me standing awkwardly outside the fence.

He turns to me. "I don't have conquests."

I fiddle with the zipper of my racquet bag. "It's none of my business."

"Yeah it is. If we're going to practice together, I don't want you thinking I'm some predator."

"Fine," I say. "Noted." I don't really care if he has conquests or not. The whole school might be in love with him, but to me he's just a guy helping me with my serve.

We end up practicing on Court Two, between Kimber and Colleen on Court One and Jade and a girl named Penn on Court Three. Penn looks like a catalog model—tall and tanned, with shoulder-length cornsilk-blonde hair secured in a braid and a thin headband taming her flyaways. She's really good, though, chasing down every ball Jade hits and directing them at the far corners of the court.

"Nice shot," Jordy says after she rockets a ball cross-court out of Jade's reach.

"Thanks." She flashes him a smile. Sliding a ball out from a pocket sewn into her tennis trunks, she goes to the baseline and prepares to serve.

I trace the movement of her long, lean form as she tosses the ball high, brings her racquet back, coils her body, and launches herself upward into the serve. The ball goes over the net and lands on the outside line of the service box. It's perfect, just like she is. Jordy is still watching her, and I wonder for a second if she got a lecture from Kimber too.

"That's how you want your serve to look," Jordy yells from across the net. He pulls a ball out of his pocket and tosses it to me.

I do a five-second check and then attempt to imitate Penn's service motion. My ball slams into the tape and rico-chets off at an angle, spiraling its way through the middle of Court One just as Kimber is approaching the net.

She stops short as my ball rolls right in front of her. "You're going to have to do better than that, New Girl." She scoops up the ball with her racquet and hits it in my direction.

Jordy jogs around to my side of the court. "You want your toss high and out in front of you." He sets his racquet on the ground, the handle almost perpendicular to my front foot. He puts a ball in my hand and then wraps his hand around mine. "Don't let go yet." He demonstrates the movement my arm should make. "Smooth. Relaxed," he says. "Use your shoulder. Don't bend your elbow or wrist. You want the ball to fall close to where the face of my racquet is right now."

I feel anything but relaxed. *Focus, Maguire.* I try not to notice Kimber and Colleen stopping to watch us. I try not to focus on the sensation of Jordy's hand still wrapped around mine, the tickle of his arm hair brushing against my wrist.

"Ignore them. There's no one here but you and me," he says. "Now just toss a few balls up to get a feel for it. Use your backswing, but don't hit them."

Trying my best to pretend the rest of the tennis team doesn't exist, I toss a ball up in the air. It lands behind me.

Jordy bounces me another ball. "Try again. Use your fingertips instead of your whole hand. That'll make you less likely to wrist it."

The next three balls land too far in front of me or too far off to the side. But eventually I toss one up that lands on the face of Jordy's racquet.

"Better." He grins at me. "Okay, now we're going to add in the whole service motion." He positions himself behind me and rests his hands lightly on my arms. He walks me through an imaginary serve.

His touch makes me blush. He smells like a mix of sweat and Christmas trees, a blend that's strangely appealing.

"Remember, you want your arm to be fully extended when you make contact with the ball. For right now don't worry too much about your aim. Just work on a proper toss."

He backs up, and I get to work. I try about twenty practice serves but only get four of them over the net. Discouraged, I swing my racquet in a vicious arc. "I'm hopeless, aren't I?"

"Nobody's hopeless," Jordy says. "Using your shoulder is going to throw you off until muscle memory takes over. But once it does you'll be fine. Keep working. I'm going to go check on everyone else."

I scan the area to make sure there's no one nearby that I might accidentally hit, no one in danger of tripping on cracks or slipping on runaway balls. Some of the girls are serving, and some are playing practice points. Everyone seems safe.

I turn back to the ball hopper. I focus on my toss and on hitting the ball with my arm completely extended. Gradually, the noise from surrounding courts fades into the background. Gradually, my serves start going over the net. They still suck, but they suck less than they did yesterday.

When Coach announces that practice is over, it hits me that for the past hour I haven't done any five-second checks.

All I've been thinking about is tennis. And it feels good.

CHAPTER 9

I take a quick shower and stuff my towel and sweaty clothes into my backpack. I slip out of the locker room, relieved to see the hallway empty. My flip-flops squeak on the linoleum and my thick black bun drips water down the back of my neck.

"Hey." Jordy appears behind me, also fresh from the shower.

"Hey." I smile and keep walking.

"The activity buses are already gone. Do you need a ride home?"

I think of the words "Ride in a car with someone besides Mom" written on the last page of my luck notebook. I'm not ready. I shake my head quickly. "It's cool. I usually walk."

"Oh yeah? Where do you live?"

I pause. If I tell him the truth, he'll insist on driving me, since it's over a mile away. Then I'll have to come up with an explanation for why I don't take rides from people. But who lies about where they *live*? That seems like plunging headfirst down the slipperiest of slopes.

Jordy whistles under his breath. "It's not a trick question."

"Yeah. I know. I just—" I just nothing. There is no logical reason for me not to answer. I sigh. Life was easier when I didn't talk to anyone.

"Wow. Yesterday I get your whole life story without even asking, and today everything's a secret?" Jordy shakes his head in dismay. "Your erratic behavior is making it difficult for me to form snap judgments."

I laugh under my breath. "Well, we can't have that, can we?" I turn and head down the long hallway that runs from the locker rooms to the gym.

"Seriously," he continues. "Do you think I'm some crazed stalker who's going to come watch you sleep?"

"No, it's just . . ."

I trail off at the sound of tennis shoes squeaking behind us. Three guys from the basketball team are heading down the hallway, still wearing their mesh practice jerseys. One of them is bouncing a blue-and-gray basketball.

"Jordo!" The guy with the ball palms it and gives Jordy a high five. "I don't know why you don't come manage us instead of hanging out with the girls' tennis team." He pauses, his lips curling into a sly smile. "Or maybe I do." He and his friends look appraisingly at me, like I'm a new phone or video game console they've never seen before.

"Is this her?" The guy tosses the basketball against the nearest locker and catches it. "The Ballbuster?"

"Shut up," I say, the words coming out harsher than I expected.

"Yeah. Shut it, Chris," Jordy says. "Don't you have anything more interesting to talk about?"

Chris passes the ball to a guy wearing a number five jersey and raises his hands in mock surrender. "Damn, Jordo. Your girlfriend is hot, but she's kind of mouthy. You might want to do something about that."

"Whatever, dude." Jordy swipes the ball from Number 5 and flings it the length of the hallway. "You guys might want to do something about your turnover percentage."

Number 5 swears under his breath and takes off after the ball.

"And I'm *not* his girlfriend," I add.

"Good to know," Chris drawls. He gives me another long look before he and his friend stroll leisurely after their teammate.

I turn to Jordy as they disappear. "Nice move. Friends of yours?"

"Yeah. They're harmless." He pauses. "You sure didn't waste any time setting them straight."

I nibble on one of my pinkie nails. "What do you mean?"

"And I'm *not* his girlfriend," he mimics. "Wouldn't want anyone to get the wrong idea, eh?" His voice is joking, but his jaw is tense. "You know, there are girls at this school who would love to be my girlfriend."

I snort. "So I've heard."

"But not you, obviously." He's looking forward, watching Chris and his friends disappear around the next corner.

Keeping my voice light, I say, "I barely know you. Plus, maybe I just didn't feel like giving people another reason to talk about me." I plaster a smile on my face. "Besides, I heard you were . . . unavailable."

"Who told you that? One of my conquests?" Jordy's voice drips with sarcasm.

"Multiple people. You don't date. All you do is play tennis. You are . . . singularly focused." We pass the cafeteria and head toward the lobby.

He sighs. "It's true. My whole life is tennis right now. Well, tennis and studying. My parents are always cracking the whip about one or the other."

"I think I'm going to go for a little singular focus myself. Maybe then I won't get cut from the team."

Jordy steps in front of me to hold the door. "You're not going to get cut," he says. "Coach is peeing his pants about you. All you need is a decent serve."

"I guess I know what I'll be doing all weekend."

"I won't be at tryouts tomorrow, but I have some time on Saturday if you want to practice. Just you and me. No Kimber rolling her eyes or Coach giving you a hard time."

I blink rapidly as I step out into the sun. "You just said you're too busy to have a life. How could you have time to practice with me?"

"Even I get a few hours of free time occasionally," Jordy says. "And it'll qualify for this week's shrink homework too, so win–win."

I want to ask him what the assignment is, but then he might ask me about mine, and I don't feel like trying to explain my curse. "Okay, if you're sure. That would be cool."

Jordy pauses at the bottom of the steps. "My parents are members at the Pacific Point Tennis Club, so I can usually get a court. What time should I pick you up?"

I've never been inside the tennis club, but I've driven by there, and the parking lot is always packed. "Is there any place less crowded we could go?" My fingers reach out to grip the wooden handrail of the stairs. I tap it three times with one finger, hoping Jordy doesn't notice.

He looks up at me, a teasing grin on his face. "Are you saying you want to be alone with me?"

I blush. "No, I just thought it might be easier to learn with fewer people watching."

"Sorry. There I go again with the slick asshole jokes," he says. "I know a place. How about if I pick you up around eleven?"

"I can meet you there," I say quickly, descending the rest of the steps so we're back on even ground.

"Oooookay." Jordy pulls a plain black key ring from the

pocket of his warm-up pants as we head for the parking lot. "So you *do* think I'm a crazed stalker. That or a bad driver maybe?"

I sigh again. He's not going to let up without an explanation. Maybe I'm the only girl in the history of ever who refused a ride home from him. "I was in a car accident when I was young," I say. "People died. Now I get freaked out riding with people I don't know."

The grin melts off Jordy's face. "Oh, I'm sorry. Your dad?"

I nod. "It's okay. It was a long time ago." A trickle of water runs from my hairline down over my temple.

Jordy reaches up and brushes it away. "It looks like it still hurts a lot."

I flinch inwardly, surprised by the softness of his touch. "People keep telling me that time heals all wounds, but it's been almost five years and I can't even make a scab grow, you know?" Tears rise up from nowhere and I turn away.

Jordy places a hand on my shoulder. "Time doesn't heal anything. It's like drinking. The best it can do is help you forget, if you're lucky."

"Guess I'm not lucky," I say softly.

But I already knew that.

CHAPTER 10
Session #6

Dr. Leed is listening to the same wailing guitar music as usual when I stroll into his office on Friday. The chords sound even darker this week, like maybe his secret second life isn't going so well.

"It's pretty," I say. "But sad."

He tucks his phone into his desk drawer and turns his chair around so he's facing me. He polishes his glasses on his shirt. "What is?"

"Your music."

"Ah," he says. "I agree. What about you? Are you sad?"

I shake my head. "I'm working on making the tennis team. Official tryouts are next week, but we've been practicing for the past couple of days."

"And?" He arches an eyebrow. "No loss of life?"

"Well, I did hit someone with a ball." I blush just thinking about it. "It was pretty awkward."

"Was she mad at you?"

"No." I decide to let Dr. Leed think it was a girl. No need to get into the details of that moment ever again. "She said she'd been hurt worse before playing tennis. And then she even offered to help me with my serve."

"So then that sounds like a good thing," Dr. Leed points out.

"Yeah, I guess. This girl, er, other girl started talking to me more after it happened, too. She's sort of becoming my friend."

"So then that sounds like *two* good things."

"Yeah, maybe."

"What's next on your list of therapy challenges?"

"Ride in a car with someone."

"Do you feel ready?"

I shake my head. "Not sure I ever will, though."

"Just remember that your first challenge is going okay, and you even made some friends. And trust your gut. You'll know when it's time."

I think back to what it was like to ride with my mom after the accident. "Can you medicate me or something to make it easier?"

Dr. Leed studies me for a moment. "Do you think you need medication?"

"Well, I just mean to get past that initial fear of getting in someone else's car." My chest gets a little tight just thinking about it.

"I can discuss medication options with your pediatrician

if you want me to, but I'd prefer not to use it as a first-line treatment in your case unless you're unable to even attempt your challenges."

"Okay," I say. "I'll try."

As usual, Jordy is reading a magazine in the waiting room. He straightens up when he sees me. "You kept the same appointment time."

"Yeah. I can make it if I come directly here after practice, but if I make the team I'll probably have to reschedule on match days."

He rolls the magazine into a cylinder with his hands. "Cool. I enjoy our little meetings."

"But you see me almost every day at practice." A terrible thought hits me. "Wait, am I getting cut?"

His eyes widen. "No, no. Like I said, we'll get your serve fixed." He tightens the magazine even further between his hands.

"Well, I should go."

"Yeah, me too," he says. "I mean, not go, but you know."

"You ready, Stanford?" The receptionist smiles brightly at Jordy from behind her desk.

I cough. "Stanford?"

"Yes, my parents named me Stanford. Jordan is actually my middle name." He sighs. "Soon you'll know *all* my secrets."

"Do you moonlight as a stockbroker or something?"

"Yeah, an elderly stockbroker. Make way for Stanford, everyone. He's coming through with his walker." Jordy makes a gagging sound. "And the nickname possibilities are epic. Stan? Ford? Either one would be irresistible to the ladies, am I right?" He continues without giving me a chance to respond. "Thank God my coach recommended I compete under my nickname. Otherwise all I'd have to look forward to would be denture cream endorsements."

"It's not *that* bad," I say.

"Yeah, well. Thanks for lying." Jordy gives me a gentle punch in the arm as he heads for Dr. Leed's office. "See you tomorrow, Maguire."

CHAPTER 11

The next day I wake up thinking about Jordy, about how he seemed hurt when I told the guys from the basketball team that I wasn't his girlfriend, about the way he seemed a little awkward and unsure of himself at Dr. Leed's.

Shaking my head, I start my morning good luck rituals. First, I lift a hand to my throat to make sure my mystic knot amulet is still in place. I slide the clasp to the back of my neck and wish for a safe, uneventful day. I knock three times on my wooden nightstand and then dab a bit of jasmine perfume from a tiny heart-shaped vial on each of my wrists. The manufacturers of the perfume claim it's made with water from a special Himalayan stream and has been blessed by Nepali monks.

Just one more ritual to complete before I slide out of bed—my daily positive affirmation. I know it sounds cheesy, but a lot of people swear that starting your day with a positive thought makes a difference, and I'm in no position to ignore stuff that works just because I feel lame doing it. Most people say something like, "Today is going to be a great day." I try to keep things a little more realistic, like, "Today isn't going to be as bad as the day of Celia Bittendorf's sleepover party when everyone but me started throwing up and Celia told her parents I poisoned the cake and then her mom called my mom and I got picked up at midnight and everyone at school avoided me for the rest of the year."

Okay, maybe that's a little long.

"Today is not going to suck," I mutter.

Standing in front of my dresser mirror, I recite a Chinese good luck prayer eight times. (Eight is a lucky number in Chinese.) I twist my hair into a bun and then cruise into the kitchen to look for food.

After managing only a few bites of fruit for breakfast, I return to my room, get dressed, and then try to read. I end up staring at the same couple of pages for about ten minutes. I trade my novel for my trig homework and do a little better with that, completing a handful of problems.

Hopping up from my bed, I tug at the hem of my new wraparound tennis skirt and stare at myself in the mirror. "Stop fidgeting," I tell my reflection. "You're going to be fine." I mean, pretty much the worst thing that could possibly happen on a tennis court already has, right?

Well, except for that one death at Wimbledon.

Which I don't want to think about.

I grab my phone and send Jade a text.

Me: Guess what I'm doing today?

Her: Studying?

Me: Ha. It's like you know me so well. That's what I was doing five minutes ago. Now I'm getting ready to go practice serving with Jordy.

Her: Where are you guys playing?

Me: Not sure. I'm meeting him at his house.

Her: Uh-huh ;) Try not to let him get you naked until at least the second "practice session."

Me: I take it back—it's like you don't know me at all! I'm not some sheep who would just sleep with a guy who snapped his fingers.

Her: Yeah, but. He's cute. He's famous. He's just goofy enough to seem harmless . . .

Me: Well I've never even kissed a guy before, so . . .

Her: OMG. You neither? I thought I was the world's last unkissed 16-year-old. That makes it even more danger-ous. You're like fresh meat and he's a tiger!

Me: LOL. He is not a tiger. More like a baby giraffe.

Her: Just keep your guard up. That's all I'm saying.

Me: Okay, Mom. Talk to you later.

My actual mom knocks gently on my doorframe and then peeks her head through the open doorway. She's got my baby brother, Jacob, balanced on one hip. He makes a sort of burping-giggling noise when he sees me.

"This boy must like you if he's willing to help you out like this," she says.

I debate explaining to my mom how Jordy is singularly focused, but I decide that might encourage a conversation I don't want to have about how I should be dating. "I have to get going," I say.

"Do you need the car?"

As scared as I am of riding with strangers, maybe it seems weird that I can drive myself places, but it's all about feeling in control. If I'm behind the wheel, I can go slow. I can establish safe space cushions and pull off crowded freeways. I can force myself to stay focused. Riding with someone else means trusting them not just with my life, but with theirs too, and with the lives of everyone else out on the road. And I've never found anyone who drives as carefully as I do.

I grab my racquet bag from the floor in front of my bed. "Yeah. If you don't mind."

"Okay." My mom leans in and gives me a kiss on the forehead. "Have fun."

"I'll try." I give Jake a little tickle under the chin and then squeeze past Mom and head for the door.

Erin is parked on the living room floor watching a TV show about dinosaurs. She's drinking pink milk from a cereal bowl one spoonful at a time. "Mack Wire!" she says. "Where you going?"

"To play tennis."

"Can I play too?" The spoon wobbles in her little hand, and a bit of milk dribbles onto the carpet.

"Maybe next time," I tell her. "Be careful with your spoon."

She glances at the damp spot on the carpet and then back up at me. She rubs at the spot with her foot, and her sock soaks up the milk. "All better," she says.

I smile. "All better." I wish I could fix things as easily as she can.

A twinge of nerves radiates through my body as I park the car across the street from a two-story house made of pale pink stucco.

I stroll up the driveway and knock gently on the door. Once. Twice. Three times. I check out the yard while I'm waiting. A row of palm trees casts spiny shadows over the front of the house. A marble birdbath sits between a pair of flower beds, bits of scattered leaves and debris floating on the surface of the water.

The front door opens with a soft creak. Jordy looks down at me through the screen door. He's wearing black mesh shorts, a T-shirt, and a visor. "You came," he says.

I wipe my hands nervously on my tennis skirt. "Were you expecting me not to?"

"I don't know." His lips curl upward, and from this close I can see the way his eyes change, the way his whole body seems to relax in tandem with his grin. I can't believe I ever found his smile manufactured. "I haven't really figured you out yet." He opens the screen door and I step inside.

I follow Jordy through a foyer with a vaulted ceiling into a living room with a white leather L-shaped sofa and glass coffee tables. There's not a speck of dust anywhere.

"Your house is really pretty." I stand frozen in place, like I'm afraid to touch anything for fear of getting it dirty.

"Thanks. But it's my parents' house. I just live here."

"Are they around?" I shift my weight from one foot to the other.

"I think they said something about a wine tasting. I didn't press for information. They feel more like jailers than parents sometimes, so any day I get to myself is a major bonus."

"Well, at least it's a nice place to be imprisoned. Do you have a tennis court here? Or are we going somewhere?"

Jordy pulls the silver cord on a set of vertical blinds and they swish to the side, revealing a sliding glass door that leads out into a backyard with a bright orange tennis court. A hopper of balls is already set up behind the baseline, waiting for me.

"Excellent," I say. "Now I can mess up as much as I want without a whole club full of people staring at me."

He lifts a fist to his mouth to stifle a yawn. "Well, chances are they'd be staring at me, but yeah, okay, if it makes you feel better."

I crack a smile. "Your arrogance is kind of refreshing."

"Thanks," he says. "Honed by years of practice. Now

let's get going. I want twenty serves over the net to start. Remember, good toss. Use your shoulder."

It takes me about fifteen minutes and forty-five tries to get the twenty good serves Jordy wants from me. He stands patiently on the other side of the net and returns each ball I manage to put in play. By the time I hit the last ball over the net I'm sweating like crazy, but my new toss is starting to feel less awkward.

He jogs around to my side of the net. "Better."

"You're a good teacher." I blot sweat from my forehead with the back of my hand.

"You're a good student." Without warning, he leans in close to me, so close I can see the sprinkling of freckles across the bridge of his nose and smell the sharp woodsy scent of his deodorant. His fingertips land on the clasp of my necklace, which has worked its way around to the front so it's next to my mystic knot. "Make a wish." He twists the chain so the clasp is in the back again.

"I wish I knew how to serve."

"Shh." His pupils dilate. "You're not supposed to tell it to me. Now we're going to have to practice twice as hard."

"How do you know about wishing on necklaces, anyway?" I spin my racquet between my palms.

"My sister likes to wish on everything." Jordy pulls a water bottle out of his tennis bag and takes a long drink. "What about you? Do you have sisters or brothers?"

Connor's face flashes before me. Green eyes. Dark hair.

Another replica of my mom. Maybe it's weird, but when I think of my brother, I think of the eighteen-year-old he would have been, not the thirteen-year-old who died. I think of the way his voice would sound now, of how we'd fight over my mom's car, of how he'd be overprotective of me and threaten to mess up any guy who broke my heart.

"I have a half sister and a half brother," I say finally. "Erin is two and a half and Jake is a month old." I fumble in my bag for my own water bottle and take a long drink.

"Cool," Jordy says. He leaves me on the side with the hopper of balls and jogs around to the far side of the court. "Start putting back in your power and angles, but don't lose your new toss. Let's try for forty more good serves. Twenty down the center and twenty out wide."

"You're a slave driver," I joke. But I do a quick five-second check and then get to work. I go from left to right and serve balls at Jordy. Slowly but surely I find the body position and toss I need in order to aim my serve in different spots. Jordy returns most of the balls softly, just over the net, so they'll be easy for me to retrieve. Occasionally, though, he cranks one cross-court or down the line, painting the outside stripe of the singles court.

"Showoff," I say after a ball blazes past me almost too fast to even see.

He cracks his neck from side to side and rolls his shoulders back. "Might as well have a little fun, right?"

After I land my fortieth serve over the net, Jordy and I

hit around for about an hour, and then we call it quits. I help him collect all of the loose tennis balls and place them back in the metal hopper.

"You're doing a lot better," he says.

"Thanks. I'm feeling a lot better."

"Awesome. We should celebrate." He pauses. "What are you doing later?"

"What?" I say, even though I'm pretty sure I heard him just fine.

"I was going to invite you to a barbecue," he says. "My parents almost never let me go out, but Kimber is throwing it and she's a friend of the family. Plus she lives right down the street."

"Kimber from the team?"

"The one and only. You should come. Lots of tennis people will be there."

"Is that supposed to be a plus?" I grin.

Jordy laughs. My insides go a little wobbly. For a second I imagine a life where I could say yes, where I could go to a party again and not worry about anyone getting hurt. That reality feels even further away than the one where I get on a plane to Ireland in three months.

"We're not all bad," he says.

I snort. "I don't think Kimber likes me. She implied I was out of shape and then offered me some free passes to her gym."

Jordy snickers. "Sorry, that's not funny, but don't take

it personally. She's just intense like that. To Kimber, if you don't eat, sleep, and breathe tennis, you're not committed enough. She's probably in better shape than I am."

"Yeah. Well, thanks for the invite, but I've got some stuff to do." Looking down, I tug on the hem of my shirt, suddenly aware of how clingy my clothes are now that I'm all sweaty.

Jordy's grin fades for a second, but he recovers quickly. "If you have a boyfriend or whatever, you can invite him too."

"I don't have a boyfriend. I just . . . can't go."

"You really don't like me at all, do you?" His smile falters again. He's clearly not used to being rejected.

"It's not that. It's—"

Jordy cuts me off before I can come up with a specific excuse. "I find that kind of . . . what was the word you used? Refreshing."

"What?"

"Most of the girls around here hang all over me, but it's only because they see me on TV and stuff. It's just nice to know there are people out there who don't care about any of that." He heads across the impeccably manicured back lawn, the ball hopper in one hand, his racquet bag in the other.

I follow him back into the living room and slide the door closed behind me. "I've never known anyone famous," I say, making air quotes around the "famous" part. "So you're just a regular guy to me."

"I'm just a regular guy, period. I wish more people would get with that program." He sets the hopper down just inside the door. "How about we have our own barbecue instead? Or better yet, do you like California burritos?"

"Are they different from Mexican burritos?"

Jordy gasps. "You've never had a California burrito? With the best carne asada and guacamole north of the border, wrapped in a tortilla and stuffed with French fries?"

"You sound like a commercial." I raise an eyebrow. "French fries in a burrito? Is that part of your athlete diet?"

"Only when my mother isn't looking. Hang out for an hour; you have to try one."

Before I can reply, he grabs a cell phone from the glass coffee table. "You have to," he mouths. I listen as he orders multiple burritos and a variety of sauces to go with them. Then he tosses his phone back onto the table and looks at me. "Thirty minutes," he says. "Thirty minutes until your life changes forever."

"Must be some burrito." I tug at the hem of my shirt again.

"You have no idea."

"Okay." I fumble in the zippered pocket of my racquet bag. "I've got about ten dollars—"

"My treat," Jordy says. "And by that I mean my parents' treat."

"But I shouldn't—"

"Yes you should." He rests his hand on top of mine and

zips my bag closed. His fingers are really warm. "Like I said, helping you with your serve is helping me with my shrink homework. And trust me, my parents are paying a lot more than the price of a burrito for therapy."

I set my bag on the carpet next to the tennis ball hopper. "You just seem so together . . ."

He flops down on the sofa. "Ha. Glad I've got one of us fooled."

I lean against the wall that separates the living room from the dining room. "No, seriously. You seem like the least likely person ever to need a therapist."

He makes a face. "I hated it at first. I swear I thought my mom picked Daniel on purpose just as one more subtle reminder that Real Jordy isn't very impressive without Tennis Player Jordy to go along with him."

"What do you mean?"

He snorts. "Oh, come on. Daniel's young. He's smart. He's successful. He's probably rich. All the girls think he's hot. And then there's me. I'm . . . young."

"Dr. Leed is almost as old as my stepdad," I say. Which is probably true; Tom is five years younger than my mom. "Besides, as far as I can tell, all the girls think *you're* hot."

Jordy sighs deeply. "Not me. Tennis Player Jordy is hot. Real Jordy tries hard, but he's just a tall goofy guy who sucks at math."

I tilt my head to the side and study him for a moment. His words feel unsure, insecure even. But the way he's delivering them so openly makes him seem more like someone really comfortable in his own skin. "Who are you being right now?"

He flips his visor around backward and rests his head in his hands. "I don't even know. How sad is that? I want to be real, but I also want to impress you, and Tennis Player Jordy is a lot more impressive." He looks away, his gaze falling on the case full of trophies and ribbons along the side wall of the living room, the mantel covered in plaques and plates from tournament victories. "That's the whole point of Daniel, to figure out how to be a professional tennis player without losing myself completely." He looks back at me. "That's my goal, you know? To decide for sure who I want to be and be that guy, regardless of what anyone else thinks."

My eyes flick from the trophies back to Jordy. It occurs to me I haven't done a five-second check in a while. I scan the living room and backyard. "I'm sure you'll figure it out," I say finally.

Jordy tosses me a remote control. "Too much heavy conversation. Let's kill our brains with TV like regular people." He gives me another megawatt smile, but this one doesn't quite reach his eyes. It's almost like he's reset himself, like I caught a glimpse of the real him but now he's done sharing.

"Good idea." I sit next to him on the sofa, praying I won't leave any sweaty spots on the leather when I get up later. Crossing my legs, I adjust my skirt for maximum coverage. I aim the remote at the TV, and the screen comes to life. I flip through a few channels and stop on Animal Planet. It's a show about the ocean.

Jordy adjusts his body on the sofa, his bare leg brushing against mine. He exhales deeply. "I sure hope this doesn't have dolphins. I *hate* dolphins." He smirks. "You know, I think you can get kicked out of San Diego for saying that."

I elbow him in the ribs. "I never said I hated dolphins. Just that everyone probably—"

He holds his hands in front of his face as a pair of bottlenose dolphins appear on the screen. "My eyes. My eyes. Make it stop."

"You're an idiot." I slap him on the leg with the remote, but I can't keep from smiling.

He drops his hands to his lap. "Finally! Finally someone sees the real me." He lowers his voice. "I think this is the part where you're supposed to run away."

On TV, the two dolphins circle around each other, clicking and squeaking. I glance over at them and then back at him.

I shake my head. "I don't want to leave."

"Oh yeah? Why not?"

I blink innocently. "Because I'm hungry."

"Oh, you're a mean one. Just for that." Jordy grabs the remote and turns the volume all the way up. The dolphin chatter is joined by the shrill call of a whale.

"Ah!" I cover my ears.

The doorbell rings and Jordy springs up to answer it.

I flail for the remote and punch the volume back down to normal.

He strolls back into the living room a couple of minutes later and drops a greasy brown bag on the glass coffee table. I glance from the food bag to the table to the pristine leather sofa. "What's the penalty for spilling on the furniture around here?"

"Death by landscaping, I think. How are you with a Weedwacker?" Jordy grins.

I cringe at the thought. "I try to avoid sharp, whirring blades. But I'm good with these." I hold up my hands.

"Yeah, but you're going to need those for tennis, and my mom has been known to work people to the bone. Hang on a minute." He disappears and returns with napkins, paper plates, and a woven Mexican blanket. He drapes the blanket across the white leather. Plucking the bag of burritos from the table, he wipes at the condensation on the glass with one corner of the blanket. Then he grabs a magazine from a nearby end table and uses it as a base for the food. "There we go. Now if we spill I can just toss this blanket in the washer."

I sit on one end of the sofa, a paper plate with a foil-wrapped burrito balanced on my lap. Jordy grabs a burrito for himself and then skims through the channels, pausing for a moment on a tennis match.

"What is it?" I ask.

"A repeat of the US Open finals."

I watch the players cover the court effortlessly as I bite

into my burrito. It's a mix of piping hot French fries, spicy meat, and cool guacamole. The different flavors and textures all meld together in my mouth. I swallow and blot my lips. "This is amazing."

"Yes it is." Jordy squirts a packet of hot sauce on his burrito and takes a huge bite.

I gesture at the TV. "So are you really good enough to play tournaments like that?"

"I made it to the quarterfinals last year. This year all my friends went without me because my parents decided I should skip it." He rolls his eyes. "I'm recovering from a knee injury."

"Seriously? You don't seem injured to me."

"I'm mostly back to normal, but they thought if I did poorly in the Junior Open it would hurt my ranking. So I'm just playing local satellite tournaments until I'm completely healed. I'm hoping once I finish the requirements for my diploma that my parents will let me turn pro."

"You're eighteen, right? Could they actually stop you?"

He sighs. "No, but there's a lot involved in being on the tour. Travel and tournament draws and ranking points and payouts. I don't know enough to handle all that stuff by myself." He trains his eyes on his lap. "I guess it sounds lame, but I need my parents."

"I don't think that's lame." I remember the big gaping hole left by my dad's absence in the months following the accident. He'd been the one who went to my parent–teacher conferences, the one who taught me mnemonics to memorize the Great Lakes and the Earth's atmospheres. Whenever I did something silly, my dad always made me feel better by telling me a story from the firehouse about someone who had done something even sillier. Sometimes you don't realize all the things a person does for you until they aren't there to do them anymore.

"Plus my future is their dream too," Jordy says. "I want to share it, but it sucks that we want different things. They want me to play collegiate tennis instead of turning pro—let my game mature, get a degree to fall back on."

"Does it stress you out? All of those expectations?"

He takes another bite of his burrito and chews thoughtfully. "Yes. Yes it does. I wish more people would ask me that."

I angle my body so I can see both Jordy and the TV. "It seems like an obvious question."

"Usually all people our age care about is how awesome it is to be an athlete. How many famous people have I met? What awesome trips have I gotten to take?" He twists his napkin into a rope and coils it around one hand. "And then the adults, they only care about my grades or how my game is or whether I'm behaving in public."

"I'm sure they care about more than that." I bite into my burrito again, trying not to drip sauce down my chin.

"Yeah, maybe." He doesn't look convinced.

I swallow another mouthful of meat, cheese, and French

fries. "So how do you handle it—all the expectations?"

"Poorly?" Jordy drops his twisted napkin onto the table and reaches for another packet of sauce. "Apparently I do things like cancel weekend practice sessions to help pretty girls."

"Jordy!" His name feels strange on my lips. "You shouldn't have skipped your own stuff to help me."

"One or two missed practices won't kill me, as long as my coach doesn't narc me out to my parents. I told him I was hitting around with one of my friends, so mostly true, right?" He drizzles more sauce on his burrito.

"I don't want you to skip practices for me," I say firmly.

"Okay, but it wasn't just for you—it was for shrink homework too. Plus sometimes I just need a break. I need to hang out with someone who I can be real with."

Before I can respond, the front door opens and the alarm system starts beeping quietly. Instinctively, I slide away from Jordy and focus my attention on my burrito.

"Probably just my sister," he says. He starts to say something else, but then the beeping turns into a shrill electronic siren.

CHAPTER 12

"Crap." Jordy jumps up from the sofa.

I follow him into the foyer, where a blonde girl in jeans and a T-shirt is busy punching buttons on a control panel just inside the door. Her hair is hanging in her face, and she's got smudges of something black on one arm. It takes me a second to recognize her.

"Jesus, Penn," Jordy says. "How hard is it to remember the code?"

"I feel like Dad changes it every week now," she hollers over the shrieking.

Jordy slides in next to her and punches a few buttons. The noise stops. A phone rings. "That'll be the security people," he says.

"I'll go call off the dogs." Penn strides across the foyer and into the dining room.

"Penn is your sister?" I hiss.

"Stanford and Penn," Jordy says. "My parents' alma

maters. Are you actually surprised?"

Penn answers the phone, nodding to herself and then pressing a few keys on the keypad. "We're good." She turns back toward the foyer and notices me for the first time. "Oh, hello." Her eyes take in every inch of me. Then her gaze flips to her brother, an unreadable expression on her face. "Didn't you tell Mom and Dad you were going to Kimber's barbecue?"

"I might stop by later," he says. "I'm assuming you didn't come from there looking like that."

Penn picks at a bit of dirt under her fingernails. "I was going to go, but then Alex from across the street said his dad was letting him rebuild a transmission. I asked if I could watch, and they let me help." She licks her finger and rubs at one of the smudges on her arm.

"I don't think we've officially met," I say. "I'm Maguire."

"I know who you are." Penn smiles sunnily. Her gaze flicks back to her brother. "Did you tell her about the time *I* hit you playing tennis?"

"You mean when you broke my nose?" Jordy swings a pretend racquet with an exaggerated follow through. "We were playing doubles a few years back. She cracked me right in the face with her racquet." He scoffs. "And then had the nerve to start crying like it was all a big accident. I know she did it on purpose."

She grins at him. "I couldn't stand the thought of you being prettier than me."

He flicks her in the side of the head with one finger. "I'm still prettier than you."

"Dream on. What are you guys eating? It smells amazing." She stops short when she sees the rumpled blanket on the sofa. "Ooh. This looks cozy. Did I interrupt something?" Her eyes gleam as she looks back and forth from Jordy to me.

"No. I mean, we weren't—" I fumble.

Jordy slings an arm around my shoulders. "We were working on her serve and then we decided to order food and not trash the furniture. I got you a burrito, but I might eat it myself if you're going to scare off my friend."

"Friend, huh?" Penn says. "Too bad. I thought maybe you were finally going to tell Mom where to go."

"One rebel in the family is enough." Jordy's still got his arm around me. His fingertips are tickling my collarbone.

A tense moment passes between him and his sister, one of those beats of silence where expressions convey whole paragraphs, where teasing is more than what it appears to be. I suddenly feel like I don't belong here.

Shaking off Jordy's arm, I fish my phone out of my racquet bag to check the time. "I should probably head home."

"Hey, don't leave on my account, *friend*. I'm going to go shower off this grease, but I'll be back for that burrito." Penn gives us a little wave and then jogs up the stairs.

"Sorry about that," Jordy says, after she disappears. "She can be a shit disturber sometimes."

"I like her," I say. "She says what's on her mind. People

like that are a little scary, but they're easy to trust."

"Yeah, I guess you're right." He flops back down on the sofa. "Speaking of trust. Are you going to tell me *your* goal?"

"Um . . . make the tennis team?"

"No, not that. Your therapy goal."

I want to tell him that it's private, but he told me his. And maybe it would be good for someone else to know. At least Jordy won't judge me for seeing a shrink. "I want to go to Ireland in December." I tell him about Grandma Siobhan and the memorial service. About how I'm not sure I can get on the plane.

"Maybe we can help each other out with our homework," he says. "What's your next assignment?"

I make a face. "Ride in a car with someone else."

"So what's the holdup?"

"I'm scared. I feel like whoever I ask might end up getting hurt," I admit.

Jordy furrows his brow. "Why would you think that?"

"I'm not just afraid of public transportation. I'm basically afraid of public everything. Bad things happen to other people when I'm around." I sigh. "It's like I'm bad luck."

Jordy rubs the bridge of his nose as he studies me for a moment. "Wait a second. That's what that notebook was about, right? Your luck notebook!"

"That doesn't have anything to do with . . ." I trail off, unable to bring myself to lie.

He squares his shoulders. "Yes it does. What's the deal

with that? And don't tell me it's a math project. I know I saw my name in there."

I slouch forward, rubbing my temples with my fingertips. "I keep track of when people get hurt around me. It wasn't just the car accident. There have been . . . other things." I swallow hard. "I know it sounds crazy, but it's almost like I'm . . . cursed."

"Cursed?" Jordy stares at me, waiting for a punch line that's not coming. "So you're *seriously* afraid that if you ask someone to drive you somewhere, something bad might happen?"

I pick at a loose thread on my tennis skirt. "The chances of something bad happening are a lot higher than if I just stay home and do my own thing like usual."

"But if you use that logic, why ever leave the house?"

The bleak expression on my face tells him everything he needs to know.

He reclines back on the sofa. "How do you live like that? How do you even go to school?"

"I tried to get my mom to homeschool me, but she refused." My finger is still working at the fraying thread. I tug hard until it pops off with a satisfying snap. "Mostly I just try to stay away from people when I'm not in class. And when I am in class, I'm always checking for potential bad things—tripping hazards, spilled chemicals, crazed gunmen running past the windows."

"Jesus," Jordy says. "I can't even imagine. Do you have

all that in your head while you're playing tennis too?"

"Sometimes," I say. "But it's weird. As I get into a point or rally I start to forget about everything else. Until something bad happens." I pause. "You think I'm crazy, don't you?"

"No. I mean, everyone has issues. So you're kind of OCD because you worry about people getting hurt?"

"Sort of. Dr. Leed thinks it all stems from PTSD due to things that happened to me when I was younger."

Jordy blinks. "It must be a huge burden to worry about so many things. It must be . . . lonely."

"I'd rather be lonely than feel like someone got hurt just from being near me." My voice cracks.

"No one could get hurt just from being near you." He reaches over and tucks a strand of dark hair back behind my ear.

"I used to believe that," I say. "But after I started keeping track of bad things that happened to other people when I was around, I realized it's definitely more than it should be."

I give him a quick rundown of the major catastrophes that occurred over the past few years, tell him how in every case other people got hurt, but not me.

"That doesn't mean you *caused* anything."

"Maybe not, but when you do something and something horrible happens, your brain links those events. And when the only thing you happen to be doing is existing, and horrible things happen repeatedly, but they never hurt you . . ."

"Okay. So maybe you're indestructible. Like a super-hero."

I nibble at one of my pinkie nails. "Believe it or not, I had that thought too, right after the roller coaster." I lift the hem of my skirt slightly so he can see the scar on the inside of my leg. "Jumped out my bedroom window, just to see. Broke my femur."

Jordy's eyes linger on my skin for a moment. "Holy crap. I bet your mom was mad."

"She was too scared to be mad. But that was my first experience with therapy. She thought I was trying to hurt myself." I smooth the fabric back down over my thighs. "I guess in a way I was."

"Have you ever tried to aim it at people?" He plucks a pillow from the back of the couch and spins it between his hands.

"What do you mean?"

"Like Kimber. Let's say she's annoying you. Can you loiter around her and cause her to fall on her face or lose a match or something?"

The image of Kimber's dress ripping in psychology class flashes through my mind. But no, that had to be a coincidence. "It's not a superpower. I can't harness it and use it against my enemies."

Jordy looks up at me, his eyes bright with curiosity. "Is Kimber your enemy?"

"No," I say quickly. "I don't even know her. But you know what I mean."

"Yeah. But it sounds like except for the fire that things have been going okay the past couple of years. Maybe whatever it was, it's ending."

"Why would it be ending?"

"Maybe you've paid your karmic dues. Maybe you outgrew it. If things have changed, who cares why?"

"Things have been going better because I've been insanely careful," I say. "I was going on seventy-six days without incident before I hit you."

"Oh come on, Maguire. You didn't maim me for life. That doesn't count as a big enough deal to break your streak. People get hit with balls all the time. Let's go driving right now, you and me. We'll be fine, and then you can cross off another challenge."

I frown. "You would risk your life just to test my curse?"

"Yes." Jordy tosses the couch pillow up in the air and catches it. "Well, no. I'm confident that nothing will happen. One, I don't believe you're really cursed. And two, I'm kind of a golden boy, you know? Things have a way of working out for me."

I glance from the tennis court in the backyard to the trophies to Jordy's relaxed posture. He does seem to be leading an exceptionally charmed life. "I'll think about it," I say. "But not right now. I should get home."

"Okay." He drops the couch pillow and stands. "I'll walk you out."

We head back into the sunlight. The street is full of cars. Kimber's barbecue must still be going strong. "You should go," I say.

He shrugs. "I might. Just so no one makes a big deal of me not coming. Wouldn't want my sister to spread any uncomfortable rumors."

"What did you mean about her being a rebel?"

He leans against the side of my mom's car. "She likes to push my parents' buttons."

"And you?"

"I get the job of diffusing the bombs so the family doesn't explode." Jordy looks down at the ground. "Just one more expectation, I guess."

It seems like a lot for any one person to handle and I'm not sure what to say. "Thanks for your help today," I finally blurt out. Anything to break the deafening silence.

"Sure." He reaches out with one hand and gives me a gentle punch in the shoulder. "So we're on? Shrink-homework partners?"

"Well, I meant your help with my serve, but all right; I guess we can give it a try and see what happens."

After I get home, I text Jade.

Me: I just wanted you to know that my purity is still intact.

Her: That's a relief. I don't want to join the convent all by myself.

Me: He did try to get me to go to some tennis party at Kimber's house, though.

Her: Probably to try to make you jealous when she hangs all over him.

Me: You really have a bad impression of him, don't you?

Her: I have two older brothers. I have a bad impression of most guys ;)

I laugh out loud, but then a pang of sadness hits me. I think of Connor again, of the eighteen-year-old boy he'd be today if he hadn't died in the accident.

CHAPTER 13

I wake up on Sunday thinking about Jordy again. I reach up for my mystic knot, twisting the clasp around to the back, for the first time considering wishing for something other than a safe day for everyone. But I don't do it. I can't. Other than hitting Jordy with the tennis ball, things have been going well lately. No point in jinxing that because of some boy's smile.

The smell of pancakes wafts from down the hall as I knock three times on my nightstand and dab my lucky perfume on both wrists. Quickly I mumble, "Today no one will get hurt." I slide out of bed and recite my Chinese good luck prayer eight times in less than two minutes. I run a hand through my tangled curls and then twist the whole mess up into a giant bun as usual.

My mom is at the stove when I head into the kitchen. "I knew you wouldn't be able to resist the temptation of my special M&M pancakes," she says.

"You were right. My mouth is watering. Do you need help?"

"Nope. I have everything under control."

"Where's Tom?" I ask.

"He's playing golf with some of his work buddies today. It's just you, me, and the kiddos." My mom smiles. "And Jake is sleeping in for once."

My sister is sitting on the living room sofa watching cartoons. She always wakes up early, so I'm sure she finished eating already. I take my usual seat and toss a little salt over my left shoulder. I slide a couple of pancakes off the serving platter and onto my plate. "Mmmm." Bending low, I inhale the warm, buttery scent.

"So that was some practice session yesterday. Five hours?" My mom's voice is light, conversational, but I can tell she's dying of curiosity.

"We practiced for about three hours, and then we ordered California burritos." I cut into the soft pancake with my fork. "They have French fries in them."

"Sounds delicious. So you like the idea of making the tennis team?" She hovers next to the table, picking at the edge of one of the pancakes while more bubble on the griddle behind her. "It was Dr. Leed who suggested you join a team, wasn't it? I wouldn't want you to do it if it made you miserable."

I savor a bite of pancake and then swallow with a smile. "No, it's fun. I actually learned how to serve. We'll have to go play again sometime, if you want."

"I'd like that. Speaking of fun, Tom wanted me to ask if you would go with him and Erin to his work picnic on Friday night. It's at Balboa Park. They're going to have food and games, even a live band." My mom flips another pancake on the griddle. "I'm going to stay home with Jake, but I think the three of you would have a great time."

Not a chance. Tom works for a big company, and Balboa Park is huge. There'll probably be two hundred people or more there. Adults drinking, kids running around unsupervised—that's the perfect setup for a catastrophe. I swipe at my phone like maybe I'm checking my schedule. "I can't."

My mom's face falls a little. "You can take two cars if that'll help."

"Well, I have practice and then my appointment with Dr. Leed," I remind her. "It'll be after six-thirty by the time I get home."

"That's still plenty of time to shower and change. You could go to the picnic later." Mom sets her spatula down on the counter.

Which would mean drunk adults and unsupervised kids running around *after dark*. Even worse. "I don't think so. You know I don't like that kind of stuff."

"Maguire, I know it can't be easy to be in a new place again, but don't you think getting out would help?"

"I am getting out, Mom. I just need to do it at my own pace."

She nods. "How are things going with Dr. Leed?"

"Good," I say. My mom didn't press me to talk about what happened after the fire, so I didn't. I don't know if she thinks I freaked out because I'm the one who left the candle burning (a rare but massive oversight on my part) or if she has any idea it all ties together, that everything goes back to the accidents. She knows I'm superstitious, but I've never felt comfortable burdening her with all my fears, especially not after she got pregnant with Erin. And now that I have Dr. Leed, I feel like there's no point. I'd rather just pull myself together and then surprise her. *Look, Mom. Normal child.*

"Have you mentioned Ireland to him?"

"Yeah. We're working on some stuff," I say. "I promise you I'm trying."

She scoops another pancake from the griddle and turns back to me. "I know you are." She reaches out to touch my hair, but I can see the resignation in her expression. She doesn't think I can do it. She's given up on me already.

"You know what? I'm not hungry anymore." Throwing down my fork, I leap up from the table and head to my bedroom. My mom opens her mouth to say something, but then she thinks better of it and turns back to the stove.

Erin peeks over at me with wide, curious eyes as I round the corner into the hallway. "What's wrong, Mack Wire?"

I force a smile at her. "Nothing. I'm fine. I promise."

I slip into my room and close the door behind me quietly so I won't wake up the baby. Flopping down on my bed, I

119

bury my face in my pillow. My mom wouldn't ask me to go to a work function with Tom if it weren't something that meant a lot to her. I swear under my breath. If only I could be normal. I look up Balboa Park on my phone. It's even worse than I imagined, with its streets and ponds and fountains. All the five-second checks in the world wouldn't be enough.

I sit up and take three deep breaths in through my nose and out through my mouth. I rap three times on my nightstand. A neat pile of library books about Ireland sits on the floor next to my bed. I checked them out to motivate myself, but now I feel like they're mocking me. I pick up the thickest one and start reading it from the very beginning.

I'm only on the fourth page when my mom knocks gently on the door.

Hopping up from my bed, I stride across the room and open the door a crack. "What?"

"I just wanted to say I'm sorry for upsetting you." She looks down at the book in my hand. "You got books from the library?"

"Yeah. I was just curious about the weather and customs and stuff. I haven't gotten very far."

She nods. "Can I come in?"

I open the door.

She slips into my room. "Do you resent me?"

"Mom, no," I say. "Why would you think something like that?"

She closes the door. "You started retreating into your

120

shell right about the time Tom and I got married and I told you I was pregnant with Erin. At first I thought it was just you becoming a surly teenager or the stress of relocating, but sometimes I wonder if you don't like being around us because you feel like I replaced your dad and brother. I can't remember the last time we all did anything together as a family."

Oh, God. I avoid family stuff mostly to keep Tom and the kids safe, and my mom has been thinking it's because I'm mad at her? "I don't resent you," I say. "I'm happy that you were able to . . . get past everything."

She sighs deeply, as if I've just confirmed her worst suspicions. "I'll never be 'past everything,' okay? Losing your dad and brother was horrible. It was like realizing I failed to protect my family, even though I know there's nothing I could have done. What happened that day affects every part of my life, Maguire. I'm terrified all the time. I'm afraid Jake is going to die of SIDS. I'm worried about Erin going off to preschool next year. I'm worried about Tom when he works late. I'm worried about you at a new school, about you driving places by yourself. Please, please don't think I just started over with a new family."

"I don't, but I didn't know you worried about all that stuff." Maybe my mom and I have more in common than I thought. I set the book about Ireland back on the stack. "How do you not go crazy thinking about it all?"

"It's hard. I try to take one moment at a time. Sometimes

when I'm feeling down, the whole world is just one terrible and scary thing after the next. That's when I try to focus on the good things that have happened to me since then." She ruffles my hair. "Like seeing the smile on your face when you came home last night."

Did I smile after hanging out with Jordy?

"You're smiling again." My mom sits on the edge of my bed. "Tell me about this guy. Is he cute?"

Kind of. "It's not like that," I say. "He's just helping me because he knows me a little bit from Dr. Leed's."

"And that does not answer the question of whether he's cute."

"Yeah, he's cute," I admit. "He's got a great smile."

"I want to see." She points at the laptop on my desk. "Google him."

Oh, Lord. That didn't even occur to me. Jordy "Everyone Knows Who I Am" Wheeler's whole life is undoubtedly on the internet for public consumption. Reluctantly I grab my computer and type his name into the search box. I click on the images tab and about two hundred smiling pictures pop up.

My mom tries to wolf whistle, but it just comes out like a stream of air. I make a face at her and then click on one of the thumbnails—Jordy in a tux. I blow it up and read the caption. It's from an Arthur Ashe Foundation benefit dinner.

"Oooh. What a babe!" Mom giggles like a middle school girl getting asked to her first dance.

"No one says 'babe' anymore," I tell her. "But he's a nice guy, and I'm lucky he's helping me."

"Is he a good teacher?"

"The best," I say. "I wish you could make it to one of our matches. He revamped my serve in only a couple of days. All he had to do was watch me and he realized my toss was off, so he helped me fix it."

Her body wilts a little. "I wish I could. It's just that Jake's so young. I hate leaving a tiny baby with a babysitter I don't know and—"

"It's okay, Mom. I understand." It would be a lot for her to handle, managing both Erin and Jake while watching one of my matches. And Tom is never home until after six, so he wouldn't be able to help.

"Maybe I can convince Tom to take a day off work."

"That'd be cool." I shut my laptop and set it on my bed. "But if not, there's always next year."

"Maybe by next year I'll feel comfortable trusting Tom alone with the kids." She grins.

"He's not so bad," I say. "And if we go to Ireland, he'll be watching them by himself, right?"

Mom gets that dreamy, wistful look in her eyes again. "Don't feel pressured into that. I know it's a lot to ask." She lifts herself from my bed and glances around the room.

Two walls are all bookshelves. I have over five hundred books, all alphabetized by author. The other walls are blank, as are the top of my desk and dresser. It occurs to me my room looks more like a library than a place where someone actually lives.

"You keep everything so clean." Mom shakes her head. "You're a much better kid than I was."

"You must've been a hellion." I give her a half smile. "Sorry about earlier. I might not make the party, but I'm trying really hard to make that plane."

"Okay." My mom brightens, and just like that I feel like crap again.

It's been two weeks since I started my list of therapy challenges, and I haven't even completed the first one. I've still got a long way to go.

CHAPTER 14

The next week passes in a blur. Wednesday, Thursday, and Friday are what Coach calls the "official tryouts." On Wednesday and Thursday, we go through a series of skill stations designed to test us on forehands, backhands, passing shots, drop shots, overheads, and serves. I do okay on all of them. On Friday, Coach has us run three miles to test our endurance, and then we play singles against each other. I win games against Jade, Colleen, and Mae, but I lose easily to both Penn and Kimber.

Jordy calls me on Saturday. "How are you doing?" he asks.

I'm crashed out on my bed, working my way through some physics homework. I set my textbook to the side. "I hurt all over," I tell him. "I tried to go for a run this morning but didn't make it very far. I have sore muscles in places where I didn't even know I had muscles."

He laughs. "Welcome to competitive athletics. I still have

those days occasionally."

"I hope I make the team."

"From what I saw you did great," he says. "I bet you're a lock."

"Do you have inside information?" I ask hopefully.

He chuckles. "Unfortunately, no."

"Well, if I do make it, a lot of it is because of you," I say. "So thanks again."

"You're welcome," Jordy says. "I like helping people with their game."

I see an opening. My pulse races a little, but I remember Dr. Leed telling me I need to push myself. "What about helping them with therapy challenges? Is that offer still on the table?"

"Sure. Are you still working on riding in a car with someone?"

"Yep."

Do you need to ride for a certain length of time? Go anywhere specific?"

"Nah. Maybe twenty minutes. Anywhere you want to go is fine."

"All right. How does Monday night sound? By then you'll know you made the team and you'll have one less thing to worry about."

"Let's do it," I say.

We hang up, and instead of going back to my homework I reach for one of the Ireland books. I flip from picture to picture, marveling at the castles and countryside. I close my eyes and imagine my mom and me there, riding horses across the moors with Grandma Siobhan. *You can do this*, I tell myself. *You just have to be brave.*

Monday is the slowest day of school ever because I'm waiting to find out for sure that I made the team. I'm fairly certain I did, but I hope Jade makes it too. I see her once in the halls between classes, but then not again until the end of the day in psychology class.

She leans back in her seat, her feet propped on the chair in front of her. "I think I'm going to be sick."

"You're going to be fine," I assure her.

"Easy for you to say, Manager's Pet. Have you been enjoying your private lessons?" She licks her lips suggestively.

"Hey." I bend down and pretend to fumble in my backpack for something so she won't see me blush. "Coach is the one who decides who gets cut, not Jordy."

"Oh, relax. I was just kidding." She clucks her tongue. "You have the best skin, you know it?"

"What?" I peek over at her as Ms. Haynes heads up the main aisle to her desk.

"It's so pale and perfect, yet blushy at the same time." She grins. "You always look like you're in love."

"Hardly," I scoff. "I'm just one of those people who always look pink."

"Uh-huh," Jade says.

Today's lecture is about self-fulfilling prophecies—how if a person expects something good or bad to happen, he might subconsciously help bring about the expected result with his behavior. Ms. Haynes shows a video clip about the power of positive thinking, and it reminds me of my daily affirmations.

"This must be the theory one hundred percent of self-help books are based on," Jade whispers. "Good news. I think we both made the tennis team, so I guess that means we both made the tennis team. Now to start thinking about my starring role in the winter play."

I smile at her, but at the same time I weigh the idea of self-fulfilling prophecies in my head. Maybe if I try to believe what Dr. Leed believes—that I'm not cursed, that none of the accidents were my fault—it'll help with my therapy challenges.

After class, Jade and I head to the locker room together and then down to the tennis courts.

Once everyone is present, Coach gives us the good news: no one is getting cut this year. I'm going to play third singles behind Kimber and Penn. Jordy gives me a slap on the back. Penn gives me an enthusiastic thumbs-up. Kimber gives me a smile that looks a little forced.

Jade is going to play second doubles, and she's thrilled about it. She prefers doubles to singles and is hoping she can move up to first doubles next year when Colleen and Luisa both graduate.

Today's practice is the best so far. I win a few points off everyone who I hit against, including Kimber, and my serve has never looked better.

Jordy calls me later while I'm working through some trig problems. "What are you doing?" he asks.

"Homework," I say.

"Me too."

"What's it like taking classes online?"

"Boring," Jordy says. "And I'm easily distracted, which doesn't help. But I should be able to get out sometime after eleven, if that's not too late."

"Sounds good." I'm nervous, but if I can pull this off, I'll have completed two therapy challenges in one day.

Everyone at my house is usually asleep by 10:30. I pretend to get ready for bed like always, slipping into my pajamas and making a point of brushing my teeth and washing my face with the bathroom door open so my mom and Tom can't possibly miss me.

Then I slide back into my room, close the door, and pull on a pair of jeans and a T-shirt. I twist my hair up into a messy bun. As I stare at my reflection, I decide I look a little more tired than usual. Digging in the top drawer of my dresser, I find a brown eyeliner pencil and pull off the cap.

Then I come to my senses.

I don't need to look good for Jordy. I don't want him

to like me like that. Right now I have to focus on me, on getting over my fears. Two of the books about Ireland are stacked on the corner of my dresser. I've spread the books around my room so that everywhere I look I see another reminder. Ireland equals goal. Jordy equals . . . tall goofy guy who sucks at math. I smile as I think of the way he described himself. Jordy equals friend.

But what if Dr. Leed fixes you?

He won't. And even if he does, that won't magically change everything. I'm only meeting Jordy tonight so I can cross another challenge off my list and get one step closer to Ireland.

And because he volunteered.

And okay, fine, because he's sort of funny and I like hanging out with him.

But none of those things require eyeliner.

I put on a little anyway.

The floor outside my room creaks as someone walks by. Quickly, I dive into bed and pull the covers up to my chin, just in case my mom got up to check on Jake and decides to look in on me.

The creaking stops, and the entire house falls silent. I curl onto my side and rest my phone next to my pillow in case I fall asleep.

Right at 11:30, my phone buzzes with Jordy's text message.

Here

I get out of bed and peek out my window. An unfamiliar car is parked across the street. I slide the window open and crawl out, narrowly avoiding the prickly pear cactus that grows along the side of the house. My blood pounds in my ears and I hold my breath as my feet hit the ground. This is the first time I've ever sneaked out. Ducking low, I dart across the grass and the street. I'm still crouching when I reach the passenger side of Jordy's car.

"Car" is actually an understatement. This is more of a street racing death machine, with two thick tailpipes and a pronounced fin on the back. It's black and sleek with green and silver stripes painted down the sides. This car looks like it's begging to get into an accident.

Jordy leans his lanky frame across the front seat and opens the door for me. "Hey." He's wearing a backward baseball cap.

"You might have mentioned you were picking me up in a race car. Didn't I see this in *The Fast and the Furious*?"

"Maybe in a chop shop getting broken down for parts."

"Whatever." God, everything about him is so attention-getting. "Did you buy it with your tennis millions?"

He snorts. "Sorry to disappoint you, but I have no millions. Mitzi here barely ran when I bought her. Not that expensive."

"Mitzi?" I ask incredulously. If this car has a name, I'm pretty sure it should be something like Diablo or Black Death.

"It's a Mitsubishi Lancer. Honestly, I would have preferred something a little less flashy." Jordy fiddles with the brim of his hat.

"Right." I cough into my fist. "Like you didn't get it specifically to be a chick magnet."

"Clearly it's a chick magnet, because my sister picked it out," he says. "She's into cars but doesn't have a license yet, so she begged me to get something she and the kid across the street could fix up. It's a sweet ride, but I'm always worried someone is going to steal it."

"Your sister . . ." I arch an eyebrow. "Penn?"

"The only sister I have. You saw her covered with grease the other day. She's all about cars, and she's going to turn sixteen soon. I've been thinking about giving it to her."

"That's nice of you."

"Yeah. I'm nice every once in a while." Jordy clears his throat. "Like now, up in the middle of the night helping my friend with her shrink homework. So are we doing this, or what?"

I pause. My eyes flick all around me, looking for signs— black cats, ominous clouds, anything that tells me this is a really bad idea. The night looks back at me, suburban, innocent, unthreatening. There's no reason to be nervous.

But I am. My breath hitches. "Wait. Have you ever been in an accident?"

"No."

"And how long have you been driving?"

"For two years. I have my unrestricted license. I've never

gotten a ticket. I even got an *A* in Driver's Ed."

"Okay. Give me a second." I rest my hands on my thighs, my knees wavering beneath me.

Jordy slides out of the car and jogs around to my side. Gently, he places his hands on my shoulders and turns my body so the car is supporting me and we're facing each other. I realize he's dressed all in black.

"Are you robbing a bank later?" I joke weakly.

"Sneaking out of my house requires a bit of effort."

"You sneaked out to do this?"

"Didn't you?"

"Yeah," I admit. "But my mom worries constantly that I'm antisocial. She'd probably be happy to catch me sneaking out."

"I'm usually in bed by now. But it feels good to do what I want for once, instead of just doing what's expected of me." Jordy reaches down and takes my hands in his, squeezes them gently. "I know you can do this, Maguire. Just think—it'll be one step closer to that trip to Ireland."

I nod. *Mom. Dad. Grandma Siobhan.* Right now Ireland feels like a dream, like it's not even a real place. "I just need a minute. I haven't driven with anyone but my mom since the accident. And with her I needed sedatives for months. Even now it's still hard sometimes."

"We can just sit in the car for a while and see if you feel any better, if you want."

"Okay," I say. We both slide into the car. Exhaling

deeply, I lean back against the leather seat and look up at the upholstered ceiling. "Thanks for helping me with this."

"You're welcome. But it's not exactly a huge expenditure of effort on my part." He shrugs. "Plus, like I said, it gives me a reason to break out of jail."

"Sorry I'm being so lame about it. I know you probably have to be up early."

"You're not lame," Jordy says. "We're all afraid of things."

I glance over at him. "What are you afraid of?"

He tilts his head to the side and thinks for a moment. Then he ticks things off on his fingertips. "Grasshoppers. Sharks. Drowning. Disappointing my parents."

I arch an eyebrow. "Grasshoppers?"

"Have you ever seen one of those up close? They look like tiny aliens." He shudders. "And nothing should be able to jump twenty times its height. That's just wrong."

"But you could squish like five of them with one of your giant feet," I point out.

"Stop." Jordy squeezes his eyes shut. "Have you ever stepped on a grasshopper? You can feel their bones or shell or whatever—"

"Exoskeleton," I say.

"Yeah, that. You can feel it crushing beneath you and then there are soft parts and then there's this pile of . . . stuff and it sticks to your shoe." He shudders again. "Let's not talk about grasshoppers anymore, please."

I crack a smile. My heart rate slows a little. "Okay. Why

do you think you're going to disappoint your parents?"

Jordy turns the key in the ignition but doesn't start the car. "Just to make the seat-warmer work," he explains. He taps one foot against the floorboards. "My sister thinks I'm a wuss, you know?"

"I'm sure she doesn't—"

"No. She does. And she's sort of right that I let my parents run my life. But they've made a lot of sacrifices for me. My dad used to be a freelance video game designer, but he took a corporate job that paid a ton more and had better benefits after I was born. I'm sure he thought at some point he'd go back to doing what he loved, but then I started playing tennis and seemed to have a natural aptitude, so instead he and my mom took out a second mortgage so they could have the court put in the backyard. My mom quit her job so she could manage my day-to-day stuff." Jordy turns to face me. "Basically, they stopped doing what they loved so that I can do what I love."

"And you love tennis."

"I do. I really do. Sometimes the off-court stuff—the interviews, worrying about image and endorsements, etc.—gets me down. But there's nothing I love more than the feel of playing." He smiles. "Except my family, of course. So yeah, it's easy for Penn to say I should demand to be in charge of my own life, but what if my parents are right? What if I insist on going straight to the pro tour and never achieve the success they want for me?"

"They're not going to judge you based on your ranking," I protest.

"No, but if I do it their way I have a college degree to fall back on. It just means four more years of having absolutely no life of my own outside of school and tennis. But if I bail on school after I graduate next year, I can focus on my game and still have a little bit of time for me."

"That's tough. I can see both sides."

"Me too. I think that's some of why I'm glad you let me help you tonight. Okay, sure. I like being around you, and this gives me an opportunity. But it's also because I think you *can* have a normal life, and you're cheating yourself out of it."

Once again, I feel a twinge of envy at his easygoing confidence. I look out through the windshield. The neighbor's trash cans are casting a shadow across the sidewalk. A gust of wind blows grass clippings down the street. "How can you just say stuff like that?"

"Like what?"

"That you like being around me."

"Why wouldn't I?"

"I don't know. What if I don't say it back?"

"You didn't say it back," Jordy points out. "But you're here, so I'm going to assume you don't mind my company." He looks over at me. "And if you blew me off totally, it'd be a little embarrassing, but I'd survive."

"How are you so okay with embarrassing stuff, especially

when what happens to you gets spread around to so many people?"

"I don't know. When I first started competing, I went to this sports psychologist. He said there were two options for handling awkward moments. A, you pretend it never happened, which is sort of pathetic and delusional, and you're really only fooling yourself. Option A means even if everyone plays along, they still talk behind your back—you give up the power."

"And option B?"

"B is when you own it, no matter what it is. You play it off, you play it up, you laugh. Everyone still talks, but at least it's to your face. Option B is all about making things work for you."

"And how's that working for you?"

"Pretty well, I think," he says. "Oh, I almost forgot. I brought you a little something. Just to make you feel extra safe." Jordy reaches around to the backseat and grabs a small black duffel bag. He drops it on my lap. "Check it out. It's the Jordy Wheeler Deluxe Emergency Kit."

I remove the items one at a time: an extra phone, a first aid kit, an emergency roadside kit, and a US Army survival guide. I have the same survival guide at home and similar kits stashed in my mom's trunk. "You really thought of everything."

"I tried," he says softly. "But if you're not ready to do

this, I'll be around for a do-over when you are."

I'm not ready, but it's like Dr. Leed says—if I want to go to Ireland, I have to push myself. I reach back and buckle my seat belt. "Let's go."

Jordy nods. "I promise I won't let anything happen to you—to either one of us."

I shake my head. "Don't say that. Don't make promises you can't keep." Some people think they can just decree that everything will be fine. The world doesn't work like that. I'm not sure the world gives a crap about anyone's promises, well-meaning or otherwise.

Sometimes the Universe just takes what it wants.

CHAPTER 15

Jordy makes a big point of buckling his seat belt, checking his mirrors, and signaling before he pulls away from the curb. I squeeze my eyes shut for a moment but then force myself to open them. I can't possibly prevent an accident if I'm not paying attention. He slowly drives to the end of my street and turns left. My entire neighborhood is dark. I exhale a heavy breath and fold my hands in my lap. So far, so good.

"You're doing great," he says.

"How far are we going?"

"Not too far." He turns again, and a pair of headlights appears on the horizon.

I slouch back in my seat and try to relax. If I'm ever going to have a normal life, I need to be able to ride with other people. That means figuring out how to handle being on the road with other people, too.

We pass the car with no issue. Jordy looks over at me. "See. No worries."

We leave my neighborhood and head toward an unincorporated area. As we turn onto a state highway, three more cars pass in rapid succession. I dig my fingernails into the flesh of my palms but manage not to visibly flinch.

Jordy exits onto a service road that winds along the side of a hill. It's still completely safe—paved, with a guardrail, well maintained. I look straight ahead. My right hand curls protectively around the door handle.

"You okay?" he asks.

"Yeah," I mutter.

But as we turn sharply on the switchback, my pounding heart starts to crowd out everything else in my chest. My stomach drops low. I fight for each breath. It's not just the hill that's getting to me; it's the sharp turns too. I've survived moving twice with only moderate anxiety because it was just Mom and me in the car and she stuck to the major roads. Big, straight highways. This road has a thousand dark corners, too many blind curves. The tall trees, the hint of salt in the air. It's all the same. I close my eyes again and I'm back in my dad's car, five years ago.

Dad's humming to himself as he drives. Uncle Kieran is in the passenger seat, alternating between controlling the radio and doing something on his phone. My brother and I are in the backseat. Connor keeps poking me in the ribs.

"Stop it," I tell him.

"No." He starts singing that playground song about boys and girls kissing in a tree, only he's inserting my name and the name of

the kid who lives down the street. "He totally likes her, Dad," *he says.* "He's always asking me if she can hang out too."

My dad laughs. My uncle turns down the radio slightly.

"That's just because I'm better at stuff than you are," I shoot back. "You throw like a girl."

"Oooh." Uncle Kieran turns around from the passenger seat to grin at both of us. "Them's fighting words."

Connor pokes me again. "She's just trying to act tough because she knows she looooooves him."

"Shut up," I say. I lean sharply toward Connor as my dad navigates the twisting mountain road.

"Make me," Connor taunts, reaching out to poke me again.

"Oh, I'll make you." I slug him in the arm. "I'll shut you up for good."

And then Dad swears loudly, the kind of language he only uses when he thinks my brother and I aren't listening. At first I think it's because Connor and I are fighting, but then I see the truck bearing down on us, in our lane, the metal grill leering like the face of a monster. There's nowhere for my dad to go . . .

A sharp gasp escapes my lips. Tears push their way out of my eyes, and I look toward the side window. The night looks back at me, dark silhouettes of Southern California pines in their feathery dresses.

"Maguire." Jordy touches my arm.

I pull away. "Both hands on the wheel." My words come out strangled and broken.

"Hang in there." Jordy makes another sharp turn, slowing the car almost to a stop to navigate the curving road. Then he pulls into a parking lot for a scenic viewpoint.

I hold my breath until he shifts into park and turns off the ignition. Then, suddenly and violently, I start to cry.

"Oh God, Maguire. I am so sorry." Jordy jumps out of the car and comes around to my side. He unbuckles my seat belt and half-drags me out of the car.

My muscles are gelatin and I start to sink to the cool ground of the parking lot. The night air is chillier up here. Goosebumps form on my skin.

"I got you," Jordy says. "I got you." I lean on him as he leads me across the lot. I don't know where we're going. I don't care. All I know is that I can breathe again.

We end up on the bench of the scenic overlook, the sky awash in tiny points of light, the ocean just barely visible on the horizon. Off in the distance, a lighthouse blinks, slow and steady. I try to match my breathing to its winking light. Gradually my sobs subside. I look down at the winding road, and my stomach twists into knots.

Jordy shrugs out of his Windbreaker and gives it to me. "You're shaking," he says.

"It's not from the cold." I let him wrap the jacket around me anyway.

"I'm so sorry." He fumbles with the zipper, the wind threatening to steal away his hat as he tries to zip me up.

I take the ends of the fabric from his hands and zip the jacket. The sleeves come all the way down over my hands.

"You don't have anything to be sorry for."

"I hate that I made you this upset." He leans forward, resting his forearms on his thighs.

"Minor panic attack. No big deal." I blot my eyes with the cuff of his Windbreaker. "It was my idea. All we did was drive to the top of a hill. I need to be able to deal with that." I look out into the night. "The road just reminded me of the accident."

"You want to talk about it?"

"No." I purse my lips, shake my head. "At least not right now."

"Okay." Jordy stares out at the ocean for a few seconds. "What does your mom think about everything?"

"What? About me being cursed?"

"Yeah. That, the notebook. Why you are the way you are."

"She doesn't know everything. I mean, she knows I had issues after the accidents and that kids avoided me for a while after the birthday party. She was there for my freak-out when the neighbors' house burned down. But she doesn't know about the notebook. I'm not sure if she realizes everything is connected."

Jordy is still looking out at the ocean. "Did you tell Daniel everything?"

"Yeah."

"That's good." Jordy's shoulders twitch a little as he tries to hide the fact that he's shivering.

"We don't have to sit out here," I say. "I know you're freezing."

"I have an idea." He hops up from the bench and jogs over to the car. He comes back with the emergency blanket from the first aid kit. He wraps one side around me and then sits next to me on the bench again, cocooning us in the crinkly silver material.

"I always wondered if these kept you warm," I say. "Not too bad."

The whine of a jet plane fills the air. I can barely make out the silhouette as it tears across the night sky, probably on the way back to the naval base at Coronado.

"As a bonus," Jordy says, "this space blanket makes us invisible to the military's thermal imaging technology."

"Really?" I turn toward him to see if he's kidding.

"Yeah. We are protected from the government's prying eyes," he says. "But just let me know if you want to leave."

"Okay." I pull my legs up onto the bench and tuck them beneath the blanket. Even though the journey was hell, it's kind of nice up here. Peaceful. I like being around Jordy, too, even if it's a little harder for me to say it. I still can't believe I told him about my bad luck, but that's the weird thing about secret sharing. As scary as it is to think of him telling other people, there's also a comfort in not being the only one who knows anymore. And even if he thinks I'm completely bonkers, he's not treating me like a crazy person.

The wind steals the corner of the emergency blanket out

of my hand and sends it flapping in the night like an out-of-control spaceship. Jordy wrestles the blanket down and drapes it over both of our laps. My head brushes against his arm as I angle my neck to look up at the sky. "Wow. You can see so many stars," I say.

"Yeah. Makes me feel sort of small." Jordy rests his head against mine.

My lips quirk into a half smile. "You're a giant."

"Nah, I'm just a speck."

"Then I'm a half a speck."

He nudges me in the ribs. "Your hair alone makes you more than half a speck." He reaches up and gently removes the elastic that's keeping my bun in place.

My hair tumbles down around my shoulders, the breeze sending thick spirals forward in front of my eyes. "What is this obsession with my hair?" My mouth suddenly goes dry.

"I don't know. It's cool, and you keep it hidden away from everyone. It makes me wonder what else you're hiding." Jordy lifts a hand to my cheek.

For one terrifying moment I think maybe he's going to kiss me, but then he flicks a strand of hair stuck to my lip back away from my face. Pulling back, I scoff. "Is that Charming Asshole Jordy I hear? He of the slick lines for the fangirls and the cameras?"

"Ouch," he says, dropping his hand to the bench. "There's nothing fake about me being here with you, Maguire. I hope you can see that."

"Sorry. I don't know why I said that. I got nervous or something."

He blinks rapidly. "Do I make you nervous?" The beginning of a smile forms on his lips.

"A little," I admit. "But so does everything." I fidget beneath the emergency blanket. "We should probably get going before one of us gets busted for sneaking out."

"Okay." Jordy walks a little behind me on the way back to the car, as if he wants to be in position to support me if I start to collapse again.

The trip back down the hill is almost as excruciating, but he talks me through it, one-tenth of a mile at a time. "It's okay," he says softly. "You're okay. We're almost there." He repeats these simple but soothing phrases until we're back on the neighborhood streets.

We pull up in front of my house a little after 1:00 a.m., and I sneak back in without being detected. A few minutes later I receive a text.

I'd call that a success. Wouldn't you?

I text him back. One word.

Thanks.

Pulling my luck notebook out of my purse, I flip to the last page. I draw a line through therapy challenges one and two. Five more to go.

CHAPTER 16

Jordy isn't at practice the next day, so I don't see him again until Wednesday, the day of our first match.

It's an away match at Lexington High, a school across town. My mom let me drive her car to school so I wouldn't have to ride the bus with everyone else. I barely survived last night with Jordy. I'm not ready for a bus full of teammates yet.

I meet up with everyone else at Lexington, where Coach informs me I'm going to be playing a girl named Silvia. She smiles and then grabs a can of balls from her coach. She opens the can and drops the silver pop top in the trash. I notice the balls are Wilson #4s. Four is bad luck in several Asian cultures. I tell myself it doesn't mean anything. *Self-fulfilling prophecy. I believe I can win this match.*

Jordy is bent over a clipboard with Coach Hoffman and Kimber. He looks up just long enough to mouth "good luck" and then turns his attention back to them. My insides are quivering with nervousness, but I try to hold my expression steady as I walk down to the third court. Since we're the away team, I get to choose whether I serve or receive first. Everyone always chooses to serve—it's a natural advantage.

Except for me. After we warm up, I hand Silvia the balls and pick my side of the court instead, the side opposite the Lexington bleachers, so I won't have to look at anyone during the next game while I'm trying to serve. Jordy jogs around the courts to my side and gestures to me as I'm heading back to the baseline to start the match.

"One second," I holler to Silvia. I jog back to the fence. "What's up?"

"I just wanted to wish you good luck again," he says. "In fact, I found something for you." He pulls a wadded-up tissue from his pocket and folds it back to reveal a four-leaf clover. "Put it in your shoe or whatever."

My cheeks get hot. Gently, I reach my fingers through a hole in the fence and take the clover from Jordy's outstretched hand. I twirl the stem between my thumb and index finger. "Thanks, that was really sweet of you."

"It was, wasn't it?" Jordy tosses his hair out of his eyes. "I'm glad you didn't accuse me of being Slick Asshole Jordy again. Maybe I shouldn't have told you about him."

"No. I'm glad you . . . shared that with me. I'm sorry again about last night."

"It's cool. I know you didn't mean it. Because I make you *nervous*." He winks. "Now hurry up and kick this girl's ass."

Before I can reply, he gives me a little wave and then heads back around to the side with the bleachers.

I should take his advice and put the clover in my shoe, but instead I tuck it inside the small pocket of my racquet bag. No guy has ever given me anything, and this is one good luck charm I want to keep.

Silvia bounces a ball repeatedly while she waits for me.

"Sorry." I jog to the baseline and take my place at the back of the service box. Quickly I scan the court, making sure there are no loose tennis balls or any obvious hazards on Silvia's side. "Ready." I bend my knees and shuffle from side to side, my heart thrumming with the anticipation of receiving my first-ever serve in a real match.

Silvia serves the ball, and I return it low and deep. We exchange several ground strokes before she finally hits a backhand into the net. I've just won my first point!

The next point goes to her when I return her serve off my back foot and the ball goes so long it pings off the painted fence. We trade points again, and then finally I win the game when she double-faults at 30–40. I can't believe it—I've just won my very first tennis game! I try to hold in a huge grin, but it slips out a little as Silvia and I change sides and I catch sight of Jordy smiling at me.

But now I have to serve. Silvia casually hits both balls over the net. I tuck one of them in the pocket of my trunks and grip the other one in my hand. Stepping up to the baseline, I get in position just to the right of the center T.

"Just concentrate. You can do this," Jordy yells from behind me.

I throw the ball up, but my toss is too low. I let it fall and catch it off the bounce. A second toss, too far behind me. I lean back and catch the ball again. Across the net, Silvia shuffles back and forth. She takes a step inside the baseline, perhaps realizing that she's about to be served up a cream puff.

"Third time's a charm," I mutter to myself. Tossing the ball up in the air, I bring my racquet back and explode upward, making contact with the ball at exactly the right time. The serve lands in the box, and Silvia struggles to return it, hitting a short shot that brings me up to net. I aim for the back corner of the court and plant my feet, ready to volley whatever she aims at me. She goes for my backhand side, and I punch the ball cross-court out of her reach.

"Nice one, Maguire." Jordy flashes me a thumbs-up as I'm heading back to the baseline.

"Thanks." I head to the left side of the court, ready to do it again. But this time my first serve hits the top of the net and lands on my side. I try again. Double fault.

Silvia smiles to herself and trots over to the right side of the court. We trade points again, but she ends up winning the second game. She wins the next game too, and then I win, making it two games apiece. We go back and forth like that, trading games until it's five games to four and my turn to serve. I glance up at the bleachers, but Jordy isn't watching me anymore. He's two courts down, talking to Kimber. I can see her scorecard—five games to five. Looks like I'm not the only one struggling. Between us, Penn seems to be winning her second set 3–1.

My new toss abandons me at this crucial moment, and I end up serving a bunch of double faults and losing the first set 6–4. I take a few minutes to stretch out and drink water before starting the second set.

Coach Hoffman jogs down to give me some pointers. "Don't get down on yourself, okay?" he says. "This is your first-ever match and you're doing fine."

I nod, but my chin droops slightly. I really wanted to win for the team, and for Jordy. I don't want him to think the time he spent working with me has been a waste. I trot back out onto the court and try my hardest, but Silvia ends up winning the second set 6–3. By the time I finish my match, Penn has already won hers, and Jade and her doubles partner are just finishing up. I'm the only one who's lost so far. Kimber is starting a third set, and we all go to sit behind her court and cheer her on.

Jordy is down talking to the third doubles team but breaks away when he sees me in the bleachers. He jogs down and takes a seat next to me. "How'd you end up?"

"4–6, 3–6," I say.

"Not bad." He claps me on the shoulder. "I lost my first match 6–1, 6–0."

"Really?"

"Really. How did you feel serving?"

"Better. I think I just got nervous when the score was close and reverted back to my old toss."

"Old habits die hard."

Jordy and I watch Kimber with the rest of the team. She ends up winning in a third-set tiebreaker. After we all congratulate her, Jordy turns to me. "Want to give me a ride back to school?"

"That's probably a good idea. Dr. Leed says I need to keep reinforcing my earlier tasks as I move through my list."

I feel a little better as the two of us head for the parking lot. Even though I lost today, in a lot of ways I kind of feel like I won. I played respectably. I served okay for most of the match. And the team won—and that's what's most important. I think about the four-leaf clover tucked inside my tennis bag and decide to leave it there for the time being. Jordy is almost like a living good luck charm.

CHAPTER 17
Session #8

"Why do you let some people call you by your first name?"
I ask.

Dr. Leed laughs under his breath. "You can call me Daniel if you want."

"What's up, Daniel?" I try it out. "Do you not want me to?"

He shrugs. "I go on a case-by-case basis. Dr. Leed feels kind of stuffy and old, but sometimes with young women it feels a little creepy to be like, 'Heeey. Call me Daniel.'"

"Ah," I say. "Makes sense." I smile. "Can I call you Danny?"

"Not if you expect me to answer." He smiles too. "So how are things?"

"I rode in a car with someone else," I say. "Finally."

"And?"

"It was horrible."

"But?"

"We survived." I give him a quick rundown of what it felt like being in the car that first night. "Then I did it again on Wednesday during the day, only that time I drove."

"Congratulations. So what's next on your list? Ready to try riding a bus or similar?" Daniel asks.

My eyes widen. "Like during the day? With other people?"

"Well, there are going to be other people on this plane, right?"

"Yeah." I bite my lip. "What about something like just hanging out in a crowded place first? You know, enough people where I can't control everything with five-second checks, but where I'm not completely trapped just in case something happens."

"You're the boss. Where would you go?"

"Not sure. Maybe the mall or the beach?" I really don't like the beach. It's bad enough keeping track of everything happening on the sand, let alone in the water.

"And what about after that?"

"Maybe then I can try the bus?"

Daniel smiles. "Sounds like you're right where you want to be."

My heart is pounding a little bit as I leave Daniel's office. I think about riding with Jordy, about how he talked me all the way through the task. I'm glad we decided to work together on some of our therapy challenges.

I lick my lips and swallow, prepare myself to smile and say hi. But today the waiting room is empty. I remember that he said something about playing in a tournament this weekend. It's no big deal. I'll see him next week at practice.

But still, I'm a little sad he's not here.

CHAPTER 18

On Saturday, I get a call from Penn. "What are you doing today?" she asks.

"I don't know." I pause. "Did your brother give you my number?"

"Oh. He has a sheet with everyone's address and phone number on the team. I hope calling you like this is okay." She sighs. "I need a favor, and since Jordy is your friend, I thought maybe you might help."

It feels weird to hear Penn call Jordy my friend. I wonder if he told her about our late-night drive. "What's up?" I ask her.

"I need a ride to my brother's match. He's playing at San Diego Tennis Complex. The semifinals of the Pacific Crest Open."

Last night I Googled Jordy's results from Thursday and Friday, so I know he's advanced through the first four rounds of the tournament, but my insides twist a little at the thought of driving Penn somewhere. It shouldn't be any different than driving Jordy, but it is, for one because she doesn't know about my phobia. "You can't get a ride with him?"

"He and my parents are already there. I was supposed to go with them, but tomorrow is my birthday and we kind of all got in a fight."

"Oh."

"Yeah. I'm the invisible child when my brother is winning. But it isn't Jordy's fault my parents care more about his matches than my birthday. I feel like crap for some of the things I said, and I want to be there to watch him." She trails off. "I guess I thought you might want to watch him too. I can get you in for free."

I think about a crowded tennis stadium. It would work for therapy challenge number three, if I can handle another challenge after the stress of driving Penn. My stomach knots even further. The first two tasks went okay, but this one would be a lot bigger—hundreds of people, way more than on a plane.

But you wouldn't be trapped, I remind myself. And Jordy will be there, and he does seem to be lucky. So far he hasn't gotten hurt from being around me—not *really*. And if I just sat in my seat, maybe everything would go smoothly.

I would love to see him play.

"Maguire? You still there?"

"Yeah, okay," I say. "I can drive you. When do you need me to pick you up?"

"His match starts in an hour," Penn says, "so the sooner the better, I guess."

Penn is sitting on the porch waiting for me when I pull up to the Wheeler house. Her blonde pigtails swing back and forth as she jogs across the grass. She starts talking a mile a minute the second she gets into my car. "Thank you so much for this. I totally owe you and my brother owes you and I'm so glad you're going to come watch him play and I know he'll be glad you're there too."

"I'm glad you called," I say.

She rubs at a stain on her T-shirt. "I probably should have changed, but I'm hoping we can avoid my parents altogether. That way I won't be yelled at for being *slovenly*." She flares her nostrils. "One of my mother's favorite words."

I sit there at the curb for a minute, trying to figure out the best way to ask her to buckle up without sounding like an old lady.

"Oh, do you need directions?" She peers at me through her sunglasses, apparently confused by my lack of motion. "First go back to the main road and make a left."

"I have to tell you something," I blurt out. "I sort of have a phobia of driving people places."

"What?" Her smile fades. She flips her sunglasses onto her forehead. "But then why did you say that you would take me?"

"I'm trying to get over it," I tell her. "But it's not easy."

"Do you want me to drive?" she offers. "I've got a permit and I'm pretty good at it."

"No," I say, imagining what constitutes "pretty good at it." "I can drive. I just—it would help if you put on your seat belt." I give her a sideways glance. "And if you were sort of quiet."

"Ooh. Understood." She clicks on her seat belt and makes a little motion like she's holding a key to her lips and locking them. She gives me a thumbs-up.

"Thanks." I do a quick check of my surroundings, start the car, and shift into drive. "I know it's weird to ask someone not to talk in the car, but that way I can totally focus on the road."

"Got it," she says. "Jordy told me about what happened to your family. Sorry. I didn't think about that before I asked you. I'd probably be afraid of cars too."

I signal as I prepare to pull away from the curb, checking my mirrors one last time. My hands are clammy on the steering wheel. "He told you about that, huh? What else did he say about me?"

"Not much. Don't be mad if it was a secret. I'm good at getting him to talk to me about stuff. My mom has scared off most of his local friends, so when he's not on the road, I'm pretty much all he has." She grins mischievously. "I think he likes you, though."

I blush. "No. We're just helping each other with—"

"Shh." She holds her index finger to her lips. "Less

159

talking. More driving."

"Right." I do another check and then pull out into the street. I force myself to focus on driving instead of what Penn said. *I think he likes you.* If anything, it's just some weird fascination with me because I'm apparently the only girl in all of San Diego who didn't recognize him on sight. I check my mirrors repeatedly, slowing down whenever I get too close to another car.

Penn sits next to me, quiet except for occasionally tapping her foot against the floorboard. I repeat Daniel's coping statement over and over in my head. *No one is going to die.*

When we arrive at the tennis complex about twenty minutes later, I pull my car around to the back parking lot as Penn directs. She ushers me through what looks like a players-only entrance. The stands are packed with people.

I follow Penn up a set of green metal stairs and then inside to an air-conditioned hallway. She opens the door to a small but lavish room with one wall made completely of glass. "It's a private box," she says. "Only for family of the seeded players."

I freeze midstep. "Are your parents going to be up here?"

"Oh no. They feel the need to sit in the front row of the stands so my mom can yell helpful things at Jordy like 'tuck in your shirt' and 'get your hair out of your eyes.' You won't have to meet them, I promise."

We each take a seat in front of the big glass window and watch Jordy's opponent—a guy named Peter Kline, according to the electronic scoreboard—go through some basic stretches. Although he's several inches shorter, he looks older than Jordy. A tattoo of a leopard protrudes from his left sock and covers most of his calf.

"So the driving thing," Penn says. "Is that why you drive yourself to our away matches?"

"Yeah," I admit. "It's not so much a fear of driving as it is a fear of being in a vehicle with other people."

"That must be hard," she says. Then her face brightens as she points down at the court.

Jordy emerges from the tunnel across the stadium, dressed in white tennis shorts and a black and green Windbreaker. An unfamiliar heat radiates through my body as I watch him jog slowly over to his seat and set his water bottle and racquet bag on the ground. There's something about the way he carries himself, about the way he looks wearing actual tennis clothes instead of mesh shorts and a T-shirt. He looks older, professional. *He looks hot.*

I can't even believe my mind just went there. I should be focused on possible hazards, not fangirling. I force myself to scan the crowd and the court for anything that appears dangerous, but after seeing nothing, my eyes come back to Jordy. Is this what happened to every girl at school, too? Did he wear them down one at a time with his exhausting mix of confidence and charm? No, this is a guy who trains five hours a day and then studies and then goes to practice and then comes home and does homework. There's no way he found time to work his magic on all the girls who are crushing on him.

Jordy strolls over to the edge of the stands where a thin blonde woman is standing. She says something to him. He pulls a headband out of his pocket and affixes it over his forehead. Then he makes a big point of tucking in his shirt.

I smother a giggle. "You weren't kidding about your mom."

Penn coils one of her pigtails around her hand. "Nope. And there's my dad next to her, in the aviator sunglasses. He's the silent partner in the tyrannical dictatorship known as the Wheeler household. And there's Jordy's coach, Mr. Sang, next to Dad."

The announcer introduces Jordy and his opponent. Apparently this is one of two semifinal matches being played today. The announcer states that Kline is ranked 141st in the world and Jordy is ranked 47th among 18-and-under juniors. The crowd applauds as the two of them begin to warm up.

I settle back in my chair, and the match gets off to a good start, with Jordy taking a 3–0 lead. His serve is incredible. He hits ace after ace, the balls being clocked at over 120 miles per hour. I can barely even see them from up here. The announcer comments on how Jordy's height gives him an advantage with serving, but the rest of his game is also pretty stellar. Peter Kline wins a game to make it 3–1, but Jordy comes back and wins two more games without even giving up a point. He's basically dominating and quickly wins the set 6–2.

He goes to his chair and mops some sweat from his forehead. Then he glances up and smiles in our direction.

"That was for you, by the way," Penn says.

"Nuh-uh," I say. "He can't see me from down there."

"I might have texted him on the way here to apologize and say good luck." She blinks innocently. "And mentioned that his *friend* Maguire was giving me a ride."

I make a move like I'm going to strangle her.

She laughs. "Do you like him?"

I think about how sweet he's been, from the serve lessons to helping with my therapy challenges. And the way he took care of me when I was freaking out and flashing back to the accident. "He's really nice," I say.

She scoffs. "Yeah, that's his biggest downfall if you ask me. He hates making waves. He tries to please everyone all the time. He lets my parents, his coach, his sponsors, random people on the internet tell him what to do and who to be. No wonder he feels like—" Penn pauses. "Well, I guess as far as annoying qualities go, it could be worse, right?"

"Feels like what?" I ask. "Like the real him is disappearing?"

"Yeah. Wow, he told you that?"

"We were sharing shrink stories," I say. "I'm not sure he meant to tell me. It just kind of spilled out."

Before she can respond, Jordy jogs back out onto the court. I do a five-second check, scanning the court and the crowd for anything that looks out of place. I can't see all of the people from where Penn and I are sitting, but it's a gorgeous, sunny day, and everyone seems to be having a good time. I lean back in my chair and prepare to enjoy the second set. But after winning three of the first four games, Jordy double-faults twice, and suddenly it's three games to two. From that point onward, he seems to slowly unravel. He wins a point, but then loses two. He makes a great shot but then makes a silly mistake. He follows this pattern for several games in a row.

"What's happening to him?" I ask Penn.

She shakes her head. "No clue. He said he's been feeling tired lately. My mom made him go to the doctor, but as far as I know they didn't find anything wrong."

A terrible idea seizes my brain. I was worried about coming here because of the crowd, because I imagined being in a public place meant someone might get hurt. What if Jordy is the one I'm hurting? What if he's losing this match because of me? I reach up and touch my mystic knot pendant, hoping the clasp is in front. No such luck. I sink lower and lower in my chair, dropping my hand over the side and knocking feebly on one of the wooden chair legs. *Please don't let him lose.*

When Jordy loses the second set 6–4, I almost ask Penn if we can leave, but I know that will look unsupportive, like I've given up on her brother.

He goes to the stands briefly. I watch his mom's lips. I can't make out any words, but they seem sharp. His coach is gesturing wildly with one hand. Behind them, Jordy's dad appears to be talking on his phone.

Jordy's shoulders droop slightly as he heads for the folding chair set up next to his racquet bag. I wish I could go talk to him and tell him he's doing fine.

"Can we text him or something?" I ask. "Encourage him?"

"Not a good idea," Penn says. "If my mom sees him on his phone, she'll have a shit fit. He knows you're here. That helps."

"Doubtful," I mutter.

"Let's get food," Penn says. "This is only a 'best of three sets' match, but we might be here for another hour or so."

"Okay." I follow her back down the green metal stairs to the ground level of the stadium where there are the usual booths selling beer and pretzels, as well as a few fancier places selling things like pasta and salads. I pause on the bottom step, a little afraid to abandon the relative safety of the staircase. People are milling in all directions, carrying too much food, talking on phones, not paying any attention to where they're going. Blue flame flares up in a skillet at the back of one of the booths. The cook shakes the pan without even looking, instead talking and laughing with the cook next to him.

The entire stadium suddenly feels tiny, like the walls are

closing in. Pain jolts through me, like someone is holding a lit sparkler in my chest. I reach up to touch my mystic knot, one hand pressing hard against my breastbone, willing my heart to slow down.

"Let's get pasta," Penn suggests, oblivious to the panic welling inside me. I do a five-second check of the pasta stand as I get in line behind her. My blood is still racing through my veins, my pulse roaring in my ears, but there are no obvious signs of danger. *No obvious danger.* I repeat the words in my head like a mantra. I breathe in for a count of four, hold my breath for a few seconds, and then exhale slowly, like my old therapist taught me to do for a panic attack. *No obvious danger.* Penn and I will be back in the safety of the box in a few minutes.

She orders manicotti and sparkling water, and I order a plate of ravioli and a large Coke. I peer around the corner as we wait for our food, scanning the masses of people. *No obvious danger.*

Just as we get our food, the announcer asks everyone to take their seats so the third set can begin.

"Come on." Penn turns toward the metal stairs, dodging around people, both hands full of food. She hits the steps running.

I'm slightly behind her, not quite as quick or agile. "Wait up." I adjust my grip on my container of ravioli so I can hold it and my soda in the same hand and use the other hand on the railing.

And then I see Penn's foot miss a step. Her toe comes down on the edge of it and slips off. She pitches forward. Manicotti and sparkling water go flying as she flails her arms to regain her balance. It doesn't happen. She lands face-first on the metal staircase.

CHAPTER 19

"Penn," I shriek. I hurry up the steps and push my way through the circle of onlookers gathering around her. "Let me through." A little voice in my head says, *You did this.*

Penn is sitting on the stairs, covered in tomato sauce and looking dazed. One hand is curled around her nose and mouth. "Ow," she says through her fingers.

I set my food on the steps next to her. "Are you all right? Let me see your face."

She moves her hand, and I can see she's got a bloody nose and a puffy red spot beneath her left eye.

"Can you see okay?" I ask. The blood trickling from her nose makes me a little woozy. I bite my lip as I struggle to focus.

"I'm not sure." She tries to close her eye but can't quite do it. A drop of blood falls from her lip and lands on her T-shirt. "Dammit," she says. "That's going to be so hard to get out." She pinches her nose closed with her thumb and forefinger.

A guy in black pants and a navy blue shirt pushes his way through the crowd. "Step aside, everyone," he says. "Just head back to your seats please." He turns to us. "I'm club security. What happened?"

"I fell," Penn says. "I was running up the stairs like a dumbass. I'm sorry about the mess."

"Don't worry about the mess. Just sit right here while I call a medic."

"I don't think I need a medic," she protests.

"Yes you do," I say firmly. "Penn, you're bleeding and half your face is swollen. You might have a broken nose."

She uses the reverse camera on her phone to check her appearance and then swears under her breath. "My mom is going to kill me." She turns to the security guard. "Look. My brother is playing. We just want to go back to the box and finish watching him. I know there's probably legal stuff you need me to do, but can I have my mom fill out the paperwork or whatever after the match?"

"You're with one of the players?"

"Jordy Wheeler," Penn says.

The guy sighs and then pulls out a cell phone. He steps away from us and mutters something into the phone.

"I'm so sorry," I start. "I shouldn't have—"

She waves off my apology. "It's not like you pushed me. I was just in a rush."

"Does it hurt?"

Penn doesn't answer. She's staring at a guy dressed like an

EMT and the blonde woman from the stands, who are heading toward the stairs. An older man with a mop and bucket trails behind them.

"Shit," she says. "Get out of here, Maguire. Go back and watch my brother. I don't want my mom meeting you like this."

"I'm not just going to leave you like—"

"I assure you, I'm in good hands. Too good. Just go, please. Jordy deserves someone to support him."

"Um . . . okay, if you're sure." I head back to the third level of the complex and watch from the landing as the medic and Penn's mom escort her down the steps.

I return to the box, realizing only when I get there that I left my food sitting on the stairs. I'm not hungry anymore, anyway. I hope Penn is okay. I wonder if Jordy knows what happened.

I get my answer a couple of minutes later when Jordy goes to the stands after a point to talk to his coach and then doesn't return to the court. He pulls his Windbreaker over his head, grabs his bag, and runs over to the umpire. Then he jogs up to his opponent at the net and shakes his hand.

Jordy disappears, and the announcer tells the crowd he's forfeited the match because of a medical emergency. I sink to the floor of the box and rest my head in my hands. This was only my third therapy challenge. I can't believe I failed already. Reluctantly, I pull my luck notebook out of my purse and make a new entry.

Sept 26. San Diego Tennis Complex. Penn Wheeler falls on stairs.

I try to think about what Dr. Leed would say. He'd point out that this is different from my previous incidents, because only one person was injured. It's not like the entire stadium collapsed. He'd undoubtedly mention that it wasn't my idea to get food and that I wasn't near Penn when she fell. And he'd be right about all of those things. I know logically I didn't cause Penn's accident. But curses, bad luck, these things aren't logical.

"Maguire." Jordy is standing in the doorway. "Are you okay?"

I shake my head. The tears surge from my eyes without warning, hot and fast. His sister is hurt. He had to forfeit. And yet he came to check on me. "Why are you here?" I ask. "You should be at the hospital."

"I'm going right now," he says. "But why are you crying?"

"I shouldn't have come here," I choke out.

"I'm glad you came." Jordy kneels down in front of me, his hair plastered to the sides of his face with sweat. He rests his hands on my shoulders. "What happened exactly?"

"We went to get food and she fell on the stairs and her nose was bleeding and she said she couldn't see out of one eye." I bury my face in my hands, taking a couple of slow breaths to get myself back under control. I don't want him to see me like this. I don't want anyone to see me like this.

I don't want to *be* like this. Ever.

Jordy pulls me into his arms, and my face ends up in his chest. His shirt is drenched with sweat, but I don't care. Beneath the fabric he's solid, a wall to lean on, and I am in danger of collapsing. I wrap my arms around his neck. His heart beats gently in my ear.

"It wasn't your fault," he says. "And it's no big deal. Penn texted me on the way to the ER to say Mom was overreacting and she was fine." He strokes my back gently. "Please don't cry."

I peek up at him. "But you were competing for money and now you had to forfeit and your parents are probably mad and I'm so sorry. I'm messing with your future."

"I didn't *have* to do anything. I wanted to because my sister means more to me than a tennis match. Plus I was losing anyway." He sits down on the floor next to me. "I'm tired, Maguire. I feel so out of it lately. I don't know what my problem is, but I would've lost tomorrow if not today. So please don't be upset."

I nod. "Go see your sister."

"I am." He squeezes my hand. "You want to come with me?"

I shake my head. "I can't. Not right now. I'm too freaked out. I don't even want to drive by myself for a little bit. Tell her I'm sorry."

He gives me a long look. "Are you going to be able to get home okay?"

"Yeah. I'm just going to sit here for a little bit and calm down."

"Good idea," Jordy says. "Call Daniel, maybe. See if he can fit you in. I think he works two weekends a month."

"Yeah, maybe."

"I'll call you later and let you know what the deal is," Jordy says.

I watch him leave and then lean back against the wall, rubbing my temples with my fingertips. Jordy shouldn't call me. He should stay away from me. And if he won't, then I should stay away from him, for his own good.

CHAPTER 20

Jordy calls me twice in the afternoon, but I let the calls go to voice mail. Then I turn off my phone. I want to call him back, but I'm afraid to, like maybe every conversation we have brings me one step closer to really hurting him. Mom made me an appointment with Daniel tomorrow. Hopefully, talking to him will help.

Only I should've known better than to think I could avoid Jordy by turning off my phone. He shows up at my house around 8:00 p.m.

I hear someone knock on the door, and immediately my stomach crashes down into my feet. I slip out of my room and tiptoe down the hallway to see Jordy standing just inside the front door. He's dressed to impress in jeans and a collared shirt, his hair looking professionally disheveled.

"I apologize for coming over so late, ma'am," he says. "My name is Jordy Wheeler. I'm friends with your daughter. Is she around?"

Ma'am? Late? It's 8:00 on a Saturday. He's kind of laying it on thick.

Mom's got Jake in one arm. My sister is sitting on the floor looking up at Jordy like he's some sort of storybook character.

I slide around the corner. "I'm here."

"You have a visitor," my mom says with a smile.

"Hey," I say.

"Hey," Jordy says.

"Why are you so tall?" Erin asks.

He smiles at her. "I'm a giant." He turns to me. "Can I talk to you?"

Erin's eyes get wide. "Like from a fairy tale?"

"Sort of," he says. "But I'm a nice giant, not a mean one that steals your gold and livestock."

"What's livestock?"

"Cows," I tell her. I turn to my mother. "Mom, we're going to go outside for a few."

"Okay." She flips on the TV to distract my little sister so she won't try to come with us.

Jordy follows me through the front door, and we sit on the porch. The sky is mostly clear, the stars glittering high above our heads. *Dear Universe,* I think. *Fight fair. Mess with me all you want, but leave my friends out of it.*

"You okay?" He bumps his shoulder into my shoulder. He smells good, like maybe he splashed on a little cologne for this occasion.

"Yeah." I stare out at the grass.

"Any particular reason you dodged all my calls?"

"I know what you're going to say, and I'm afraid hearing it won't help."

"Fair enough. I don't have to say anything." He taps one foot repeatedly. Now we're both staring at the grass. "Go for a walk with me," he says after a couple of minutes. "Just around the block."

"Okay."

We get halfway around the block before Jordy finally breaks the silence. "Like I said, my sister is fine. So if you're blaming yourself, you can stop."

And just as I thought, hearing that doesn't make me feel better. "Yeah, but she still got hurt. And you had to forfeit your match."

"I didn't have to. I *chose* to." He sighs. "Why are you so upset about me forfeiting, anyway? It's just a tennis match."

"Because I'm sick of people getting hurt in my presence. I'm sick of feeling like I can't do anything or go anywhere without having it end in some kind of disaster."

"Too bad," Jordy says.

"Too bad what?" I snap.

"I was hoping you were going to say you got so upset because you like me." He jams both hands in his pockets. His shoulders slump forward.

"You know I like you," I protest. "You, Penn, and Jade are basically my only friends."

His eyes latch on to mine, and for a few seconds neither of us speaks. "You know that isn't what I mean," he says finally.

I look away, feigning interest in something across the street. Weird tingly moments and wobbly stomachs aside, I can't handle the idea of Jordy really liking me. I don't want to hurt him by rejecting him, but I don't want to hurt him with my bad luck either. Plus he's not allowed to date and I'm not interested in being . . . whatever. *He still manages to get plenty of action.* What does that mean? Why do I even care?

"How'd you get out of the house?" I ask. "I thought you weren't allowed to go anywhere."

He flushes. "I told my parents I was going to the drugstore to get stuff for Penn."

"Oh."

"I already got it. I just wanted to stop by and make sure you're okay."

I kick at a pebble on the sidewalk. "I'm okay."

"There's something else—something I have to tell you," Jordy says.

A red convertible pulls up to a stoplight nearby, and the driver looks over at us. Farther down the block, a couple of kids on skateboards are heading our way and show no signs of slowing down. Jordy steers me off the sidewalk and into the parking lot of a gas station. It's not very private, but at least we won't get mowed down by middle school kids.

I cross my arms. "What is it?"

Jordy turns me to face him. He rests one hand on my waist. I tense up a little as I wait for him to speak.

"This has never been so hard before." He rakes his other hand through his hair. "Probably because I know what you're going to say, and it's not going to make me feel better." He forces a smile. "I like you, Maguire. I like you a lot."

"Jordy . . ." I trail off. A lock of hair blows in front of my face, and he brushes it away. He leans in, resting his jaw against my temple, his lips somewhere in my hair. I can't feel them, but I know they're there. All I have to do is turn my head, lift my chin, and he'll kiss me.

No one has ever kissed me before, but that's not the real reason why my chest hurts and my hands are shaking. "I like you too," I say finally. "You've been great to me, and you make me laugh. You make me forget the things I worry about. But what if I'm not ready to forget, you know? I've been okay by myself for so long and now I'm doing this therapy stuff and it feels like maybe even that's too much for me and . . . I'm scared." I pull back from him and train my eyes on the ground.

"I know you're scared," he says. "I want to help you."

"I don't know if you can. I think I have to do some of this stuff on my own. I'm sorry."

He nods. "Okay. I understand."

Wordlessly we both turn back toward my house.

My brain takes note of every single thing we pass. A fire hydrant. A Navy guy walking a dog. Three girls wearing suede Ugg boots with short skirts just like Kimber did the first day of tryouts. A handful of leaves blows down the sidewalk. I watch them tumble end over end, my stomach matching their motion. This isn't a five-second check. This is an endless check, a way not to have to feel the disappointment radiating off Jordy. We get back to my driveway, and he pauses at the end of it.

"Nothing else to say, I guess?"

I glance over at him. "I don't know what you want from me."

"Forget it," he says. "It's probably just a stupid crush. I'll get over it."

Crush? On me? I am so completely unprepared to process this information that I blurt out the first thing that pops into my head. "What about Kimber?"

"What about her?"

"I thought you two . . ."

"No," he says sharply. "You thought wrong. We kissed once, but that's it."

The idea of this near-perfect boy having a crush on me is almost laughable. Not that there's anything wrong with me, aside from my curse, but Jordy could have almost anyone. Why not pick from the pool of willing girls instead of go for the one who's too screwed up to let herself care about anyone? He's a competitive athlete—it has to be about the challenge. But what if it's not that? What if he really *likes* me? "Maybe we should stop helping each other."

"I don't think we should." He crosses his arms. "And I don't think you do either."

"I don't know," I say. "I hate the thought of hurting you."

"You didn't—"

"So you say. But next time could be different."

"I'll take my chances." The wind blows his hair forward into his face.

Behind him, the moon shines almost full in the sky, its glow illuminating the sloping edges of the nearby roofs. Across the street, Jordy's car is a glimmer of black on black.

He fishes his keys out of his pocket and turns to me. "Look, whatever. If you don't want my help anymore, then I'll back off. But don't give up on your therapy challenges over what happened at the tournament, okay? I can already see changes in you, Maguire."

"Like what?"

"Like you drove my sister across town, and she said you did fine."

"It was scary. I had to tell her about my phobia to make her be quiet," I say. "But yeah, I do feel a *little* less scared about driving with other people."

"I'm glad," Jordy says. But he doesn't sound glad. He sounds hurt.

I hate knowing I'm the one who did that to him.

That night I dream I'm in psychology class, and Jordy is there too. Ms. Haynes starts talking about survival instinct, about how we'd all behave differently if we were in a plane crash together. How some of us would find inner strength and others would succumb to baser instincts and weaknesses.

Kimber raises her hand and says that in order for anyone to survive, the weak people would have to be left behind. "Like Maguire," she says. "She's so scared of everything. All she'd do is bring everyone else down." Jordy is sitting next to her in Colleen's usual chair. He turns around to look at me and nods in agreement. His expression is exactly the same as it was when he left me in my driveway. Disappointed. The whole class starts nodding and pointing at me—even Jade. Ms. Haynes makes two columns on the whiteboard: "SEEK RESCUE" and "LEAVE BEHIND." She writes my name in the second column. She starts writing everyone else's name in the first column.

I wake up, relieved to find myself tucked beneath my comforter. It's still dark so I try to go back to sleep, but I can't stop thinking about Jordy, about what I gave up because I was afraid. I remind myself that I'm supposed to be focusing on Ireland, not boys. On getting stronger so I can honor my family. But still, the look in Jordy's eyes reminded me of my mom's look when we talked the other day. I hate knowing that I'm letting people down. Curling onto my side, I squeeze my eyes shut again. But the tears come anyway, silent and then louder.

There's a soft knocking sound. My eyes flick open as my bedroom door creaks inward. Tom is standing in the doorway wearing plaid pajama pants and a Doctor Who T-shirt.

I sit up in bed. "What is it?"

He steps inside my room and closes the door halfway behind him. "I got up to feed Jake and I heard you from the hallway."

"Oh."

He rubs at his beard. "Do you want me to wake your mom?"

"No, I'm fine." I wipe at my eyes with the back of my hand. "Just stupid girl stuff."

Tom pulls the chair from my desk over to the bed and sits down so we're eye to eye. "I've never been very good at stupid girl stuff," he says. "But I can try. Your mom told me you had a visitor tonight. Does someone need to kick that kid's ass?"

It's weird, Tom being here like this. He's the polar opposite of my dad in so many ways. Bearded, broad-shouldered, nerdy, a little overweight. He met my mom when she backed into his car in the parking lot of a grocery store. I wonder if it was this gentle, comforting side of him that won her over. "Apparently someone needs to kick *my* ass." I bury my head in my hands.

"Why's that?"

I peek at Tom through my fingers. "Jordy is a good guy. No, he's an amazing guy. And he told me he likes me."

Tom clears his throat. "So I *do* need to kick his ass."

I drop my hands to my lap and smile. "No you don't.

Because as soon as he said that, I basically pushed him away."

"Yessss." Tom pumps his fist.

I frown. "Not helping."

"Sorry. That's just every dad's dream answer."

I don't say anything for a second. Hearing Tom refer to himself as my dad always tears me up inside. On one hand, I feel like no one but my real dad should ever get to say that. But I know with Tom it comes from a good place, that he's trying to make me feel included, that he doesn't want me to feel like an unwanted piece of the past that everyone else is stuck with.

"And now I worry I've offended you," he says softly.

"No. It's okay. I . . . like it. Does it offend you that I call you Tom?"

He rubs the bridge of his nose. "I mean, I prefer 'Sir,' but I can live with Tom."

I smother a laugh. "No being funny at two a.m. We'll wake everyone up."

"Seriously, though, Maguire. If you ever have tips, I'm all ears."

"You mean like stop wearing black socks with white shoes?"

Tom snorts. "Now who's being funny?" He pauses. "I'm always worried I'm being not enough of a dad or too much of a dad to you, that no matter what I try I'm doing it wrong."

"You realize I'm going to use this weakness against you now, right?"

"Noted," he says.

"But FYI, you're doing great." I smile at him. "You should get some sleep before Jake wakes up again."

"Good idea." He stands up and quietly slides the chair back under my desk. He pauses just inside the doorway and turns back to me. "It's hard to let yourself be happy, isn't it?"

I ball the fabric of my comforter in my hands. "What do you mean?"

He leans back against the door. "Your mom. You, Erin, Jake. I have everything I ever wanted, but someone had to die for me to get it." Even in the darkened room, I can see his broad shoulders slump inward a little. "I figure maybe it's similar for you."

My eyes fill with tears again. I slide out of bed, cross the floor to him, and throw my arms around his waist. He's almost as tall as Jordy, and my head fits right beneath his, my chin quivering in the general vicinity of his chest.

He pets my hair. "Shit. I guess I should've quit while you were making fun of my socks."

I hug him even tighter. I never once considered that the past hurt Tom too, but it makes sense. Of course he would struggle with knowing that my mom never would have married him if my dad hadn't died, that so many of the things he loves are a product of tragedy.

"It is hard to be happy," I whisper. "It's like I'm betraying them. Like I got to live, so that should be more than enough. Like wanting to feel good is almost greedy. God, you're one of the only people who gets it. I had no idea."

He pats my back tentatively. "Yeah, I don't think we've ever talked like this before."

I shake my head. "Me neither."

"Maybe we can do it again sometime when it's not two a.m."

"I'd like that," I say. And I mean it.

CHAPTER 21
Session #9

"I can't believe you do sessions on Sundays," I tell Daniel.

He turns off his music. "I don't have a receptionist on the weekend, but when your clients are kids and teenagers, you have to work around a lot of school schedules." He takes a sip of coffee. "I'm glad I could fit you in, because your mom made it sound urgent. What's going on?"

I swallow hard and start to tell him about what happened to Penn, but tears form in my eyes and I can't get the words out.

He hands me a box of tissues. And waits.

"Tell me about your music," I say suddenly. I blot my eyes and then ball the tissue in my hand.

"You're not here to talk about my music."

"I know, but I need a minute. I need to think about something other than me. So that guitar music you're always listening to—is it you?"

"It's my girlfriend," Daniel says.

"Is she sad? It always sounds so sad."

"I don't know," he says. "I guess that's why I'm always playing it, trying to find her in the chords, trying to understand her. I'm not very creative. Sometimes I feel like our brains are wired completely differently."

"You don't play too? But you have those music magazines. I thought maybe you had a secret second life."

"I think everyone has a secret second life." A smile touches his lips. "But no. I don't play. Reading music magazines is just my way of trying to see the world through her eyes. She gets mad when she catches me. She thinks I'm analyzing her." He makes air quotes around the word "analyzing."

"Are you?"

"Maybe?" Daniel shrugs. "I like to think of it as trying to appreciate something that means a lot to her."

I nod. "That makes sense."

"So what happened yesterday?"

I take a breath. "This girl on the tennis team invited me to go watch a tennis match. Jordy's sister, actually," I admit. It seems pointless to keep hiding the fact that I know Jordy from Daniel. It's too hard to be honest if I have to keep half of everything a secret.

"And?"

"It started out okay. I told her about being afraid to drive with other people. She was really cool about it and we made it to the tennis complex just fine. Jordy won the first set easily. Then he lost the second set. We went downstairs to go get food." My lower lip trembles. "She tripped on the way back up. Her hands were full. She landed on her face."

"Ouch," Daniel says. "Is she okay?"

"She said she is, but there was all this blood." I shudder just thinking about it. "Her mom took her to the hospital, and Jordy forfeited so he could go with her." I inhale deeply. "And I feel like both of those things are my fault."

Daniel drums his fingertips on the edge of his chair. Then he says basically everything I thought he would say about how what happened was unfortunate but wasn't on par with a fire or a major accident or eight people getting sick at a slumber party. "It sounds like she slipped because she had her hands full and was hurrying."

"I know you're probably right," I say. "But I can't help but think if I hadn't driven her, she wouldn't have gone. She wouldn't have gotten food. She wouldn't have gotten hurt. Jordy wouldn't have had to forfeit. It's just not fair."

"Well, first off, your thought process is flawed," Daniel says. "If you hadn't given her a ride, maybe she would've borrowed her parents' car and tried to drive herself and gotten in an accident. She could've gotten hurt worse."

"I guess," I mumble.

"No section for that in your luck notebook, is there? All the bad things that might have happened that you actually prevented?"

"I can't quantify things that don't happen," I protest.

"Then it seems like your data is incomplete, which brings

188

me to my next point. Are you familiar with the concept of selective attention?"

"No."

"So if I asked you to write down everything you've done in the past week, it'd include going to six classes a day for five days, tennis tryouts, going to and from school, dinner with your family, other stuff, I'm guessing, right?"

"Yeah?"

Daniel taps some notes into his tablet. "And nothing bad happened during any of that stuff."

"True."

"But something bad happened at the tennis tournament, so that's all your brain can focus on." He continues before I can respond. "I am not trying to say what you went through when you were younger wasn't unusual or excessive. I'm simply saying this might be different. After all, it isn't like everyone else got hurt and you were the only person who didn't suffer. It just feels like that because Jordy and his sister are your friends."

"Maybe." I sigh. "Why am I like this?"

"I have my thoughts," Daniel says. "But that answer needs to come from you."

"How do I figure it out?"

"Keep going with your therapy challenges. You can do number three over if you want, but keep in mind that it's unrealistic to expect all of these to go off without a hitch. No one died. No one got seriously injured. That's what matters.

And I have an idea for number four: get angry at the Universe. Can you do that?"

I think about walking around the block with Jordy last night. How unfair it felt that I couldn't do anything without someone getting hurt. "That's my challenge? Get angry? Done."

"Good," Daniel says. "Now you need to take back something the Universe has stolen from you."

"What do you suggest?"

"That's up to you."

I think about all the things I've lost, all the things I've given up. My family, my friends, my hobbies . . . my personality. I'm not the person I would have grown up to be if I hadn't been in those accidents. The Universe has taken almost everything.

I like the idea of taking something back.

CHAPTER 22

Back at school on Monday, I find myself dreading the end of the day and tennis practice.

Part of me needs to see Jordy, but part of me wants to avoid him forever. I try to put him out of my head.

But I fail. I fail in first hour and second hour. In third hour we have a test, so I manage to replace the hurt in his eyes and the tightness of his voice with trigonometric functions for about forty minutes. I'm just settling in on the steps outside of the school with my lunch and a book about an Irish girl who finds out she's part faerie when I see his car pull into the parking lot.

I half-expect him to avoid me, but he strolls up the steps in his warm-up pants and T-shirt almost like nothing happened. I want to look up at him, see him smile, hear him say that everything is fine. But instead I concentrate really hard on my sandwich, because that's easier.

He drops his backpack and tennis bag on the ground and

sits next to me on the steps. "Why do you always eat by yourself?"

"I like eating by myself. Gives me time to read." Without having to monitor everything.

"I won't stay long then." He nudges my flip-flop with his tennis shoe. "Are we cool?"

I look over at him. He's backlit by the sun so his form is shaded. He looks unreal, like a photograph of a shadow. It's impossible not to think about my face against his chest, and then, later, his jaw against my temple, his mouth in my hair. It is impossible not to stare at his lips and wonder.

Crap. He's waiting for me to answer, and I'm sitting here gawking at him like a freshman girl. I swallow hard as I try to figure out what to say. I want us to be friends.

I want more than that, but I know I can't keep pulling him close and then pushing him away when I get scared. "Well, from what I hear, you're cool," I say finally. "I'm more of a work in progress."

"You'll get there. You're still young." He grins. "Sorry I went all sensitive guy on you. It was sort of an intense week-end."

"Don't apologize for being you." He's working so hard to hold on to his identity. The last thing I want is for him to feel like he has to censor himself around me.

He gasps in mock outrage. "Are you calling me a sensi-tive guy?"

"Don't worry." I bump my knee against his "Your secret's safe with me."

"You're the only girl who knows all my secrets. Well, you and my sister." He snatches my sandwich right out of my hands and takes a bite out of it. "I've got to go barely pass a geometry exam," he says through a mouthful of roast beef and cheese. He hands the sandwich back to me. "See you at practice."

Coach ramps up our physical conditioning today, so we have to run a mile. I run with Jade as usual. We make our own pace—one quick enough to satisfy Coach but slow enough that we can talk without getting short of breath. I can't help but sneak a peek at Jordy as we run by the spot where he and Coach stand chatting.

Jade bursts out laughing as we round the far corner by the football goalposts for the third time. "You have got to be kidding me."

"What?" I ask, my footsteps and heart pounding in tandem.

"You too?" She glances over at me, her dark eyes wide with glee. "I thought I had finally . . . met someone else . . . immune to Jordy's charm." The words come out in small gasps.

"I'm immune," I say, struggling not to think about Saturday, about what it felt like to be wrapped in Jordy's sweaty embrace. To hear him say that he likes me.

"Please. You look in his direction every time we pass. You are so not immune."

I give Jade a little push as we pass the home team bleachers. "Am too."

"Then why are you grinning like you just won Wimbledon right now?"

"Maybe I'm having fun," I shoot back.

"No one has fun running. It's unnatural."

I laugh. "Maybe I'm having fun with you."

Jade starts to speak and then stops as Colleen and her doubles partner, Luisa, pass us on the inside. She slows until they're a few yards ahead of us and then says, "Maybe you're having fun with Mr. Off Limits." She leaps over a crack in the asphalt. "You'd tell me, wouldn't you?"

"There's nothing to tell," I say firmly, feeling the slightest twinge of guilt. No need to start up a bunch of team gossip, especially not with Kimber acting like Jordy belongs to her.

"Well, he sure did a number on your serve," Jade says. "Just be careful. Like I said before, he's got a bit of a reputation, and it's obvious he likes you."

We finish our last lap and slow to a walk. "So what have you heard exactly?" I ask.

"Nothing specific. Just that he's been known to hook up with girls at parties and then make like it never happened afterward. Probably an overblown rumor, like everything else."

"Girls including Kimber?"

"Maybe. Don't they seem awfully tight to you?" Jade threads her fingers together behind her head and takes big gulps of air. "I swear Coach is trying to kill us with all this conditioning."

"It's helping though, right?" I say absentmindedly. I'm trying to reconcile the Jordy I know with the kind of guy who hooks up at parties and then pretends it didn't happen. *We kissed once.* It's a struggle. Nothing about the way he acts makes me think he would treat a girl like that.

"Helping me think I should have gone out for softball instead," Jade mutters.

Coach Hoffman is standing right inside the gate as we enter the tennis courts. His clipboard has a list of hitting partners. Almost everyone else has paired off already. "Go ahead and get to work," he says. "Everyone should play as much of a set as they can in the next hour."

Jade gives me a little wave and then meets up with her doubles partner. I'm assigned to Penn, but she showed up late and is still finishing her mile run. I take a seat on the far side of the court and do a little extra stretching while I wait.

I fold one leg behind me and lie back on the ground. It's a beautiful day as usual, the bright sun warming the asphalt beneath me, fluffy white clouds floating in a perfect blue sky. I switch legs and then lie back again, inhaling deeply. A butterfly floats by—a monarch with brilliant orange wings. I reach for it, but a gust of wind pushes it beyond my fingertips.

I close my eyes and listen to the sound of shoes squeaking, the rhythmic thwapping of tennis balls.

It occurs to me that this is nice, that occasionally the Universe gives me a serene and peaceful moment. Then I open my eyes and sit up. I do a five-second check, just in case.

"Hey, sleepyhead!" Penn shouts

I bounce to my feet as I see her approach. I suck in a sharp breath as she draws near. Half her face is swollen; the skin around her eye is an ugly bluish-green color.

"Oh my God. Can you see out of that?" I ask.

"Yeah," she says. "It looks worse than it is."

"I still can't believe you fell."

"I can't believe Jordy forfeited just to come to the hospital." She swishes her braid back over her shoulder. "He is the best brother ever."

"Yeah, that was pretty great of him."

She pulls a ball out of a pocket in her trunks and bounces it repeatedly on the strings of her racquet. "You don't know the half of it. My mom yelled at him for like an hour for doing that, and for once he didn't apologize to her. He just took it and then asked me what I wanted to do on my birthday. Which was the best birthday ever."

"You had the best birthday ever with a broken face?"

"Girls. Less talk, more play," Coach calls from the next court.

"I'll tell you later," Penn says. She hits both tennis balls in my direction. "You serve first."

I try my hardest, but Penn is a lot better than I am, and she quickly wins our set 6–2. Still, I manage to squeak in a couple of service winners, so I'm not completely bummed about losing. Despite starting late, we're one of the first pairs to finish, so Coach has us do some extra calisthenics up on the field while we wait for everyone else.

We each do twenty-five push-ups and then hold each other's feet while we do fifty sit-ups. Penn cranks out her first forty-five at high speed. Then she collapses back to the ground, breathing heavily. "So anyway, about my birthday." Her tanned skin is flushed red as she slowly rises up to touch her elbows to her knees again. "There was this band I wanted to see play up in LA, but my parents said no way since my friend only has a provisional license and wouldn't legally be able to drive us. But then Jordy totally agreed to play chauffeur since he didn't have anywhere to be."

Her expression goes from concentration to joy as she completes her last sit-up. She lowers her head to the grass and mimics taking a nap. "And before that I practiced driving with him and my dad. And Jordy and I went to lunch with my parents and hit the climbing gym for a couple of hours. I had so much fun."

We switch positions and I begin my sit-ups. "That sounds like a very busy day. Weren't you still sore from falling?"

"A little bit, but my brother is always out of town for my birthday. It was so cool to have him home that I didn't want to waste it. The whole family took turns picking stuff to do."

"So you guys are into rock climbing?" I can't keep the envy out of my voice. I've driven past the climbing gym a couple of times since we moved here and always wished I felt safe enough to give it a try.

Penn tosses her hair back from her face. "More him than me. My mom hates it because she says it's dangerous. He hardly ever goes anymore."

"That's too bad," I say. My abs are beginning to burn, but I'm not even halfway finished. "Your parents like to control everything, huh?"

She adjusts her hold on my shoes. "They like to control Jordy for sure. Forget arranged marriages; my brother has an arranged life. I guess he feels like they made a lot of sacrifices for him, so now he owes them."

I nod. Luisa and Colleen join us on the field, with the second doubles team right behind them. Penn looks over her shoulder at her brother. "Those two must be playing a whole match. There's no way he hasn't smoked her by now."

I watch Kimber run back and forth from corner to corner, refusing to give up as Jordy drills shot after shot back across the net, seemingly with ease. She manages to win the point when he aims for the sidelines and hits the ball just wide. She does a little cheer, and Penn rolls her eyes.

"You're supposed to cheer when you hit a winner. Not when someone else screws up," she says.

Coach whistles and motions for everyone to gather around Court One. We all jog back down the hill and onto the first court, where Kimber is mopping the sweat from her brow.

"You went easy on me," Kimber tells Jordy. "I've never won more than one point in a row off you before."

"Not that easy," he says teasingly. "What can I say? You're finally getting good." He slings an arm around her shoulder, and she smiles; it's maybe the happiest I've ever seen Kimber.

I wonder about their relationship again. It's obvious she's crazy about him. But if he hooked up with her while having no intention of dating her, why would she still like him so much? Kimber does not strike me as a girl who would let herself be manipulated or used.

After Coach dismisses us, part of the team heads for the parking lot and the rest of us head for the locker room. I'm walking with Jade and Penn, with Colleen and Luisa right behind us.

"Maguire?"

I turn to see Jordy loping across the blacktop. "Yeah?" I say.

He stops a few feet back from us. "Can I ask you something?"

Jade gives me a sideways glance, her mouth curling into a smile.

I shoot her a glare in response. "Catch up with you guys

in a few," I say. I fall back alongside Jordy. "What's up?"

"So are you still going to let me help you with your shrink assignments?"

"I'm not sure if that's a good idea."

He slouches a little. "Oh. I was going to ask for your help again with mine, but you probably don't want to do that either."

"What did you have in mind?"

"Just hanging out sometime."

"Jordy, come on. Your therapy challenges are not to hang out with me."

"Well, technically I'm supposed to hang out with someone who makes me feel stronger."

I laugh out loud. "And that's me? Why? Because I'm so weak?"

He slugs me in the arm. "Yeah. You and your home run ground strokes. That's you because I don't feel like I'm constantly letting you down."

I don't respond right away. I'm staring at the silver carabiner clipping his water bottle to his tennis bag. I hear Daniel telling me to take something back. I haven't rock climbed since the car accident. And Jordy—he's fun to be around. I like him. I don't want to have to avoid him. I don't want the Universe to steal him too. What about taking back two things? "Do you want to go rock climbing with me?" I blurt out.

Jordy's eyes light up. "Seriously? I would love to."

"Penn told me you guys went on her birthday, that it's something you really like." I shrug. "I haven't gone in years, but I have all the gear."

He fiddles with the strap of his backpack. "The gym actually has everything we'd need."

"Forget the gym," I say. "Have you ever been to Joshua Tree?"

"Yeah. Penn and I drove through with my parents. The scenery is beautiful, but I don't know enough to rig climbs there."

"I know enough," I say. "My dad and uncle used to bring my brother and me with them to parks all over California, but I quit climbing when they died. I'm supposed to take back something the Universe stole from me. Maybe we can help each other at the same time."

OCTOBER

CHALLENGES

1. ~~Make the tennis team.~~
2. ~~Ride in a car with someone besides Mom.~~ Jordy.
3. ~~Spend a day in a crowded place: Tennis tournament.~~
4. Take something back from the Universe: Rock climbing.
5.
6.
7.

GOAL

Plane ride to Ireland for memorial service.

CHAPTER 23

We had to plan around Jordy's tournament schedule, so it's the second weekend in October before the two of us get to go rock climbing.

On Saturday morning, I watch for his car out the window and head for the living room when I see him pull up.

My mom looks up from changing Jake's diaper. "Are you going to be home in time for dinner?"

"Probably not," I say.

She unsnaps a container of baby wipes with one hand. "What are you guys doing again?"

"Just hiking and stuff." I dropped two duffel bags full of gear straight outside my window so my mom wouldn't see. She's still adjusting to me being able to ride in a car with someone else. I don't want to worry her by telling her I'm driving halfway across the state to go rock climbing.

Tom enters from the kitchen. "You want something to eat before you go? I'm making French toast."

"Sounds amazing," I say. "But we're kind of in a hurry."

"Am *I* ever going to meet this guy?" he asks.

I think back to our late-night conversation. "I don't know. If you do are you going to kick his ass?"

Tom chuckles. He pounds his right fist into his left palm, looking about as threatening as a baby polar bear. "Maybe."

My mom looks back and forth between the two of us as she finishes with Jake. "Why would you kick his ass?"

Tom winks at me. "Inside joke," he tells her.

"Whatever." She heads toward the nursery with my little brother. "See you tonight. You guys have fun and be safe."

"Will do." I step out into the warm sun and pull the front door closed behind me. Ducking down below the living room window, I cut across the grass and grab the gear bags.

Jordy pops the trunk of his car and I stow everything inside, hoping that my mom is too focused on Jake to spy on me through the window.

"Damn. What is all that?" Jordy asks.

"A rope, two harnesses, shoes, webbing, chalk, and the necessary cams and carabiners," I say.

"That's a lot of gear."

"That gear will keep us safe," I say with a smile. "You have no idea how good it felt to drag it out of the depths of my closet."

"And your mom was okay with it?"

"I told her we were just going hiking. What about your mom?"

Jordy smiles. "I said I was going rock climbing with a friend."

"I thought you always had to lie or sneak out."

"I do usually, but I told her I'd be getting exercise today and that I'd do a double practice session tomorrow. I also told her maybe what I needed was just a break—a day to not think about competing for once."

"And that worked?"

"She told me if I left the house I was grounded." He shrugs. "But next week's shrink homework is to do something for Real Jordy and not lie about it, so I figured I'd get ahead for once. I swear to you, I'm getting better at not letting them run my life."

"That's awesome. I'm happy for you," I say. "I mean, not about the grounded part."

"I'm happy for me too," he says. "And I'm basically grounded all the time, right? What else can my mother take away from me?"

"Well, I don't want to be the reason she's mad at you."

"You're not," he says. "What about you? How was your session with Daniel yesterday?"

"Good," I say. "Daniel is psyched that I'm climbing again."

"Cool." Jordy starts the car and then tosses me a tube of sunscreen from the center console. SPF 50. "Apply liberally. It'll take about three hours to get there, but we can switch off driving if you want."

"You'd trust me with your car?"

"No one is safer than you."

"True," I say. "But I'll try to make it the whole way."
I start working on my sunscreen as we head north on the
15, pausing occasionally to do a five-second check. We pass
through the outlying suburbs of San Diego and then some
smaller towns.

We turn east, near Riverside. Gradually the trees and
wildflowers give way to layers of brown and tan. Sand blows
against the windshield and tumbleweeds bounce across the
highway. This is the part of California that never makes it
into the movies. The hot, dry part where most people don't
want to live. But there's something almost magical about the
slender saguaro cactuses and beautiful Joshua trees that stand
sentry along the road.

Jordy closes his window and turns on the AC. About
twenty minutes later, we enter the park at the West Entrance
Station. The road is paved, but occasionally a deep crevasse
snakes across the surface. Jordy drives carefully, navigating
around the cracks and divots as best he can. On either side
of us, piles of boulders rise up like forgotten cities. Between
them are patchy scrub grass and Joshua trees—some alone,
some so close together that their twisted branches actually
intertwine.

We follow the road for a few miles and then pull into a
parking lot for a picnic area. Beyond a sandy patch with a
barbecue grill and a couple of picnic tables is a massive wall

of rock. The parking lot is full of cars, some of them from other states like Oregon and Arizona. Splashes of neon rope are visible against the brownish gray of the rock.

I feel something building beneath my skin—a fluttery sort of pressure. It's nerves, but for once it's not all about the bad things that might happen. I spent the past few days practicing my knots and researching routes, and part of me—a huge part—is dying to get back into my shoes and harness.

Well, Connor's harness. Mine doesn't fit anymore.

I suck in a breath of dry desert air as we get out of the car. The heat sears my nasal passages and sizzles in my lungs. The sun is white-hot against my pale skin.

Jordy pops the trunk and I grab the harnesses, the rope, and a string of cams and carabiners. He grabs the rest of the gear and slams the trunk. With one hand he holds up a small black duffel bag. "I even remembered the Jordy Wheeler Deluxe Emergency Kit."

"You're such a Boy Scout," I say. We cross the sandy area and approach the wall of rock.

"So you've climbed here before?" Jordy asks.

"Just once, on a family vacation. I was only ten, but I researched everything last week. Don't worry. I got this."

He grins. "I'm not worried."

I use a guidebook I got from the library to locate a climb that's medium difficulty. "Here. This is a good top-roping spot." Top-roping is the safest type of rock climbing, where the rope is doubled and one person climbs at a time. The other person belays, or keeps control of the rope's slack by pulling it through a special device.

We drop all of our gear on the ground. I look up at the wall. Fifty feet looks higher than I remember.

"You okay?" Jordy slips his feet into the leg holes of his harness and starts fastening the straps.

I'm glad he has his own. I brought my dad's for him, just in case, but seeing Jordy wearing it would have felt weird.

"You look like you're about to faint," he continues. "I promise you, I'm going to be fine."

"You can't promise that," I remind him.

"Fair enough, but just think about Ireland. Think about getting on that plane in a couple of months. If you can do that, you can do this."

It's a great thought; if only I was sure I could get on a plane. "Yeah, okay." I grab everything I need to set up the climb. "I'll be back." I head to the end of the clearing, where there's a walk-up, a pile of boulders I can climb over to make it to the top of the cliff. I find the spot right above where Jordy is now lying back on the gravel and looking up at the sky. I use the gear to create multiple safe anchors and then pull hard on the rope until I'm satisfied it's secure. Then I do a few perfunctory stretching exercises while I survey the scene below.

A girl in hot pink capris and a black tank top is clinging to the cliff, her legs spread wide and one hand stretched way above her head. Her other hand feels back and forth across the rock, searching for something to hold on to. I trace the path of her rope up to the top of the ridge and back down again, where it's hooked to a guy who looks like he's in college. He's got both hands on the rope, his eyes watching every move the girl makes. Three other groups of climbers have similar setups.

Beyond them, two kids are leaning up against a hatchback in the parking lot and smoking a cigarette. I sit on the ground and stretch my hamstrings, looking back and forth from the climbers to the kids every few seconds until they finish the cigarette and grind the butt hard into the gravel.

I think of Daniel telling me to take back something the Universe stole from me. I feel like I'm on the edge of a huge moment.

Below me, Jordy appears to be taking a nap.

"Hey," I say.

"Hey yourself," he calls up to me. "Are you having trouble?"

"Nope. Just scoping out the whole area. Seeing what's what." I hold the coil of rope out from the cliff. "Heads up."

He hops to his feet and backs up as I toss both ends of the rope over the edge. Sliding on my harness, I double-check the straps and then clip into one side of the rope. I give it another sharp tug and then begin to lower myself down the face of the cliff in small bursts, one foot kicking out from the rock as I go. I land gracefully at the bottom with a grin. I'd forgotten how much fun it was to rappel.

"That was hot." Jordy pushes his sunglasses up on his forehead. "You look really good in your gear, by the way."

"No one looks good in a harness," I say quickly. Pretty sure it's true. The nylon straps tend to make whatever fat you have bulge out at unflattering angles.

"You do." He shrugs. "Sorry. This is Real Me. We can hang out as friends, as shrink-homework pals or whatever, but I'm not going to pretend you're not hot."

My face goes red. "Why do you have to make everything so impossible?"

He winks. "Because it's fun. And you're cute when you blush." He grabs the rope and clips into the belay side. "Are you ready to climb or what?"

"One sec." My muscles are still twitching with nerves. I shake out my arms and legs, grab my water bottle, and take a long swig. Then I blot the sweat off my face with the sleeve of my T-shirt. "Now I'm ready. Just let me double-check the setup." I step in close to Jordy to make sure his belay device is properly functioning. We're so close that I can see his eyelashes, his freckles, the tiny grooves in his lips. *His lips!*

"You're still blushing," he says.

"No I'm not."

"Yes you are." He clips a fist-sized cloth bag to one of the loops on the back of my harness, his hand lingering on my hip for a moment. "Don't forget your chalk."

Chalk. Right. I'm already sweaty from the combination of heat and nerves. And Jordy.

My eyes are drawn back to his lips, to his smile. To his whole face—the slightly crooked nose, the brown eyes, the shock of brownish-blond hair sticking up behind the sunglasses that rest on his forehead.

Cursed, I remind myself. I do one last five-second check of the surroundings. It's as safe as it's going to get.

Jordy tugs on my side of the rope. "Belay on, already."

I step up to the wall and prepare to climb. "Climbing," I say.

"Climb on."

It takes me a couple of tries to get started. Once I find a little ridge that my foot feels secure against, I reach high above my head and locate an outcropping that I can wrap my whole hand around. I step up, my free hand searching for a third point I can use to secure myself. I find a crack my fingertips fit in and flatten my body against the wall, the muscles in my arms going rigid. I take a couple of deep breaths and then step up with my other foot, my hands sliding across the rock face in search of new holds. I glance back over my shoulder. I'm only a few feet in the air, but exhilaration is already buzzing inside of me.

Jordy pulls his side of the rope through the belay device. I lean back from the rock to test him. The line is snug. If I slip, I won't fall. I bring my right knee up toward my waist, the tip of my climbing shoe finding another ridge to support my weight. I step up again, my body pressed so tightly against the stone that its rough surface scrapes layers off my skin. My free hand finds a new point of anchor.

Slowly, I repeat this process. Once. Twice. Three times. My fingers ache and my forearms are burning, but it's a good kind of pain, like my entire body has been frozen for years and I'm finally starting to thaw. By the time I'm halfway to the top, one of my nails is broken, a thin line of blood visible beneath the jagged edge. I barely notice. I feel . . . good, like I'm becoming part of the cliff. For once my brain has shut off.

For once I am only thinking about this moment.

I can see bands of lighter rock interspersed in the sandy beige. Tiny spiderwebs are nestled in cracks. Dead leaves cling to the face of the cliff. Mindful of where I put my hands, I slide my fingers upward until I locate another hold. I swing my leg out wide until the tip of my shoe catches against a lip of rock. I find a secure spot and rest for a second, breathing deeply and shaking out my arms. I reach back behind me and dip the fingertips of each hand in my chalk bag.

A few moves later, I see the top of the rope. Grunting, I make one last move, and my fingers hit the locking carabiner at the cliff's edge. "Made it."

"Congrats. Ready to come down?" Jordy calls from below.

"Yep." I smile so big it hurts. I forgot how good rock climbing could feel. I forgot what it was like to do something and not be distracted by a hundred dark thoughts.

Jordy starts letting out the rope in smooth three-foot

gaps, and I drop in quick but steady bursts.

"Well?" he asks as I touch down on the gravel.

"I feel like a superhero," I say. Impulsively, I throw my arms around Jordy's neck. "Thank you for coming."

He squeezes me gently. "Thank you for inviting me." His words tickle my neck and earlobe.

I reluctantly pull back from the embrace. "Ready for your turn?"

He tosses his sunglasses back toward his backpack. "Hell yeah."

We switch places so that he's ready to climb and I'm hooked to the belay device. I gnaw on my lower lip as I watch him approach the wall, being careful to make sure there's no slack in the rope. I wasn't worried about my own safety, but Jordy climbing is a whole different story.

"Hang on a sec," I say. I double-check both of our setups again and then scan the entire clearing, going from climber to climber to make sure everyone seems secure. Okay. "Belay on."

Jordy anchors the toe of his shoe against a small outcropping of rock and steps upward, his hand finding a hold above his head. Immediately the rope goes slack, and I quickly pull it through. He steps up again, and I tighten the rope once more.

One move at a time, he ascends the wall. His height makes it easy for him to find holds for his hands and feet. I have a feeling he could be doing this even faster if he weren't concerned with giving me enough time to keep the line taut.

"You okay?" I ask when he reaches the halfway point and pauses for a moment.

"I'm good," he calls down, the fingers of his right hand dipping into his bag of chalk. "Just relax."

But I can't relax. Right now there is no knocking on wood. There are no five-second checks. There is just me, and a rope tied to a setup I made, holding Jordy in the air. As he nears the top, I inhale deeply and hold my breath. My brake hand is gripping the rope so tightly that the nylon fibers are digging into my skin. Jordy touches the carabiner and then looks down at me. "You look scared."

"I am scared," I admit.

"So then let me down so you won't have to be scared anymore."

I slowly belay him back to the ground. His feet hit the gravel and he turns to me, his fingers white with chalk, his hair sticking up in sweaty peaks. "So you did it. Took back something the Universe stole from you. How does it feel?"

I close my eyes. My muscles are quivering. The sun is searing the back of my neck. The wind is kicking up just enough sand to sting my legs as it blows past. But all of that is nothing. The shouts of the people around us are nothing. Tomorrow and yesterday are nothing. All I know is that I put my climbing gear in a box five years ago and never thought I'd pull it out again. "It feels amazing," I tell him. "Like nothing else in the whole world matters except for this moment."

Jordy unclips from the setup. He takes my hands in his and considers the red welts across my palms, marks from where I gripped the rope too tightly. "You were really scared for me, eh?"

"Yeah."

"Because you like me."

"Maybe," I admit.

The wind blows his hair back from his face. "Are you scared now?"

My heart is beating hard, but for once it's not about fear. I shake my head.

He rests a hand on my waist. My face is just inches from his chest. I crane my neck to look up at him. He slouches a little bit as he looks down. "What about now?"

"No?"

Wrapping one arm around my neck and the other around my legs, he picks me up and carries me off toward the face of the cliff.

I squirm. "Jordy! What are you doing? Put me down."

"As you wish." Jordy sets me down on a wide, flat rock near where the end of our rope is hanging. It's just tall enough that for once we're eye to eye. He grins mischievously. "Sorry, I just want to be part of the moment."

Suddenly I realize what he's doing.

Suddenly I'm scared.

"Your eyes are pretty," he says.

My mouth goes dry. I lick my lips and manage to mumble, "Thanks."

Jordy rests his cheek against mine. His sweat is slick and his beard stubble prickles my skin. His breath is hot in my ear. A wave of tension rushes through my body. Every part of me goes tight, contracted. The air floats silent in my lungs until I realize I'm holding my breath. I exhale slowly.

"I'm scared now," I say.

"Me too," he says. "But do you think fear is good sometimes? Like it motivates you to be stronger?"

"Yeah."

He presses his lips to my jawbone, right below my ear. "You think this is one of those times?"

"Maybe," I whisper. "I just don't know if I can do it."

"Maybe neither one of us has to do it. Maybe we can just let it happen." He pulls back just far enough to press his forehead to mine, aligning our eyes.

Aligning our lips.

He's so close that I'm seeing double. "Is this the real you?" I ask.

"Maguire. This is more real than I have felt in months."

We both breathe out at the same moment, and our breath mingles. His eyes are a desert of browns and golds. I can barely feel his hands on my waist, balancing me. The heat, the shouts of the other climbers, the sharp smells of sweat and chalk—everything fades to a blur again. His eyelids flutter shut. Mine do the same.

I don't know who closes the gap between us.

All I know is that my entire body goes weak when we finally kiss. My fingers begin to shake as he presses his lips harder against mine. I tighten my grip on his waist to quell the tremors. He coaxes my lips apart with his tongue. His breath warms the inside of my mouth. I try to mimic what he's doing. I hope he can't tell that I've never kissed anyone before.

My mind races, one thought after the next, about how weird it feels to be connected to another person like this, about how good it feels, about what it means, about what it doesn't mean, about how much time has passed since Jordy finished climbing. I pull back, my eyes flicking around the area nervously. No one is paying us any attention. Everyone seems to be safe.

Jordy runs the back of his hand down the side of my face. "You okay?"

"Yeah, I just forgot where we were for a second."

He grins. "Good."

My stomach does one of those Olympic triple-loop ice-skater jumps. I force a smile. "So," I say.

"So." Jordy brushes his lips against mine again. "You want to climb more? Or you just want to keep doing this? Because I'm good either way."

I hop down off the rock and stride across the gravel to

our gear. "I'm suddenly really hungry."

"Me too," he says, "but not for food."

I swat at his chest playfully and dig a couple of energy bars out of my bag. "We can eat these now, and I have food for us to cook for supper. Or we can just get something on the way home."

"Whatever you want."

I have a feeling he's talking about more than just food. I toss him an energy bar. We both sit on the ground, chewing in silence. I'm actually not hungry at all. My stomach is still going for a gold medal. But I choke down the gritty chocolate as best I can, scanning the area for possible hazards as I chew.

My eyes look everywhere but at Jordy. I can't believe he kissed me. Or did I kiss him? I don't even know. I don't know if it's going to happen again, if it should happen again. I'm seized by the strangest urge to reach up and touch my lips, to make sure they're real, they're normal, that they haven't swelled up to three times their size.

Laughter from down the way interrupts my thoughts. As I glance down at a trio of guys who are packing up their gear, I remind myself that Jordy and I are climbing and it's dangerous and I can't freak out over the fact that we kissed, even though part of me needs to.

After we finish our snack, I set three more climbs for us, but on the last one Jordy decides he's done.

"I'm getting sort of worn out," he says.

"What's up with that?" I ask. "You train five hours a day. Shouldn't you be one of those people who never get tired?"

"I should." He chuckles. "Maybe I'm getting old."

"Your sister said you went to the doctor, right? Did they find anything?"

"Nah, they took some blood and asked me a bunch of questions, but I'm wondering if it isn't just stress—Real Me versus Tennis Me, fighting my parents, this whole thing with going pro versus going to college."

"It's a big decision, I guess."

"Yeah." He looks serious for a second. "I don't want to think about it right now." He points at the cliff. "Last chance. Go for it."

Almost everyone else has left by now. There's only us and one other group—the girl in the pink capris and her boyfriend, about a hundred feet away from where we are. The guy is at the top of the cliff, preparing to rappel down after setting their climb, while the girl waits at the bottom. I step up to the wall, closing my eyes briefly to focus myself.

That's when I hear the girl scream.

CHAPTER 24

I can't immediately tell what's wrong. The guy appears to be halfway down the wall but is just hanging in the air. The girl is digging in a gear bag. She pulls out a phone, looks at the display, and then swears.

"No signal," she hollers up. "Hold on, Chad."

I unclip and race down toward the other climbers. Jordy is right behind me. "What's going on?" I ask. I try to quell the dread that's gathering in the pit of my stomach. *Don't panic*, I tell myself. *It might be nothing.*

But it's definitely something.

"He didn't center the rope and now he's stuck. If he goes any farther he'll rappel off the end of it."

"Crap. You guys didn't tie safety knots?"

"I guess not," the girl says. "We were in a hurry to squeeze in one more climb before dark."

"Don't panic, Allison," Chad shouts. "I can just unclip and free-climb down."

"You can't see the holds below you," she yells. "You won't know where to put your feet."

"A good climber uses his sense of feeling more than vision," Chad responds.

"A good climber doesn't rappel off the end of his rope," I mutter under my breath. Then I look up at Chad. "Hang on. I'll run up and set a top belay and throw the rope down so you can clip in and climb up."

"Oh my God," Allison says. "You are a lifesaver. Literally."

I scramble back up the cliff and unhook our setup. I rig the gear over next to where Chad is, double-check that everything is secure, and toss my rope down to him. He unclips from his own setup and onto mine with only a little wobble. Slowly he climbs his way back to the top of the cliff as I belay him from above. Once he reaches the top, he crawls over the edge and lies on his back for a moment, looking up at the darkening sky.

"He's okay," I call down to Jordy and Allison. "We'll be down in a few."

Chad covers his face with his hands. "Man, I really screwed up." His voice wavers. "I could have broken my neck."

"Yeah." I sit cross-legged next to him. "But you're okay now."

He sits up and takes a deep breath. Exhaling slowly, he

says, "Thanks. I didn't catch your name."

"Maguire."

He smiles. "I like it."

"Me too." I start to remove my anchors, dislodging a couple of cams and unknotting a loop of webbing I had secured around a big boulder. Once I've got all my gear together, I start working on Chad's.

"I can get that," he says.

"I know. But take a couple minutes to pull yourself together. It's no big deal. This is what climbers do for each other, right?"

"I'm not sure I'm going to be able to climb again after this." He tilts his head left and then right, like he's working kinks out of his neck and shoulders.

"Sure you will," I say. "Your fear will make you better if you let it. And next time you won't skimp on the safety precautions."

"That's for damn sure," he says. "Let's get down before it gets any darker."

As the sun falls behind the mountains on the horizon, we gather all of our gear and make our way down the walk-up.

Jordy and Allison are waiting at the bottom. "Thanks again, Maguire." Chad raises his hand for a high five.

I slap it. "Take care."

Allison gives me a hug, and then she and Chad head for the parking lot. She starts screaming at him for scaring her before they're halfway to his truck.

I collapse at a nearby picnic table. "That was seriously scary."

"You totally rescued that guy and made it look easy," Jordy says. "They're just lucky . . ." He stops and clears his throat. "*Lucky*," he repeats, "that we were still here."

"Yeah. Even I can't argue with that." There's a tiny nagging voice in my head that wonders if maybe Chad wouldn't have gotten in trouble in the first place if I hadn't been here, but I had time to act, and everything turned out fine. That doesn't feel like bad luck on anyone's part.

I lay my head on the picnic table, reaching up to flip my braid back over my shoulder. The hair at the nape of my neck has come loose and matted into a ball. "Ugh. I'm going to have to spend like two hours untangling this mop."

"Just leave it tangled," Jordy says. "Who cares?"

"Easy for you to say, Mr. My Hair Looks Perfect At All Times."

Jordy snorts. "Well, if it does, it's no thanks to me. Some stylist recommended this haircut. And the phony highlights to go with."

"I knew those blond streaks were fake." I snicker. "You really let some stranger pick out your hairstyle? Does she pick out your clothes too?"

"Don't be ridiculous." He scoffs. "My mom picks out my clothes." I laugh. "She does, too," he says seriously. "The tournament outfits. I don't care what I wear on the court. It seems like an easy way to make her happy."

"That's sweet," I say. "A little pathetic, but sweet."

"You're just scratching the surface of pathetic probably," Jordy says. "I'm sort of a people pleaser, if you haven't noticed. Penn's always on my case about being a wuss."

"She just wants what's best for you."

"Everyone wants what's best for me, but no one seems willing to give me a little time to figure out what that is."

It's going on seven o'clock, and the stars are coming out—more stars than I've ever seen. More stars than I even knew existed. Small clouds of sand blow across the picnic area, the tiny grains biting into my bare skin like sandpaper. We should head home, but I'm still a little shaken up from Chad's close call. I pull a thin zip-up jacket out of my backpack and put it on.

Jordy hops up on the top of picnic table. He dangles his feet off the end. "You should come up here."

I arch an eyebrow. "Oh yeah?"

"I know it probably looks scary from down there, but trust me, the view is amazing."

I laugh. "It's kind of a steep climb. Should we get the gear back out?"

He holds out his hands. "It's okay. I won't let you fall."

I step up onto the bench and sit on the top of the picnic table next to him. We both look up at the sky. "It *is* different," I say with a grin. "Look how much closer we are to the stars. Like almost a whole foot."

"Hey, that's the difference between winning and losing in tennis."

We both lie flat on the tabletop. "This view is even better," I say. "More of the sky without that bothersome crick in your neck."

Jordy adjusts himself so that our hands are even, his fingers twining between mine. He makes small circles on my palm with his thumb. "I can't believe you spent the whole day with me. What'd your mom say about that?"

"I think she's just happy I'm getting out and doing things."

"How long have you been hiding from the world?"

"Since I was twelve. That's when the roller coaster accident happened and people started to talk. I thought it was weird too—everyone but me dying, everyone but me getting seriously injured. But it wasn't until the food poisoning thing at my friend's birthday party that I really started to believe what they were saying might be true. Then I started thinking back, about other, less serious things that had happened. That's when I started keeping the notebook."

"So then you've never . . ." Jordy clears his throat. "Had a serious boyfriend?"

"No," I say. "You're the only guy I've ever kissed."

He rises up on one elbow and turns to face me. A piece of his hair flops in front of one eye. "You're kidding, right?"

"Why?" I say, a little defensively. "I'm sure there are plenty of sixteen-year-old girls who have never kissed anyone."

Jordy laughs. "No, I just meant because you're so *good* at it."

My face burns. "Oh be quiet. You're just saying that."

"No I'm not."

"I was just trying to imitate what *you* were doing," I admit.

"Well, then it's good to know I'm an epic kisser," Jordy says. "But I feel kind of guilty. If I'd known it was your very first kiss, I would've tried to make it a little more . . . sweet."

"It was plenty sweet." Plenty hot, anyway. I blush just thinking about it.

"Yeah, but your first kiss is a big deal. I hope you didn't feel pressured into it. Or awkward because there were a lot of people around."

I shake my head. "No. It was good."

"I generally aspire to a higher standard than 'good.'" Jordy adjusts his body slightly so that he can look me in the eye. "How do you feel about a do-over?" A slow smile spreads across his face. "A second first kiss?"

"Jordy, I don't need a do-over." My words sound unconvincing even to my own ears. I might not need one, but some part of me wants one. I don't know if I should give in or not. My feelings for him are all confused, a swirly vortex of desire and fear, currently located somewhere between my heart and my stomach.

Instead of replying, he traces both of my eyebrows with his index finger. Then he runs it down past my temple to my chin and up the other side of my face. My eyes flutter shut. There's a rushing feeling inside of me, like a wave hurrying for the shore. Jordy's finger traces the bridge of my nose and then makes a lazy loop around my lips. He pushes a lock of hair back from my face. The rushing feeling gains intensity. Now my insides are a spaceship blasting into hyperdrive.

He pulls me close, one hand low on my back and the other cradling my head. Our noses brush and then his lips fall softly onto mine, parted slightly. My body collapses against his as he kisses me again. This time is less urgent, but it isn't any less hot. Our mouths connect, disconnect, reconnect, each tiny kiss leaving me wanting more. His lips find my cheek, my earlobe, my neck. He trails kisses down it and across my collarbone. I tremble, but then an image blinks on in my brain: Jordy halfway down the side of the cliff, about to rappel off the end of his rope. Me at the bottom, unable to warn him in time.

My eyes flick open. I slide out from underneath him and hop off the picnic table. The ground feels unsteady under my feet. I stare off into the night, at the scary silhouettes of the Joshua trees, at the wide-open desert, at the mountains I can't even see but know are there. "Just because today turned out okay doesn't mean anything," I say.

"Maguire." Jordy's hand is gentle on my shoulder. "I know you're scared, and I know why. I told myself I wasn't even going to touch you today. But I also know you like me, and I like you too. You ever feel like something is eventually going to happen, no matter how hard you try to fight it?"

Without turning around to look at him, I nod. "Yeah. But for me that something has always been a bad thing."

CHAPTER 25

It's about 8:00 p.m. when we head home. Part of me doesn't want to leave. Part of me wonders if it was a mistake to even come. I completed another therapy challenge, but somehow things feel more complicated and dangerous now. I can't just kiss Jordy and then ignore him, even if that's the best thing for both of us.

I can't even stop thinking about him.

But I need to, because we're not just driving three hours to get home. We're driving on a lot of dark, deserted roads. As usual, he goes through a thorough check of his seat belt and mirrors before he even starts the engine. He turns to me before he pulls the car out of the parking lot. "Sorry if I made you uncomfortable earlier."

"You didn't," I insist.

"I probably shouldn't have kissed you in the first place. If my parents found out I was dating they would—"

"Are we *dating*?" I blurt out. A shock of fear moves through me.

Jordy's body sags a little. "I didn't mean to sound presumptuous. I just meant that even if we *wanted* to date, it would have to be a secret, and I wouldn't want to ask that of you. Now you probably think I'm some possessive psycho."

"I don't think that at all," I assure him. "This is just sort of new for me. I just . . . I'm kind of confused."

"Me too." He makes a point of signaling before leaving the park and pulling out onto the highway.

We fall into an easy silence—him focusing on the road, me focusing on the shadowy parts of the night and what they might hide. Halfway home, we stop for food, but otherwise the drive is uneventful, aside from the fact that three voice mails from my mom pop up simultaneously once we get back into cell coverage area. I send her a text and let her know I'll be home soon.

About an hour later, Jordy pulls the car over across the street from my house. Then he turns to me, his hand reaching out for one of mine. "Look, I know I don't own you because we kissed. You're free to kiss whoever you want." He sighs. "But I don't want you to kiss anyone else, which I know is selfish. I just—right now my folks would freak about me getting distracted, and I don't know what to do."

"I get it. You're singularly focused," I say. "Seriously. I'm not mad. I'm not ready to date anyone." Maybe I'm making baby steps toward being able to get on that plane in a couple of months, but a relationship? That's an everyday thing.

Jordy squeezes my hand. "I have never felt so flustered around a girl before." His lips twitch. "Are you sure you don't have magic powers?"

"I'm sure."

"Right." He nods. "So then we're friends?"

"Absolutely." A tiny pang hits me at the word *friends*, but I remind myself that a few weeks ago I didn't even have any of those. Daniel told me getting better was a process. I need to recognize the progress I've made.

Jordy unbuckles his seat belt. "Come on. I'll walk you to the door."

"You don't have to do that."

"I want to," he says, sliding out of the car before I can say anything else.

We grab the gear out of the trunk and walk side by side across the street and up my parents' driveway, our hands bumping twice on the way to the porch. When we reach the front steps, Jordy drops the bag with the shoes and harnesses on the ground and turns to me. "You know, I'll be getting my mid-semester grade report in a couple of weeks, and I should be doing fine in my classes. So maybe after that I'll man up and tell my parents they can't run my personal life. That is, if you'd ever want to date or whatever." He shifts his weight from one foot to the other. "It's cool if you don't," he tacks on quickly.

My heart expands inside of me at his words. Smooth-talking Jordy looks completely out of his element, his eyes flicking nervously around, his hands tucked deep inside his pockets. This is the real him, not the polished performer his parents want him to be.

But unfortunately there's only one me, a cursed me, and I'm not convinced that'll be drastically changing any time soon. "Oh. I, um . . ." Crap. Didn't we just agree to be friends like two minutes ago? *Is that all you want?* I don't know. Or maybe I do. Sure, it'd be great to date someone like Jordy, but that just doesn't feel like real life.

But the look on his face is so hopeful, so . . . vulnerable. I can't bring myself to reject him again. Not when deep down we want the same thing. "I'll think about it," I say finally, forcing a smile. "Maybe I can add it to my therapy challenges."

"Okay." A huge grin sweeps across his face.

Wrapping my arms around his waist, I pull him into a hug. I don't want this day to be over.

He holds me for a few seconds and then bends low and kisses me on the cheek. "Have a good night, Maguire." He turns and jogs down the driveway. I watch him slide into the Lancer and pull away from the curb. Hopping down off the porch, I venture into the damp front lawn far enough so I can watch the black of the car meld with the black of the night. Red brake lights fade slowly, and then all at once, as Jordy's car disappears over the crest of a hill.

It's a little after eleven when I slip inside the house and shut the front door behind me. Tom is waiting up, a tablet computer on his lap, the TV playing silently in the background. "Must have been a good hike." He points at my gear bags. "What's all that?"

Crap. I forgot to leave those outside my window. "We went rock climbing," I admit. "I didn't want my mom to worry. Is she asleep?"

He nods. "Did you have a good day?"

I smile. "I did. Sorry I didn't call sooner. We went to Joshua Tree. I couldn't get a signal."

"Maybe tell us where you're headed next time if you're going to be out of range? Or at least tell your mom?" he suggests.

"You're right, Tom. I'm sorry. I will." I point toward my room. "I'm pretty tired. I'm going to crash."

But when I crawl beneath the sheets a few minutes later, I can't fall asleep. First I grab my luck notebook and cross off another challenge. After thinking about it for a few seconds, I decide to add the part about Chad almost rappelling off the end of his rope under the section for bad things. But I give it an asterisk, and at the bottom of the page I note how I was able to help him and everything was fine.

Slipping my notebook back into my purse, I grab my phone from my nightstand and text Jade.

Me: Guess what I did today?

Her: Is it tall and slightly clumsy with great hair?

Me: Funny. We went rock climbing!

Her: Seriously? That's very cool.

Me: I haven't gone in years. It was amazing!

Her: I think that's more exclamation points than I've ever seen you use. Do you have any salacious tidbits to report?

Me: No. Come on. You know we're just friends.

Her: Friends with benefits?

Me: No! Well, we might have kissed. But that's it.

Her: Aww. So like grade school friends with benefits ;) Please describe said kiss in detail.

Me: No.

Her: You're so mean to me. You're lucky I like you. This is juicy gossip that I'm sitting on.

Me: Not THAT juicy. Random question. Do you believe in bad luck?

Her: Why? Did you break a mirror or something?

Me: No. Sometimes I just feel unlucky.

Her: Why?

Me: Stuff that happened in the past.

For a moment she doesn't respond. And then she calls me. "What kind of stuff?" she asks in a low voice. I'm guessing that if her mom catches her on the phone this late she'll get in trouble.

"My dad, brother, and uncle died in a car accident when I was eleven."

Jade pauses. "I'm sorry. I didn't know."

I swallow back a lump in my throat. "It's not just my family. Bad things seem to happen when people are near me. I don't want anything to happen to Jordy."

"So you like him, and that scares you."

"Yeah. I have this phobia of other people being hurt when I'm around—it's why I don't ride the team bus, why I don't eat in the cafeteria, why I go to the therapist. Before I started at Pacific Point, I was basically a loner."

"Whoa," Jade says. "That's intense."

"That's a nicer word than I usually use to describe it."

"Well, you can't help how you feel," she says softly. "A lot of fears people have are irrational on the surface."

"Yeah. Jordy actually told me he was afraid of grasshoppers."

Jade snorts. "It doesn't get much more irrational than that." She pauses. "Have you read the psych homework yet?"

"No." Normally I have most of my homework done on Saturday. I'll have to catch up tomorrow.

"It's about attribution errors. Most people take credit when something good happens, but blame others or their environments when something bad happens. Maybe you're just flipped around. Do you ever remember to take credit for the good things you do?"

It reminds me of what Daniel said when he was talking about selective attention, how my brain zeroes in on "evidence" of my curse without noticing all the times I don't seem to have bad luck. "What good things?"

"Well, you seem to make Jordy happy, for one. If you quit doing that just because you're scared he might get hurt someday, both of you lose out." Jade sighs dramatically. "At least that's how I see it. My mom won't let me date until I'm twenty, so I probably shouldn't be giving relationship advice."

As usual, Jade manages to make me feel better. And she's right—if I run away now, both Jordy and I will probably regret it. "Don't worry. Your mom won't be able to keep you from dating once you graduate."

"You don't think? She wants me to live at home and go to UCSD."

"So tell her no?"

"Clearly you've never met my mother."

"Wow. Your mom sounds like Jordy's mom. Penn told me some people have arranged marriages, and he has an arranged life."

Jade laughs out loud and then swears under her breath. Lowering her voice again, she says, "Yeah. That about sums it up. But if I can get into NYU, she'll have to let me go, so that's my goal."

"My mom is the exact opposite. She wants me to go

away to school. 'Have the authentic college experience,' she's always saying."

"Your mom sounds perfect."

"Yeah, kind of," I say. "Sometimes I forget just how cool she is."

CHAPTER 26

After I hang up with Jade, I spend at least an hour unknotting my hair and thinking about Jordy. What if by some teensy chance I successfully complete all of my therapy challenges and get on that plane to Ireland? If bad things stop happening around me, could I actually see myself dating him? Closing my eyes, I fall back onto my bed and imagine his lips on mine.

But then I think of what Jade said the day I met her: *Jordy still manages to get plenty of action* . . . Sighing, I sit up, grab my computer, and type his name into the search box. Hundreds of hits come back, more than I could ever possibly go through. I skim the listings looking for anything about a girlfriend, but they're mostly just recaps of Jordy's matches. I switch to images and click through several pages of thumbnails. There are pictures of him with a few different girls. The only ones I recognize are Penn and Kimber. One girl shows up repeatedly, a pretty brunette with a pixie haircut. I enlarge one of the pix of the two of them. The caption says, "Jordy Wheeler and Alyssa Gordon meet fans at the CAJR Tennis Open."

Feeling like a complete stalker, I Google Alyssa Gordon. She graduated from Pacific Point and is now a sophomore at Florida State and a member of their tennis team. I flip through a few articles about her, but I don't see anything mentioned about Jordy. Next I type Jordy's and Kimber's names into the search box and get several pictures of them too, but none of them look anything but innocent. *Enough, Maguire.* I put my laptop away and try to get some sleep.

On Tuesday we have a match at a high school across town. I wear my uniform to class, something a lot of the team does on days when we have away matches. As Jade and I are strolling out of psychology class together, I say, "I'll see you at Dustin."

Whistling to myself, I head out into the parking lot. A couple of girls from my classes nod or smile at me as I pass. I smile back, looking forward to today's match. It's a crucial win for us, since Dustin is in our district and they beat us last year. I'm feeling as confident as I've ever felt.

Until I reach the bottom of the school's cement steps and catch a glimpse of my mom's car.

"Son of a . . ." I hurry across the parking lot, bending down to verify my worst fear. One of the back tires is completely flat, like I ran over an entire box of nails on the way to school.

Swearing under my breath, I check my phone. Ten minutes until the bus leaves. I race back into the school and find Coach Hoffman in his office. "I don't know if I'm going to be able to make the match today," I say breathlessly. "I have a flat tire."

Coach arches an eyebrow. "So ride the bus like everyone else. You have to be there today, Maguire. We need every single win we can get to beat Dustin."

"But I—"

"A win today means a higher seed at districts," he says. "I know you like to drive yourself, but you're just going to have to suck it up for once."

I lift a hand to my throat, my fingers clutching my mystic knot pendant through the fabric of my uniform polo. "What if I can't?" I ask. "I have an . . . appointment right after the match, and I need my car to be able to go straight there."

Coach nods, his blue eyes studying me carefully. "Well, if you can't come, we can put an alternate in your spot. Maybe Missy or Alexandra."

Missy and Alexandra are freshmen. Neither of them would stand a chance against the girl from Dustin. "What about Mae? You could move Luisa or Colleen up to fourth singles and then—"

"I'm not rearranging my doubles teams," Coach says

firmly. "Like I said, we need every point we can get in today's match." He looks pointedly at me. "Including yours. Perhaps you can call whoever you're meeting afterward and say you might be a little late. Or maybe they can pick you up?"

"Okay." I drop my chin to my chest. "I'll see what I can do."

Coach checks his watch. "Bus leaves in five. Hope to see you on it."

Slinking out of Coach's office, I turn the corner into the next hallway and rest my back against the wall. There's only one person I know with a car who might drive me. But just as I pull my phone out of my backpack and start to call Jordy, I think about my latest therapy session. I'm supposed to be riding public transportation by now. If I can't get on a bus with my team members, then how can I get on a plane full of strangers?

Penn and Jade slide out of the locker room together. Jade sees me and raises a hand in greeting. "What's up? You change your mind? Slumming it on the bus today?"

"I don't know," I say. "I have a flat tire."

"Where's Jordy?" Jade asks.

"Yeah. Where's Jordy?" Kimber repeats, coming up behind the three of us. "You two seem inseparable lately. I'm expecting that serve of yours to be excellent."

"It's gotten a lot better," I say cooly, refusing to let her intimidate me.

"My brother is meeting us at Dustin," Penn says. "He's

going straight there after a meeting with some potential agent."

"Agent, eh?" Kimber says. "Good for him."

"What does that mean?" I ask Penn.

"It means he's thinking about taking control of his own life," she says. "Someone must have really inspired him."

Kimber gives me a long look, the tiniest flicker of amusement in her eyes. "Must be that therapist he's always talking about." She turns and saunters toward the back exit.

"You need help with your tire?" Penn asks.

"Just take the bus," Jade says. "Otherwise half our singles players will be late." Her face pales. "Oh, sorry. I forgot about your thing."

"We can help you if you *want* to ride with the team," Penn says. "It can be like when you drove me to Jordy's match."

There's still a tiny bruise under her eye from her fall at the tennis complex. "I'd prefer it not be like that," I say.

Penn bounces up and down on her toes, her blonde braid swishing back and forth. "I meant just the driving part. I promise not to fall on my face on the bus."

"I'll help any way I can." Jade pats herself on the chest. "After all, Jade is good luck!"

I smile. I remember thinking that same thing the first day of tryouts. I look back and forth between the two of them. I take a deep breath and let it out slowly, bit by bit. *You can do this*, I tell myself. *No one is going to die.* It's only about ten miles of flat roads. It's a school bus. Even if we get in an accident, a school bus almost always wins, right? And once I survive I can cross off therapy challenge number five and start to think about what I want to do for the last two. "Okay. I'll take the bus."

"High five!" Penn holds up her hand.

I slap it weakly. "Maybe we should wait until we get there to celebrate."

"Nah. You got this," Jade says. "Let's roll."

The three of us head around to the back where the bus is parked.

"All aboard." Coach makes a circling-the-wagons gesture with the hand that isn't clutching his clipboard. I get in line with everyone else and make my way up the stairs and onto the bus.

I haven't been on a school bus since I was eleven, and the blast of stale air that hits me in the face as I head down the aisle brings back memories of being smashed into a seat with Connor. I push the memory out of my head and quickly turn into an empty seat. Jade flops down next to me. Penn sits right in front of us.

"Glad you're joining us, Maguire," Kimber calls from across the aisle.

I'm not sure she's ever called me by my name before. Go figure. Maybe she's one of those girls who only lords it over people who act meek in her presence. Well, that's not going to be me anymore. And if Jordy and I do start dating someday, I'm not going to let her give me a hard time about it.

Once we're all on, Coach counts us. "Penn," he barks.

"Yes?" She coils her braid around one hand.

"Will your brother be joining us today?"

"He's meeting us there."

"Got it." Coach takes his seat right across from the driver.

Penn sits sideways so she can see me, her legs stretched out on the seat, her back against the bus window. "Is it best if I don't talk again?" she asks.

"Anything is fine," I say. "I'm just glad you're here."

"Okay." She tucks her earbuds into her ears and closes her eyes as we pull out of the parking lot, a serene smile playing at her lips.

I try to match her Zen by tucking my own earbuds into my ears and closing my eyes too. But every second of darkness feels like relinquishing the limited control that I have. *You have no control.* Not technically true. Even a few seconds of being able to prepare for an impending disaster can change the outcome.

Just not my family's outcome.

I turn and watch the road through the smudgy side window. The bus gets caught in a snarl of traffic, and for about ten minutes my heart clenches up each time our driver slams on the brakes. But the good thing about gridlock is that it's hard for anyone to get hurt when we're all only traveling ten miles an hour.

Still, I have to slide my fingertips under my legs to

keep my hands from shaking.

The driver hits the brakes again, and I pitch forward slightly. I glance around to make sure everyone is okay.

Jade looks past me, out the window. "We're halfway there." She pats my arm. "I'm glad you told me. I got your back."

After a minute, she digs in her racquet bag and comes up with a shiny cellophane packet. She opens it and pulls out a handful of thin green rectangles. "Salted nori," she says. "You want some?"

I shake my head. My stomach is doing those figure skater maneuvers again. As Jade crunches her pregame snack, I go back to watching out the window. The bus turns off the highway, and the traffic finally thins out. My heartbeat slows, but we've still got a few miles to go. I continue to imagine exactly what I would do at each moment in time if something were to happen. I would call for help. Then I would do a quick survey of the girls and see who was hurt the worst. I would put pressure on bleeding wounds. I would make sure anyone with neck or back injuries stayed still. I would help everyone else out the back of the bus or one of the windows.

I repeat these thoughts over and over in my head to stay calm, but I think what helps more is having Jade and Penn next to me. I figured they'd both think I was crazy for having a phobia of riding the bus, but it seems to be no big deal to either one of them. I don't know if it's surviving the therapy challenges or confiding in my new friends, but I feel stronger.

I like the person I'm becoming.

"I want to be this person," I murmur.

"Hmm?" Jade smiles at me.

"Nothing. Just . . . thank you." The bus makes a sharp turn into the parking lot of Dustin High School. "We're here," I say, joy and relief threading through my voice.

"Let's get this done." Kimber strolls up from the back, giving each of us a fist bump on the way out. She pauses at my row, a smile quirking her lips. "Don't let us down," she says.

"I'll do my best."

My opponent is an Indian girl named Naima, who Kimber says normally plays second singles. Apparently the Dustin coach rearranged their lineup to sacrifice first singles in an attempt to win second, third, and fourth. It's a shady move, but it's legal. I'm more determined than ever to win after I hear that.

As Naima and I warm up, I start analyzing her game. She has a solid topspin serve, weak but consistent ground strokes, and the footwork to get to absolutely everything.

Everything.

We each take a few practice serves and then get started. Naima wins the first game easily. Her serve shoots out wide or jams me inside on every point. She returns each forehand I pound at her as a topspin lob so that I have to wait for it to fall. It's like she's my exact tennis opposite. I find myself down zero games to three before I know it, just because of stupid errors I make. Jordy and Coach flag me down as Naima and I change sides.

"You're playing into her hands," Jordy says. "She doesn't have your strength. She doesn't have your cross-court angles. All she's doing is hitting back your shots and waiting for you to make a mistake."

"Which you keep doing because you're impatient," Coach says. "I know you said you have someplace to be later, but give them a call between sets and tell them you're going to be late. And then settle down and let *her* make the mistakes for a while."

Jordy gives me a questioning look, but I shake my head. "Okay," I say. "I will. You guys are right about me being impatient. I hate waiting for those stupid lobs to fall."

"Some of them are short enough that you can pick them out of the air if you want," Jordy says. "Slam them right at her if you need to, just until she stops hitting ten or twelve of them each game."

I frown at him. "I'm not going to aim for her. You know that."

"Then aim at her feet, or angle your shots so far into the corners that she'll have to run down to Court One for a chance to return them."

I chew on my lower lip. "Okay. Thanks for the tips."

Kimber has already won her first set, and Penn is currently winning four games to one. Dustin's top two doubles teams both went to state last year, so chances are they'll win those matches. My match could make a real difference here.

I keep Coach's words in my head and slow down, returning each of Naima's strokes in a controlled manner, not going for winners until she hits something I can easily put away. I make my way up to the net a few times and Naima falters, attempting to lob over my head but coming up short. I take Jordy's advice and pick the lobs out of the air, overhead-slamming them at the far corners of the court.

She still wins the first set six games to four, but I've made things a lot closer.

I win the second set six games to four. Looking around, I'm surprised to see that everyone except our third doubles team has finished playing. We have two wins and three losses. Third doubles is up in the third set, but I have to win or it doesn't matter.

"Don't get psyched out," Jordy tells me during the break between sets. "The tide has turned in your favor. You've got the momentum."

"Momentum," I repeat, liking the way the word sounds in my mouth. Jordy rests his hand against the chain-link fence, two of his fingers curling through one of the diamond-shaped holes.

I reach up to touch his hand with my own. "But what if I lose?"

He chuckles. "Then you lose. And you get her next time."

My chest tightens, and I'm suddenly conscious of the muscle fibers twitching in my legs. I'm conscious of everything—the soft jingling of the fence as one of our doubles players hits a ball against it in frustration; the murmuring of the rest of the team, who are now all in the first row of the bleachers; a single drip of sweat making its way down the back of my neck. I have never wanted to hug Jordy as much as I do now. I lean forward and rest my forehead against the metal for a moment, my fingers squeezing his. Then I look up at him again. "Thank you," I say. "That's exactly what I needed to hear."

"You're welcome. Now go get her."

I jog back to my place on the baseline with renewed energy. I dance back and forth, head up, shoulders back. I can do this. I know it.

Naima serves a ball into the net. I take a couple of large steps into the court. Ready. Waiting. She serves a second ball into the net, and I cross to the left side of the court. This time she hits a solid serve and I have to lunge to return it. We rally back and forth, both of us covering the entire court.

Eventually Naima hits the ball into the net, and I win the point.

And then the next point.

It takes a while, but I win the game.

I'm up 5–4 and 40–15 when I approach the net on a soft-service return. Naima goes for a passing shot instead of one of her trademark lobs. I leap for it, watching the ball all the way to my strings. It ricochets off my racquet and lands just barely on the other side of the net. There's no way Naima can get to it before the ball bounces twice.

I win the match.

We beat Dustin.

Clapping erupts from outside the fence. I turn to see not just Jordy and Coach but the entire team lined up behind my court. Even Kimber is clapping.

Coach shakes hands with the Dustin coach. Jordy finds me after the rest of my teammates finish congratulating me. He scoops me up into a hug and lifts me off the ground, spinning me in a slow circle. Then he sets me back down and kisses me. A couple of the girls hoot and holler.

"Jordy," I murmur between kisses. "What are you doing?"

"Kissing you," he says. "And I don't care who sees."

Coach clears his throat. "All right, you two. This is a school-sanctioned event, remember?" He gives us a meaningful look and then wanders off with his clipboard.

"Coach said you had someplace to go right after the match." Jordy lowers his voice. "Do you need a ride?"

Before I can answer, Colleen wedges her body between us. "Oh no you don't, Lover Boy," she says. "The MVP is coming with us."

"Right." Kimber loops her arm around my shoulders like we're best pals. "Party at my house."

I look around at the other girls, some of whom are still hugging and high-fiving each other. I can't believe no one is making a big deal out of Jordy kissing me. I can't believe they called me the MVP. For the first time in a long time, I feel like part of something. I shake my head. "There's nowhere else I need to be."

CHAPTER 27

The bus ride back to school is its own kind of surreal. I take my same seat and pop in my earbuds, planning to keep watch out the window and be ready in case of an accident, but Kimber and the rest of the team have other ideas.

First I'm forced to pose for several selfies with Kimber and Jade, which are immediately put online with captions like "Maguire for the win!" Then it turns out that Kimber and Colleen recorded some of my weak points during my third set, which they insist on replaying for me so they can give me tips.

"See how your body is sort of facing the net when you start your backswing here?" Colleen shows me a slow-motion clip. "Try and remember to get yourself sideways, even for an overhead."

"Got it," I say, nodding to her. "I'll try to remember that."

"You did all right, though," Kimber says. "I didn't think

you had it in you to come back after you lost the first set. You should be proud."

"Thanks." I'm pretty sure "all right" is high praise coming from Kimber. Maybe Jordy was right and she never had an issue with me. Maybe it was always all about tennis for her.

Jordy is waiting for us back at school. "I was going to offer to give you a ride home, because of your tire," he says.

Penn hops off the bus behind me. "I can put her spare on. She's not going home, remember? We're all going over to Kimber's house. Impromptu celebration." She glances back at Kimber and Colleen. "I'm not sure if boys are allowed."

Kimber strolls over. "No boys, but he can come because he doesn't really count." She reaches up and ruffles his hair. "Not to me anyway."

"You guys go." Jordy tosses his keys to Penn. "I'll put Maguire's spare on and drive her car over to Kimber's."

Penn bounces up and down on the balls of her feet. "Holy crap. You're going to let me drive Mitzi?"

"If Maguire is okay with that," he says. "Otherwise maybe let her drive?"

"I have no desire to drive Mitzi," I say. "But what if we get pulled over?"

"I got my provisional license last week," Penn says breezily. "I'll tell them I'm driving other people under the medical-necessity exception. One of you will just have to look extra sick."

"On it!" Jade doubles over and clutches her stomach. "We didn't want to break the law, officer," she says in a thick Southern accent. "But I do declare, I'm feeling quite under the weather."

They both burst into giggles. I roll my eyes at Jade and turn back to Jordy. "I think I can trust her to go a couple of miles, but I can call my mom about the tire. It's not your job to fix it."

"I don't mind," he says. "It won't take me that long."

Penn looks suspiciously at her brother. "You sure you won't drop her car on your foot? I don't want Mom and Dad to blame me if you do."

"Just go." He takes my keys. "Have fun. I'll see you in a bit."

I watch the road and the mirrors as Penn drives Jordy's car back to their house. Jade sits in the backseat, shaking out her hair and using her phone's reverse camera as a mirror to apply eyeliner.

"Why are you putting on makeup?" I ask.

"No reason," Jade says. "No reason at all."

Penn glances in the rearview mirror. "You got a thing for Kimber's brother or something?"

"Kimber has a brother?" Jade asks innocently.

"Darius," Penn says. "Freshman at San Diego State."

"Darius. Hmm. I think he might have been in my French class last year." Jade puts the eyeliner away and pulls

255

out a lipstick. "Is he single?"

"No idea." Penn pulls Jordy's car up onto their driveway. "See. Safe and sound."

It feels like another accomplishment, one I didn't even have on my challenge list. I can barely believe that I've gone from not feeling safe in the car with my stepdad to riding with a brand-new driver. And now I'm headed to a party.

The three of us get out and walk up the street to Kimber's. On the way, I think about Ireland. I can almost see myself in an aisle seat, watching attentively while the flight attendants go through the safety precautions.

Music blares from inside Kimber's house. I knock gently on the door and then, when no one answers, a bit more firmly. After a few seconds, Colleen opens the door, a red plastic cup clutched in one hand.

"Ladies! Welcome." She gives each of us an entirely too-friendly hug. I can smell alcohol on her breath.

Kimber's living room is arranged similarly to Jordy's, with a pair of leather sofas flanking a big screen TV, a brick fireplace adorned with tennis trophies off to the side. "Everyone is outside," Colleen says. "Come on."

I do a quick check of the living room—there's no fire in the fireplace, no electrical cords stretched across any walkways, no obvious hazards that I can see. So far, so good.

Jade tugs me toward the sliding glass door that leads out onto the deck.

Kimber, Mae, and the rest of the doubles players are

seated at a big round patio table. Behind them, the sun is setting, casting a warm glow over the grassy lawn. A giant tree takes up one corner of the yard, a tree house perched in its major branches. I try to reconcile Kimber with being the kind of kid who hung out in a tree house, but I can't. I slide into an open seat across from her and next to Penn.

"I ordered pizza," Kimber says. "Meat and vegetarian. It should be here in twenty."

"Cool," Jade says. "I am starving. And thirsty."

There's a stack of red cups and a pitcher of what looks like limeade but smells like alcohol in the center of the table. Penn and Jade each pour themselves a drink. Jade grabs a cup for me, but I shake my head.

"I don't drink."

"Aww. Something else you two have in common." Colleen nudges Kimber, who gives her a glare.

"There's bottled water and soda in the fridge," Kimber says. "I'd get it for you but . . ." She gestures to her left and right. "I'm a little trapped back here."

"No problem. I'll grab it." I glance around the table. "Anyone else need anything while I'm up?"

"I'll take another sparkling water." Kimber pulls the ponytail holder from her hair and shakes out her dark brown tresses.

I head back inside and screech to a stop when I see that the kitchen is full of boys. Three boys, to be exact, all in jeans and T-shirts. They look a little bit older than me. They're all clustered around the fridge.

The tallest of the three turns around. He's got the same dark skin and piercing gaze as Kimber. "Who might you be?" he asks.

"Hi. I'm Maguire. I'm a friend of, I mean, I play tennis with Kimber."

One of the other boys laughs. "I love how no one actually describes themselves as your sister's friend."

"She doesn't have friends," the tall boy says. "She's got opponents. Maybe a few assistants on a good day." He winks at me. "I'm Darius. And this is Shawn and Kyle. Please tell me you guys ordered food. Everything in the fridge is labeled low fat or low sodium."

"That's child abuse," I say.

"Right?" Darius grins. "A growing boy needs his fat and sodium."

"Your sister said something about pizza."

"Excellent," Darius says. "You guys chilling out on the deck?"

"Yeah."

The boys head for the door, and I start to follow them. Then I realize I forgot the water, so I double back to grab a couple of bottles.

By the time I get back outside, my original seat is taken, and I end up sitting next to Shawn. The boys chat about stuff going on at college while Kimber talks about our upcoming matches. I mostly nod and smile, trying to keep track of both conversations but not really engaging in either. My eyes scan the table, the deck, and the yard at regular intervals. Eventually, somebody suggests playing a drinking game. Darius heads back inside to find some cards, and I slide out of my chair and walk to the far end of the deck. I pull the ponytail holder out of my hair and rub my scalp with my fingertips. Leaning my arms on the wooden railing, I close my eyes and let the cool breeze wash over my skin.

"Hey," a deep voice says.

I open my eyes. Shawn is standing next to me, and I get a good look at him for the first time. He's broad-chested, with short, rusty-colored hair and bright green eyes. When he smiles, I notice that one of his front teeth is a little crooked. It's the kind of flaw that would bother me if it were mine, but somehow it works with the rest of his looks. "I brought you a drink," he says. He has the faintest hint of a Southern accent. He holds out a red plastic cup.

"I don't drink," I say. "But thanks."

Shawn puts the cup on the railing between us. "How come I've never seen you around before, Maguire?"

"I just moved to Pacific Point this summer."

"Ah. I graduated last year. I used to play on the boys' team. And also the junior tour. Kimber and I went to a lot of the same events."

"So you probably know Jordy too, then," I say.

"I do." Shawn hops up on the railing and sits facing me. "Are you one of his many female fans?"

My cheeks redden. I have no idea how to respond to that. "He helped me with my serve," I say finally. I stare down at the backyard. Shawn seems completely stable, but if he fell backward he'd fall about fifteen feet. "You're making me nervous sitting up there."

"Aww. Worried about me? That's cute." He hops down and leans against the railing. "So how do you like it here?"

"It's not bad."

He bumps his forearm against mine. Next to his sun-kissed skin I look like I'm made of vanilla ice cream. "I'm guessing you spend all your free time at the beach?"

I smile. "Not really."

"How are you enjoying being part of the team?"

"I'm having fun, but I'm not doing so great. Right now my record is fifty-fifty."

"It's a tough district. No shame in fifty-fifty. Maybe we could hit around sometime, if you want?"

"Oh." Once again I am completely caught off guard. "I don't think I'd be much competition for you."

He shrugs. "You never know till you try. Either way, one of the best ways to improve your game is to hit with someone at a higher level."

He's basically repeating things Jordy has said to me. I can't tell if he's flirting or honestly just interested in helping me with my tennis game.

"Give me your phone," he says.

"What?"

"Give. Me. Your. Phone," he repeats, as if maybe I'm a little slow.

I can't figure out how to refuse him, so I fumble in my pocket for my phone and hand it over. As Shawn accesses my contacts menu, someone knocks on the front door. *Saved by the pizza*, I think.

But it's not the pizza.

Shawn glances up as Jordy strolls out onto the back deck. "Hey man, what's up?"

"Not much," Jordy says. "How's college treating you?"

"Not too bad," Shawn says. "You know where you're going to go?"

"I don't even know *if* I'm going to go . . ." Jordy trails off. He's staring at the phone in Shawn's hand. My phone.

"Shawn!" Darius hollers from the other side of the deck. "I found the cards. You in or what?"

"I have to go school some people," Shawn says, handing my phone back to me. "But it was nice meeting you, Maguire."

"Yeah. You too," I say. Glancing down, I see that Shawn has added himself to my embarrassingly small contacts menu as "Shawn Kane—the hot guy you met at Kimber's house."

He crosses the deck, stopping halfway to turn around and mouth "call me." Then he slides into a chair next to Darius.

Jordy pulls my car keys from his pocket. He sets them

on the wooden railing of the deck, his jaw going tight. "Did Shawn Kane just tell you to call him?"

"Yeah," I say. "He offered to practice with me."

"Oh. Your car is parked across the street from my house." Jordy slides my keys toward me, but he doesn't say anything else.

I lower my voice so no one else can hear. "I'm not going to. But he seemed nice and I didn't know what to tell him."

Jordy gestures at my untouched drink. "What are you drinking?"

"I think it's a margarita or something. I'm not drinking it, though. I don't drink."

"Can I drink it?"

"Sure."

Jordy takes a long drink from the plastic cup. Looking straight ahead, he says, "I mean, you can call him if you want. He's a decent guy, and a solid tennis player too."

"Is he better than you?" I ask curiously.

"Not at tennis." Jordy swishes the remaining liquid around in his cup. "I've beat him all three times we played each other."

I nudge him in the ribs. "Not at tennis? What's *that* supposed to mean?"

He looks down at me, the flecks of gold in his brown eyes evident in the soft glow of the fading daylight. "It means this is harder than I thought."

"What is?"

He lowers his voice. "Sharing you." Before I can reply he continues, "I'm glad you felt comfortable enough to come to this party. I want you to get over your fear of being around other people, but man, I hate watching other guys hit on you."

"I don't think he was hitting on me," I protest.

Jordy snorts. "Come on, Maguire. We both know that he was."

"Jordy," I say softly. I reach out and touch his arm.

He turns to face me. "Do you want to go for a walk? I need some air."

We both know that there's no more air on the sidewalk than there is on Kimber's deck, but I nod at him. "Let me just tell Jade where I'm going." I look over at the round table, but she's not there. She must be in the bathroom or something.

Jordy drains the rest of the drink from the red plastic cup while I send Jade a text and tell her I'll be back in an hour. He leaves the empty cup on the deck and heads for the sliding glass door. We cut back through Kimber's house.

I do a five-second check as we step outside, looking for anything strange or out of place. All I see are the quiet silhouettes of the upper-class neighborhood—sloping roofs, spiky palm trees, manicured lawns cut short into submission.

Our walk takes us exactly where I expect it to—Jordy's house.

The driveway is bare. The lights are all off. I've been alone with Jordy plenty of times, even at his house before. But something feels different about tonight, like everything is getting ready to change, whether I'm ready for it or not.

CHAPTER 28

I follow Jordy inside, waiting while he punches in the security code.

He turns away from the blinking panel and heads for the stairs. "Come on," he says. "My room is on the second floor."

My heart starts pounding as I follow him; sweat beads on the back of my neck. I don't think it's from climbing the stairs.

The door to Jordy's bedroom opens with a soft creak. He reaches an arm around the doorframe and flicks on the light. There's a desk and chair, a set of shelves that runs the full length of one wall, a big screen TV, and a video game console, its wires twisting across the floor. And then there's his bed, queen-sized, unmade.

I force myself to look away from the tangled sheets. The shelves are full of trophies—big ones, small ones, ribbons, plaques. I pretend to concentrate on them and not on the fact that Jordy has invited me into his private space. He didn't even feel the need to tuck away his dirty laundry or scattered papers and magazines.

"What are we doing?" I whisper.

He loops his hands around my waist and pulls me into a loose embrace. "Hiding from the rest of the world."

"Why?"

"Good question. I'm so tired of my parents and the secrets and everyone's expectations. All this stress is like dragging around an anvil. No wonder I'm feeling exhausted."

I run one hand up and down his arm. "I don't have expectations for you."

He presses his lips to my forehead. "I know. Sometimes I feel like you're the only one."

I rest my cheek against his chest and inhale his scent—a complex aroma of soap, cologne, and alcohol. He's upset—I can feel it, but I don't know how to fix things. "So you manage to find time for video games, huh?" I say, gesturing at the console.

"Very little," Jordy says. "Sometimes I play before I go to sleep. It's weird—it helps me wind down. Do you play?"

"Not really," I admit.

"Do you want to?" His voice catches in his throat.

"Sure."

Jordy flicks off the room light and turns on a small desk lamp, bathing everything in comforting shadows. He does a belly flop onto his bed and pats a spot on the mattress. "Get comfy."

I settle uneasily on the edge of his bed and take the oval-shaped controller he puts in my hand. He flicks a button on the remote, and the start-up screen for a game called Killdead Enterprises appears. "Basically the idea is to kill all the zombies. Don't kill the hostages. The left and right arrows turn you. The forward and back make you go forward and back, and the trigger button shoots," he says. "There's more, but that'll get you started."

Jordy presses a button on his controller, and the screen changes to what looks like a military base. The zombies come slowly at first, and then quicker. I find myself getting into the game, enjoying the challenge of spotting and targeting each threat as it appears. When we get to the end of the level, there's a zombie cyborg creature that Jordy explains is the boss. "We have to shoot him like a hundred times."

"Fun." Biting my bottom lip, I target the boss and start firing, mashing buttons as fast as I can. He dodges left and right, occasionally retreating behind what looks like a small water tower. When the boss disappears from the screen, I fire a blast of machine gun bullets at one leg of the tower.

"What are you doing?" Jordy asks.

"Wondering if we can crush him with this tower thing."

"That's not a bad idea." He shoots at another leg of the tower, and it teeters dangerously. "Wait till he comes back on-screen."

When the zombie boss appears again and starts throwing axes at us, I fire rapidly on him while Jordy takes out the second leg of the water tower. It's enough to send it crashing to the ground, right on top of the boss, who promptly dies. The end-of-level scene appears, and Jordy and I get a huge point bonus.

He pauses the game and turns to me. "I never even thought of that. You are smart." He holds his hand up for a high five.

"Not that smart." I slap his palm.

"Yes, you are." Jordy catches my fingers and squeezes them gently.

I exhale slowly, my eyes locked onto his. I pull my hand free from his grip and shake it out. "I think I might have sprained something," I joke.

He reaches for my hand again. "Lucky for you I'm currently enrolled in a class called Sports Medicine."

"Does it include information on video game injuries?"

"Most repetitive motion injuries are similar." He massages my palm with both of his thumbs. Then he uses his thumb and forefinger to massage the area between each of my fingers.

It feels so good that my whole body relaxes. I drop my head forward and let my eyes close. "I give you an *A*," I say. "You're practically making my mouth water."

"Really?" He stretches the word out. "I like the sound of that." With his other hand, he reaches out and lifts my chin. He drags his thumb across my bottom lip. "You're amazing, you know it?"

"Because I killed a zombie?" I ask weakly.

He laughs silently, his eyes still locked onto mine. "Because you're smart, and funny, and talented, and kind."

"And cursed," I remind him, my voice hoarse.

He traces my jawbone with his knuckles. "I don't care about your curse." Without warning, he leans in close. His mouth brushes mine gently. One hand slides under the bottom of my shirt. His fingertips caress the bare skin of my back.

I lean into him, my lips urgent against his. The next thing I know we're both lying on his bed, our arms and legs tangled together. His soft mattress threatens to swallow me whole. I kick off my shoes and curl onto my side so we're facing each other.

Jordy reaches across me to stroke my hair. "I just keep seeing the look on your face when Shawn gave you his number."

"And what look was that?"

"Surprised. Sort of flattered."

I move closer to him. "That's exactly how I felt. But that's it—nothing more. I don't need to hang out with him or anything."

"It just made me realize how stupid I'm being about my parents, thinking they'll be easier to persuade after I show them my mid-semester grades. They want me to go to college and be all about tennis and studying." He brings my hand to his mouth and brushes his lips against each of my knuckles. "But I want to date you and I want to go pro next year, and no matter when I tell them, it's going to be a big, nasty confrontation. I need to just man up and face it."

"How are you so sure this is what you want?" I'm not sure if I'm talking about his feelings for me or going pro.

"I just am. I know how I feel." He rests his forehead against mine. "Do you know how you feel?"

I know how I feel, but what I don't know is whether my feelings are strong enough to overcome my bad luck, whether caring about Jordy is a good thing or a bad thing. I can't explain that to him, though. Not here, with our noses brushing and bodies just inches apart. I should get up, move away, but I don't. It's like when you stand too close to the edge of a cliff and part of you really wants to jump. You know it's crazy, but once the idea takes hold of you, it's hard to break away from it.

"Here's what I feel like." I roll onto my back and pull Jordy on top of me. Brushing his hair back from his eyes, I run one fingertip around his lips. His scent, the weight of his body, the look in his eyes—all of it excites me. Suddenly I don't just want to jump off that cliff anymore. I want to dive headfirst into the swirling waves, even though I'm not sure if I can swim. "Kiss me," I whisper.

Jordy's mouth crashes down onto mine. I taste the mix of sweetness and alcohol from whatever he drank at Kimber's house, but I don't mind. He bites gently on my lower lip. My hands slide under the fabric of his shirt, my fingertips gently exploring his stomach and ribcage.

He tugs his shirt over his head. He drops it on the floor and kisses me again. My fingers crawl upward, stroking his pecs, his shoulders. I feel the soft prickle of chest hair. Beneath my palm, Jordy's heart beats slow and steady. I don't know how he can be so calm when everything feels so electric, so turbocharged. My body is asking for things it's never wanted before.

Jordy's hands trace their way up my hips, tugging my shirt up just far enough that the bare skin of his stomach is brushing against mine. I kiss his jawbone, run my mouth along his neck, listen to the soft noises escaping from his lips.

His eyes snap open. He rolls to the side of me. "Screw dating. What does 'dating' even mean? I want you to be my girlfriend." He laces his fingers through mine. "Say you'll be my girlfriend right now, tonight, and I'll wait up for my parents and tell them everything."

"Jordy," I say weakly. "If this is just because you saw me talking to Shawn . . ."

"It's not," he says. "You make me want to be brave—to face the stuff that scares me."

"Some of which scares you for good reason," I say. "Let's stick to the plan. You focus on school and tennis. I'll finish my therapy challenges. Then . . . we'll figure it out. You know how I feel about jinxing things."

"I do," he says. "But sometimes I feel like maybe you're just using your fears as an excuse not to get close. That you'll

271

blow me off no matter what happens."

"That's not . . ." As I struggle to formulate a response, his mouth traces its way up the ridge of muscle in my neck. He reaches down to stroke the skin of my bare leg. "Jordy." I can hear the pleading sound in my voice, but I'm not sure if I want him to quit or keep going. "I'm pretty sure you know how I feel," I whisper. Every sensation seems amplified by a million.

"I can see how you feel about *this*," he murmurs, his lips finding the sensitive places on my neck again. "I'm asking how you feel about *me*. Be my girlfriend, Maguire."

I pull away and sit up in the bed, threading and unthreading my fingers in front of my body. For most other girls, this would be easy. But I know that even if I survive all my therapy challenges and make it to Ireland and back, that won't mean I'm not cursed, it won't mean I won't someday reflect bad luck on Jordy or his family, it won't mean I won't regret whatever decision I make here.

But I also know this isn't a choice I can put off forever.

I want this, whatever it is. I want to see where things go. I want to let myself *feel*. But just as I'm about to tell him yes, that I'll be his girlfriend, a car door slams outside.

"Shit." Jordy flinches so sharply we both almost fall off the bed. He leaps up and strides across the room to the window.

I sit up slowly, finger-combing my disheveled hair. My

whole body is warm. Everything feels a little cloudy and unreal. "What is it?"

He swears under his breath. "My parents."

I snap out of my haze. "We should get downstairs."

"Right. Except it's too late. They'll be inside before we can get back down there."

"What will they do if they catch you with a girl in your room?"

"Lecture me for hours. Ground me forever. Possibly ask you to take a pregnancy test." He grabs his shirt from the floor and pulls it back on.

"What—"

"Sorry. Stupid thing to say. I'm panicking." He tosses his hair back from his face. "You know what? Screw it. I said I wanted to tell them. This is a sign. I'm going to tell them right now. We're together. I'm going pro. That's how it's going to be. I want them to be part of my career, but if they can't live with that then I guess I'll have to start paying for my own coaching and tournaments, which I'll be able to do once I can score some bigger sponsors."

"No, wait," I hiss. "These aren't the kind of decisions you make in two seconds."

"I've been thinking about this stuff for months," he says firmly.

"Okay. But I can't meet your mom like this." I rake my hands through my hair again. "What is she going to think?"

"She's going to think we were up here fooling around. Big deal. It's not like we're naked."

"Jordy! I don't want your mom to think of me like . . . whatever. This is not a sign. It's a cosmic beatdown waiting to happen. Hide me," I beg. "Sneak me out later. Tomorrow we can figure everything out when we're both thinking clearly."

"I am thinking clearly," Jordy says. "And I'm sick of hiding,"

"I'm not!" I give him my best pleading look.

Suddenly there's a knock at the door. "Stanford?" A woman's musical voice calls.

I lie down and pull the quilted comforter over my head. As hiding places go, it's not much, but it's the best I've got.

"Jesus, Maguire," Jordy mutters. "Fine. But that is not going to work if she turns on the overhead light."

I roll onto my stomach and flatten myself out as much as possible, willing my body to sink into the mattress, willing the comforter to fall around my frame in indecipherable, non-girl-shaped folds.

"Stanford? Are you in there?"

"Come on in," Jordy says, his voice seemingly relaxed.

I hold my breath as the door to his room creaks open.

CHAPTER 29

"I thought I heard voices. Who were you talking to?" Jordy's
mom asks.

"What? Oh. Chris. I was on the phone."

"Mmhmm." She makes a clicking sound with her tongue.
"This room is a mess. When did you get so slovenly?"

"Sorry. I'll clean it tomorrow," Jordy says.

I hear her footsteps cross the floor.

Toward me. *Oh my God, oh my God, ohmygod.*

"Why is your shirt on inside out?" his mom asks.

"Uh . . . it's a style thing."

"I see." She sniffs. "Why do you smell like alcohol? Also
a *style* thing?" Without waiting for a response, she yanks back
the comforter with one hand, exposing me. Sighing deeply,
she looks away from the bed. "Stanford. Not again."

Jordy looks back and forth from me to his mom, a defiant
expression on his face. "This is Maguire. Maguire, my mom,
Eileen."

"Hi," I manage to choke out. I can't look at her. I can't look at anyone. I glance around the room, half-hoping for a containable electrical fire or a small-scale earthquake. Where's a good minor catastrophe when you need one?

"How do you do?" his mom asks, but she's not looking at me either. Her eyes are glued to Jordy. "How many times are you going to make this mistake?"

My face burns. I'm fully clothed, but somehow I've never felt more naked. I ball the fabric of Jordy's sheet in my hands. Mistake? How many times? What does that mean exactly?

"She's not a *mistake*, Mom," Jordy says. "She's my girl-friend. Or I was asking her to be my girlfriend when you knocked."

Mrs. Wheeler's eyes flick momentarily to mine. "You should probably go, dear." She turns back to Jordy. "Where's your phone. Deactivate the front-door alarm for her."

"No. She's not leaving," he says. "We weren't doing any-thing wrong."

"It's okay, Jordy." I stare at my hands. "I'll go."

"I think that would be for the best," his mom says.

He shakes his head. "Don't leave."

His mom turns her attention to me completely. Her eyes are a cool ice blue, almost gray. "I'm sure you're a lovely girl, but right now is an important time for Stanford and his career. The past few weeks he's been recovering from an injury, but he's also seemed . . . unfocused. Distracted. He's struggling in matches that should be easy for him."

"Oh my God, Mom. She is *not* the reason I've been losing." Jordy turns to me. "You're not. I swear."

But his mom's words are like a blast of machine gun fire to my gut. It never even occurred to me that I might have caused Jordy to lose with something other than my bad luck. Is just *thinking* about me affecting his game? His career? His whole future? If so, then it doesn't matter if I'm cursed or not. Caring about me is bad for him. I can't bear that.

"Maybe your mom is right." I slide out from under the covers and smooth the wrinkles from my skirt. I start pulling my shoes back on.

"What?" The blood drains from Jordy's face. "No. Don't let her run you off like this, Maguire."

"No one is running anyone off," his mom says. "But if she cares about you, she won't want to—"

"If *you* care about me, you'll let me make some decisions for myself," Jordy says.

"I don't want to be the one who messes up your future," I say hoarsely. I twist my hair back up into a bun.

"Then don't leave," he says.

My eyes flick to his for a moment, but that's all I can take. There's so much pain in his expression. "It seems like you guys need to talk."

"We *all* need to talk," Jordy says.

"Okay," I say. "But you guys should talk first." I give him one last look and head for the hallway.

The tears come as I hit the stairs. Behind me I hear

Jordy's mom yelling. "We had an agreement, Stanford. Don't you remember what happened the last time you let yourself get distracted?"

"You can't keep me from having friends. That's not living."

"It's not *friends* I'm worried about."

"I'm sick of you telling me what to do and who to be!"

I plug my ears with my fingertips. I don't want to hear it—any of it. I almost crash into Penn in the foyer. She must be just getting home from Kimber's.

She grabs my arm as I go for the front door. "What is it?" she whispers. "What happened?"

"Your mom happened," I say. "I've got to go. I'm Jade's ride."

Penn follows me outside. "Hold up. I'll walk you back to Kimber's."

"You don't have to do that. I'm fine."

"You don't look fine. You looked wrecked. My mom has that effect on people. Did she . . . interrupt you guys or something?" When I don't respond, Penn keeps talking. "He's crazy about you. He'll talk some sense into her, okay? Just don't feel bad, because this conversation has needed to happen for a while, and it's more about the two of them than it is about you."

"I don't know." I pause in front of Kimber's house. "Your mom made it sound like I'm the fifth girl she's found in his bedroom this month."

Penn gasps. "That is not true, Maguire. My brother isn't a saint, but he's not some sleazy man-whore, either. You're the only girl he's even talked about in over a year."

I want to believe her, but that's just my ego. What Jordy is or isn't doesn't really matter if their mom is right and thinking about me has caused him to lose matches. "You should get home so you don't get in trouble too. And you might want some gum or something. She smelled alcohol on him right away."

"Thanks." Penn reaches over and gives me a quick hug. "Jordy will fix this."

"Yeah," I say. But I'm not sure this can be fixed.

I knock on the front door of Kimber's house. No one answers, so I let myself inside. The living room is empty. Kimber and Darius are in the kitchen cleaning up.

Kimber folds a pizza box in half and tucks it into a trash can. "Sorry, New Girl. I didn't hear you knock," she says flatly.

I can't help but wonder what I did to get myself downgraded back to "new girl" status. "I'm just looking for Jade."

"She's outside."

"Thanks." I head for the sliding glass door.

"Actually, I need a word with you." Kimber grabs my arm, her fingers clamping down on my skin tight enough to cut off the circulation. She pulls me down the hallway and into a bathroom, shutting the door behind her. Who knew a six-foot by six-foot cube filled with fluffy pink rugs and towels could feel so dangerous?

"I'm not in a very good mood right now," I say. "What is it?"

She leans against the door. "You need to stop messing with Jordy."

God. I guess that's the theme of the evening.

"You're not the boss of me," I say. "And I'm not *messing* with him."

"Really? Because I watched you kiss him a few hours ago, and then I find out you gave my brother's friend your number, and then you apparently ran off with Jordy again a few minutes later. I'm not going to tell you how to live your life, but don't jerk around one of my best friends, okay?"

"I didn't give Shawn my number. He gave me his. I have no intention of calling him."

Kimber crosses her arms. "Then why did you take his number?"

"I guess because I'm not any good at being a bitch." *Like you*, I think.

Her lips purse, and I'm pretty sure she read my mind on that last part. I don't even care. I blame myself for enough things as it is. I'm not going to let other people blame me for stuff I didn't even do.

"It doesn't matter anyway," I tell her. "Jordy's mom just kicked me out of their house. Pretty sure she's not going to let him see me ever again." My voice cracks. The tears surge up from nowhere. I step back, grab a tissue from a pastel pink tissue-box holder, and blot my eyes.

"Oh, wow." Kimber cocks her head to the side and studies me. "You really like him."

"Yeah." I sniff. I'm a little surprised that fact hasn't been obvious to her.

Her dark eyes bore straight through me. "Not just because he's cute or famous?"

"No! Why would you think that?"

She starts ticking things off on her fingers. "You show up out of nowhere and work really hard to get his attention. You're clearly good at tennis but still ask for extra help. You seem distracted at practice. You seem nervous enough at your matches that he feels the need to spend most of his time supporting you."

"Yeah, and?" I ask. "Did it ever occur to you that might actually be who I am? That maybe I have reasons for being distracted or nervous? Did you really think I faked not knowing how to serve so he'd spend time with me? That I hit him with a tennis ball to get him to notice me in the first place?" I am practically yelling by the time I finish.

"Okay, okay. Calm yourself," Kimber says. "But believe me, I've seen shadier things done."

"Not by me. Jordy has been so amazing. You have no idea." I blink back another round of tears.

"Oh, I have an idea. We've been friends since we were kids." A smile touches her lips. "I know how great he is. I also know he has a big heart. I just didn't want to see him wasting time on someone who didn't appreciate everything he has to offer."

"I appreciate him." I ball the tissue in my fist.

"I can see that now." She pats me awkwardly on the shoulder. "Sorry for giving you a hard time. And don't worry about his mom. Her bark is way worse than her bite. If you stand your ground, she'll accept you eventually."

Too bad I did the exact opposite of stand my ground.

I catch a glimpse of my reflection in the mirror. My eyes are red, my skin is blotchy, and hair is pulling loose from my bun, frizzing out in all directions like a storm cloud. Kimber is probably wondering what Jordy even sees in me.

I tuck a rogue spiral of hair behind my ear. "Why are you being nice to me?"

"Why wouldn't I be nice to you?"

"Well, you and Jordy. I thought you two used to hook up or something . . ."

Kimber bursts out laughing. "Who told you that? Because I know it wasn't him."

"It's just something I heard," I say, not wanting to betray Jade. "I mean, anyone can see how much you like him."

"Ah, rumors. Well, you got that part right at least. I do like him, but only as a friend."

"But he told me you guys kissed."

"Yeah, in middle school. It's a long story, but trust me, we were never together. I know that as a sophomore he made the decision with his parents to put his social life on hold to focus on tennis. At that point, it seemed like what he wanted to do. But things change. Jordy is a big boy, and anyone can see how much he likes you. If he's happy, I'm happy."

I think of the look on Jordy's face as I slinked out of his bedroom. Too bad he's not happy, and neither am I.

There's a soft knock on the bathroom door. Kimber opens it, and Jade peeks her head in. "Oh look. It's my ride home," she teases.

"Drive safe, you two," Kimber says. She heads back into the kitchen as Jade and I turn toward the front door.

"Sorry," I tell Jade. "I didn't mean to strand you."

"No bigs." Jade leans in. "Are those tears? What were you doing locked in the bathroom, crying with Kimber? You didn't even drink anything, did you?"

"Nope." I step back out into the night. Jade and I start walking down the street to where Jordy parked my car. I can't help but peek up at the Wheeler house. It's all dark except for a light on the second floor. His room. "I went to Jordy's for a little bit. His mom caught us up in his room."

Jade waits for me to say more.

I unlock the car and slide into the driver's seat. "We were just kissing and stuff, but God, the way his mom looked at me. She called me 'a mistake.'"

"Ouch. What did Jordy say?"

"Well, he said I wasn't a mistake. But then they started yelling at each other, and she accused me of being the reason he's been off his game."

"Double ouch."

"Yeah. She told me to leave. He told me *not* to leave. I left. Everything is messed up."

"Relationships are messy," Jade says. "But when two people like each other, they work it out." She clicks her seat belt and then reaches over to pat my hand.

I shake my head. "I think it's better if I leave him alone. I don't want to be the reason he's losing."

CHAPTER 30

Jordy isn't at practice the next day or at our match on Thursday. Penn says he's playing a tournament in Brazil. I wonder if his mom squeezed him into some international matches just to get him away from me. I search for him online and see that he's advanced to the third round of something called the Santa Caterina Cup. Good for him. As much as I miss him, I'm glad he's back doing what he loves. I think about texting him, but decide that I should let him focus on tennis while I concentrate on my own goals.

I spend Thursday and Friday reinforcing my therapy challenges. I ride the team bus, give Penn a lift home from school, and hit the mall with my mom to pick up some stuff for Jacob. I almost hop onto the San Diego Trolley that goes from the northern part of the city to the Mexican border, but as I'm standing on the platform I start to hyperventilate. I try some relaxation exercises and think about the coping statements Daniel taught me, but I just can't bring myself to board when the train cruises to a stop and the automatic doors open. At first I feel like a failure, but Daniel told me to trust my gut so that's what I do.

On the weekend, I wake up early each morning and go for a long run around the neighborhood. I spend the afternoons doing homework and going through the Ireland guidebooks, taking notes on the city where my grandmother lives and the surrounding area. I look up the various types of planes that fly internationally and study their safety features.

My trip to Ireland is finally starting to feel real.

On Monday, Penn flags me down at practice to be her hitting partner.

"How's your brother?" I ask.

"He's good. He made it to the semis. He and my mom got back last night." Then she says, "He told me you took her side. Is that true?"

I sigh. "I guess I did."

She bounces a ball on the face of her racquet repeatedly. "Why would you do that?"

"What if she's right? What if I *was* distracting him from his game?"

"Then that's Jordy's problem to deal with. Not hers. And not yours."

"But I don't want to be Jordy's problem. I would rather leave him alone so he can focus."

She arches a blonde eyebrow at me. "You think bailing

on him did him a favor? That he's not even more distracted now because he's sad? And because he misses you?"

"I don't know," I say. "I figured being apart would be helpful, give both of us a chance to work on our issues."

Penn coils her braid around her hand "I don't know why you want to do it alone instead of together, but whatever."

I start to respond but she holds up a hand. "You know what? It's not my business. Forget I mentioned it."

If only it were that easy.

I try to forget, but I keep thinking about how Penn said Jordy was sad, that he missed me. I check my phone about fifty times on Monday night, hoping for a text that never comes.

Jordy shows up to our home match on Tuesday, but he arrives after I start playing and leaves before I'm finished. If it weren't for my five-second checks, I might not have even noticed him. He doesn't say a single word to me the whole afternoon. I tell myself it's because other people needed his help more—I won easily 6–2, 6–1—but deep down I know that he's avoiding me.

On Wednesday, Penn informs me that Jordy gained last-minute entry into another international tournament when a seeded player had to withdraw. He's going to be gone the rest of the week.

Jade tries to get me to go to the Homecoming dance with her and a couple of friends from theater class, but I beg off. Even before I decided I was cursed I never had any interest in school dances.

Penn tries to get me to go to the football game, which sounds like a lot more fun. Daniel and I talk about it in our Friday session and he says it's a good idea, not just going to a crowded place, but going to one with friends. Maybe that's why I couldn't bring myself to get on the trolley—I was all alone.

Still, the football game is a big step for me since the last sporting event I attended ended in Penn being transported to the emergency room. I spend some time on Saturday morning doing relaxation exercises and an extra set of good luck rituals.

An hour before the game starts, I meet Penn, Jade, and two girls Jade knows from theater class in front of the school. The five of us sit high in the bleachers, cheering on our Pacific Point Porpoises who unfortunately lose 41–6. I do a five-second check after each play. No one gets injured, unless you count our quarterback's pride. He completes only eight passes all game and throws three interceptions.

"We could've put on pads and done a better job than that," Jade mutters as our football team slinks off the field.

We head to the parking lot as a group. Jade and her friends sit on the steps in front of the school to wait for her mom to pick them up. Penn and I turn toward the student parking lot. Jordy's car is parked in the far corner and for a moment I think maybe my good day is going to get even better. And then Penn pulls a set of keys from her pocket and I realize she drove herself. My chin drops to my chest and my shoulders slump forward.

"What are you doing next weekend?" she asks.

"You mean for Halloween?"

"I was actually thinking about Sunday."

"No plans. Why?"

"My friend and I are going to Belmont Park. You want to come? You could bring Jade if you want." Penn glances back at the school steps.

"What's Belmont Park?" I pause in front of my mom's car.

"It's this amusement park at Mission Beach. It's kind of small, but it's got rides, games, a kick-ass roller coaster."

"Roller coaster?" I ask.

"Yeah. The Big Dipper. No, the Giant Dipper. That thing is like a hundred years old."

"Is it scary?" An idea starts to form in my brain, revealing itself a fold at a time like an origami flower. It takes a few creases for me to even accept that I'm being serious.

"It is ridiculously scary," Penn says. "It's old school—no loops or upside-down parts, but it's so fast that you practically lift right off your seat on the hills. People say it goes up to sixty miles an hour."

I imagine what it would feel like to get back on a roller coaster. That slow climb to the top of the first hill, your heart beating three times for each jerking movement. That moment before you plunge downward. And then whatever comes next—the parts I won't let myself remember and the parts I've never experienced. My chest gets tight just thinking about it. My hands start to sweat. I'm pretty sure it would be horrible. But it would also be the ultimate victory over my fears.

I force a smile. "Yeah, I'll go."

Maybe it's time I give the Universe a sign of my own.

CHAPTER 31
Session #14

Daniel sets the remnants of a burger in a wrapper off to the side as I enter his office.

"Dinner of champions," I say.

He laughs lightly. "Happy Halloween. Got any big plans for tomorrow?"

"As you can probably imagine, Halloween isn't really my thing." I slide into my usual seat. "I've got some big plans for Sunday, though."

He leans back in his chair. "Oh yeah? Feel like sharing?"

I fiddle with my mystic knot pendant. "Well, I did okay at the football game but I still felt kind of lame for not being able to ride the trolley. I was thinking I would try again, but bring one of my friends along."

"Sounds good," Daniel says.

"But then I got an even better idea." I swing my legs back and forth.

"What's that?"

I look up at him and force a smile. "The roller coaster at Belmont Park."

"Wow," Daniel says. "Really?"

I shrug. "Go big or go home, maybe? I haven't asked my mom if I can go yet, but I'm pretty sure she'll say yes because she's happy I have friends now."

"Maguire." Daniel rubs his forehead. "After what you've been through, no one is expecting you to ever get back on a roller coaster if you don't want to."

"I know," I say. "I never really liked roller coasters much in the first place. It just feels like something I have to do."

Daniel nods slowly. "Well, then you should do it. But not by yourself."

"I've got a couple of friends who will be with me. They don't know what I have planned yet. They just think we're going to the amusement park."

"But they're supportive and trustworthy?"

"Absolutely."

"Then I'm excited for you. I can't wait to hear how it goes. That's number six, right? What's after that?"

"I don't know yet," I say. "I feel like my last challenge should be something big. Maybe taking a train or a plane somewhere?"

Daniel nods. "That's a good plan if your family can swing it. If not, consider doing something where you have no control over the situation at all."

"What do you mean?"

"Your good luck rituals, your constant five-second checks—these are just ways for you to try to seize control of your environment, right? To maintain order in your world. To not feel powerless."

"I guess," I say.

"You're going to feel powerless on that plane. Maybe let someone else—your mom, a friend, whoever—plan your last challenge. That way you'll experience what it's like to be truly at the mercy of the Universe."

My stomach feels like it's already on a roller coaster as I slip out of Daniel's office. I still haven't talked to Jordy since the night of Kimber's party

He's sitting in his usual spot, only today he's wearing khaki pants and a button-up shirt. His hair is slicked back on the sides but sticking up a little on top. He taps the heel of his dress shoe against the carpet as he swipes at his phone with one finger.

"Look at you," I joke. "Is that your stockbroker costume?"

"Ha. I came from a meeting."

"Are you doing anything fun for Halloween?"

"Nope." He still hasn't looked up from his phone.

I try again. "How was Brazil?"

"Brazilian," he says flatly.

"Are you mad at me, or did your parents just force you to quit talking to me?"

"Seriously? You want to do this here?" He slides his phone into his pocket. "Fine. I'm mad at you."

"What?" I reach out for the arm of the nearest chair to steady myself. "Why?"

"You told my mom she was right. That caring about you was a mistake." His voice hardens slightly. "What were you expecting? Some grand gesture where I beg you to change your mind?"

"Jordy. I just said whatever to get out of there. I was mortified."

"I don't believe you, Maguire. You were the only person who knew how hard I was working to take back control of my life. And then when I finally get the guts to stand up for myself, you take my mom's side, and then you run away." He shakes his head. "I asked you to stay. I *needed* you to stay. And you left."

"I just don't want to be—"

He holds up a hand. "Spare me. I get it. You want what's best for me. But just like everyone else, you think you know better than I do."

"It's not that I—"

He cuts me off again. "Who knows. Maybe you're right. Maybe *everyone* but me is right. Maybe I just need to commit one hundred percent to tennis right now."

"Jordy. I don't . . ." My words fall away when I notice he's staring at something over my shoulder. I spin around. Daniel is standing in the doorway, watching us.

"You two need a minute?" he asks.

Jordy shakes his head. "Nah. We're good. There's not really anything left to say."

CHAPTER 32

When I get home from Daniel's, my whole family is in the living room watching a TV show about the solar system. Mom and Tom are cuddled together on the couch with Jacob between them, and my sister is sprawled on her belly on the floor, a recently abandoned coloring book tucked under her elbows to protect her from the scratchy rug.

"Hi, honey," my mom says. "You okay?"

"Yeah." I try not to think about Jordy. He has every right to be mad at me, and there's nothing I can do about it because I can't be the girl he needs right now. Maybe the two of us were just supposed to help each other face our fears.

Erin looks up with a huge grin. "Mack Wire!" She pats the floor next to her. "Come watch. We're learning about planets."

I scoop her up into my arms and swing her around in a circle. "Whee! Look, you're a planet revolving around the sun."

She squeals. "Mack Wire! Faster!"

"If I go any faster, you might spin off into space, like an asteroid or a crazy meteor!" I twirl her one last time and then set her back on the ground, where she holds her arms out at her sides and continues spinning like a top.

"I'm Jupiter!" she shouts.

"No way. You're too little to be Jupiter!"

She stops spinning and almost falls over. I reach out an arm to steady her, and she looks up at me with her huge blue eyes. "Mom always says I'm tall for my age."

Tom laughs.

"You're very tall for your age," my mom says.

I nod. "She's right. You are definitely going to grow up to be Jupiter."

Erin giggles. "Hey, Mom. Can I be Jupiter for Halloween tomorrow?"

My mom shakes her head. "No, because I already made your costume. You said you wanted to be a tennis player, like your sister." She turns to me. "Is it okay if she borrows your racquet for a quick trip around the neighborhood?"

"Of course." As I look into my little sister's face, I am overwhelmed with affection for her. To her, I am a big sister. She doesn't care that we have different dads, that we look different, that I'm a lot older than her. The way little kids love is so pure and powerful. I throw my arms around her and give her a hug. "But maybe Mom should get you your own racquet. I could use someone to practice with." I wink.

Erin giggles again. "I want a racquet, Mom."

"Maybe next year," my mom says with a smile.

"Did you have a match tonight?" Tom asks.

"Nope. But I had a really helpful session at Dr. Leed's. I think you can go ahead and book those plane tickets."

"Oh honey, that's fantastic." My mom lifts herself off the sofa, carefully so as not to jostle Jacob. "This calls for a celebration." She heads for the kitchen and then stops. "Did you eat anything for dinner?"

"Yeah. I got a sandwich between practice and my appointment."

"We'll just do ice cream then." My mom hums to herself as she begins gathering bowls and toppings.

Erin looks away from the TV. "Did you say ice cream?"

"Yes, indeedy." Tom winks at her. "Even though it's for Maguire, I guess we'll let you have some too."

Erin's eyes get wide. "You better!"

Tom chuckles. "I know better than to get between my girls and their ice cream."

Mom returns with a tray laden with two flavors of ice cream, four bowls and spoons, a can of whipped cream, and jars of chocolate and caramel sauce. "Remind me after the kids go to bed, and I'll forward you the email with the flight information." She starts to scoop some strawberry ice cream into a bowl for Erin, who quickly informs my mom that she wants mint chip.

I flash back to the day Jordy bought me ice cream before

I knew who he was. *I'm more of a mint chip guy.* . . . "I'll take the strawberry. It's fine." I accept the bowl Mom hands me and add a little whipped cream to the top. "But wait. You still have to buy tickets, don't you?"

Mom smiles. "I bought them a few weeks ago. I could see the changes in you. I knew you'd be able to do it."

"You're the best," I say. "Speaking of changes, can I go to Belmont Park on Sunday?"

Erin turns to me so fast she almost drops her bowl of ice cream. "A park? I wanna go," she says, her eyes wide.

"This is just for older kids," I tell her patiently. "We can go sometime as a family too."

"Wow." My mom picks up Jacob, who blinks sleepily and makes a little cooing sound. She hands Tom a bowl of ice cream. Balancing the baby on one hip, she starts to scoop her own bowl. "You told me you'd never go to another amusement park again."

"And you told me to be social and get out there," I remind her. "So are you going to let me go or what?"

"You and who else?" she asks, a gleam in her eye.

"*Girls* from the tennis team," I say. "Some of the ones I went to the football game with."

"What happened to your special practice buddy?"

"Nothing happened to him. He's just focused on his tennis, like I said." I tamp down a pang of sadness.

"Well, of course you can go, if you're sure you want to." Mom hands Jacob to Tom and gives me a hug. "Honey, I'm so proud of all that you've accomplished."

I can't remember the last time I saw her look so happy. As I swirl my spoon around in my bowl of strawberry ice cream and watch the rest of the TV show with my family, I decide it's time for me to figure out how to be happy too.

Later that night, while Mom is putting Erin and Jake to bed, Tom peeks his head into my room. "Can I talk to you for a minute?"

"Sure."

"So about Ireland," he starts.

I'm sitting cross-legged on my bed, flipping through one of the travel guides, stopping mostly on pages with churches or castles. "Yeah?"

He steps into my room and shuts the door halfway. Lowering his voice he says, "I just want you to know, it's okay if something happens and you change your mind. I know you don't want to let your mom down, but if it comes to it, I can go with her. I already took the time off work so I could watch Jake and Erin."

I fiddle with the corner of a picture of something called the Rock of Cashel. "You don't think I can do it?"

Tom leans against one of my overflowing bookshelves. "I think you can do anything. I just don't want you to put too much pressure on yourself. It might be a little awkward for me to be there with her and all of your dad's family, but I'd do it for her, and for you."

"Thanks," I say. "But I think I'm going to make it."

"Well. Either way. I'm proud of you for trying so hard."

I shut the travel guide and set it on my nightstand. "Hey, Tom?"

"Yeah?"

"I'm sorry if I was ever a bitch to you. Mom found you kind of soon after Dad died. That hurt me more than I realized at the time. But I never meant to take it out on you." I thread and unthread my fingers in front of my body. "For what it's worth, I'm glad she has you."

Tom gives my shoulder an awkward squeeze. "Just remember, she's not the only one who has me, okay? I know your therapist has you completing specific challenges to help you work your way up to that plane ride. If there's anything I can do to help, let me know."

"Yeah?" I look up at him. "How do you feel about a road trip at some point? Or even better, a train trip?"

"Like a dry run for your plane?"

"Yep."

"I have to go to San Jose next month for a business meeting. I was going to drive, but I bet we could catch Amtrak up there. Or if not the train, then a bus. It should actually be perfect—about ten hours, the same as a plane ride to Europe."

"You'd do that for me?"

"Of course. It'd be nice to have the company, if your

mom will let you miss a day of school. We could even take the bus there and fly back, if you think you're ready for a plane."

"That would be perfect." I frown. "But what if something happens or I freak out?"

"Then we just rent a car," Tom says with a smile. "Easy breezy."

"Seriously?" I hop off my bed. "I'm going to hug you again."

Tom lifts me about an inch off the floor as he squeezes me. "I love you, kid," he says. "I hope that's okay to say."

"It is," I say. And this moment, this new alliance I never imagined happening, takes a bit of the sting out of losing Jordy.

NOVEMBER

CHALLENGES

1. ~~Make the tennis team.~~
2. ~~Ride in a car with someone besides Mom: Jordy~~
3. ~~Spend a day in a crowded place: Tennis tournament.~~
4. ~~Take something back from the Universe: Rock climbing~~
5. ~~Ride public transportation: Team bus~~
6. Face a specific past fear: Roller coaster
7.

GOAL

Plane ride to Ireland for memorial service

CHAPTER 33

Part of me thinks getting back on a roller coaster is the worst idea ever, but it's a good challenge, and like Daniel suggested at the start, it's me pushing myself. The bus ride went fine, and hopefully my mom will let me go to San Jose with Tom, but that's not for a few weeks. Maybe this is the next logical step—facing a fear specific to my past.

I pick up Jade first, and then we drive to Penn's house to get her and her friend. I figure Jordy should be in the middle of a practice session, but I don't feel like running into him, so I pull my car over to the side of the road and send her a text.

She comes out of the house a few minutes later, with Jordy right behind her.

"What is he doing?" I peer over at Jade. "Is she *bringing* him?"

Jade holds up her hands, displaying a set of perfectly manicured fingernails. "I have no idea."

Jordy seems equally thrilled when he sees my car. He pauses on the porch, and Penn leans in to tell him something. He shakes his head. She looks up at him, reaches out, touches his arm. He shakes his head again, turns back toward the house. She slips between him and the door. I can't hear what they're saying, but they're both throwing around a lot of violent hand gestures.

"This is not what I need today," I mutter.

Apparently Penn wins the fight, because Jordy plasters a smile on his face and follows her down the driveway.

"This should be interesting." Jade hops out of the passenger seat, and Penn slides into the back. Jade gets in beside her, leaving Jordy standing awkwardly next to the car.

He squats down to talk to me through the open window. "I'm sorry, Maguire. When my sister begged me to go to Belmont with her, I didn't know you were going too. I'll just let you guys go and have fun."

"Come on," Penn says from the backseat. "You told Mom you were taking a day off, and you should take it."

"Right. I will. But I've got homework and stuff I can do."

"What is wrong with you, Jordy? I thought you were done letting them take away everything that matters." Penn's voice is shrill.

"You should come," I say suddenly. My heart feels like it's crowding out the rest of my organs, pressing on my ribs, closing up my throat. "I'm going to ride the roller coaster. I'll take all the moral support I can get."

"Maguire." Jordy sounds shocked. "No one expects you to do that."

"Daniel and I decided it was okay. I want to. I mean, I definitely do not want to, but I want to, if that makes any sense." I pause. "Please come."

"Yeah, please come," Penn echoes.

He glances over at Jade. "Are you going to chime in too?"

"Nah. I don't like you as much as these two do." A slow grin spreads across her face. "I was hoping Penn's friend was going to turn out to be Kimber's brother."

Penn pokes her in the arm. "Kimber has a brother?" she mimics. "I knew you were into him."

"Darius is a punk," Jordy says with a half smile. And then, "All right. I'll come. Do you want me to drive?"

"I'm good," I say.

He slides into the passenger seat and everyone buckles their seat belts. I do a five-second check and then pull away from the curb. I scan left and right as I drive, watching the houses go by, soft pastel stucco blurring into a muted rainbow. Children with their parents frolic on front lawns, dancing in and out of jagged shadows cast by palm trees high above their heads. I brake as I come up on a slow-moving pickup, a chocolate Labrador hanging over the truck bed with its tongue flapping in the breeze.

"Cute dog." Penn leans forward for a better look.

"I want a dog," Jade says. "But my mom won't let me have pets. She wouldn't even let me have a goldfish when I was little."

"Sounds like our mom," Penn says. "She thinks animals are dirty and require too much upkeep."

I make a couple more turns and then merge onto the highway. Jordy sits quietly next to me, his thumb swiping at the screen of his phone occasionally, his eyes flicking from the road back to his lap.

My anxiety builds as we near Belmont Park. By the time I drive through the entrance, my skin is cool and clammy and my heart is beating like a runaway horse. The lot looks like an explosion of confetti, shiny cars and brightly dressed kids everywhere. I pull the car into a spot and shift into park. My eyelids fall shut for a moment, blocking out all the colors and motion. Maybe this was a terrible idea.

No one is going to die, I remind myself.

"Are you going to be okay?" Jordy asks. "I know how much you hate amusement parks."

Jade sighs. "How can you hate amusement parks? That's unnatural."

"One of those phobia-causing issues from my past was a roller coaster accident," I tell her. "The car jumped the track at the bottom of a hill. A lot of people got hurt."

"Whoa, I take it back," she says. "And you seriously want to ride the Dipper?"

No. "Yes." I nod. "I don't want you guys to come with me, but maybe you can all hang out close by with your phones just in case."

Penn shrugs. "Wherever you need us."

"We got your back," Jade says.

"I want to ride with you," Jordy says.

I shake my head. "I'd rather have you a safe distance away, but ready to help if anything goes wrong."

"Let's get in line and get our wristbands," Penn says. "Then we can figure out who is doing what."

Penn and Jade do their best to keep me away from the roller coaster for the first hour. Maybe they think I need a chance to get acclimated to the park to feel safe, or maybe they think the day is going to be wrecked for everyone after I try to ride it.

I fall quickly into my normal routine of looking out for possible hazards. In a place like Belmont Park, that is basically a full-time job. Ninety-five percent of the people here are looking at their phones or each other instead of watching where they are going. There are little kids dangling from ropes on the rock climbing wall and park employees threading their way through the crowds at too quick of a speed. Not to mention every carnival ride we pass seems to be corroded with rust. *This could not be any worse*, I think. And then a man on stilts wobbles into view. *I stand corrected.*

"Earth to Maguire?"

Crap. Apparently Jordy's been talking to me and I

haven't heard a word he's said.

I force myself to look away from Stilt Man, but my eyes fall on a row of darts with shiny metal tips lined up on the counter of a dart-toss game. "I'm sorry. What?"

"I said do you want to play something?"

"Nah, but you guys can."

Jordy does a quick lap of the midway to check out the possibilities and stops in front of a basketball game called Fantastic Free Throw. The contestant has to make three baskets in a row to win, but the hoops are smaller than regulation size and higher than for a normal free throw.

"This isn't going to end well." Penn shakes her head.

Jordy makes two but then misses the third. He tries again and only makes one. "You suck, bro," Penn says. "Give it up."

He grabs her and puts her in a headlock. "Why are you so mean?"

She twists her way out of his grasp. "Because it's fun."

"One more try," Jordy says. This time all three of his shots miss the mark.

"Come on," Jade says. "Maguire doesn't want you to win her any crap anyway."

"My dad would be so embarrassed by my performance." Jordy scans the game booths again. "I suppose a game involving tennis is too much to hope for?"

"You are such a one-trick pony," Penn teases. "Let me school you on this." She hands over some cash and takes the set of three basketballs from the attendant. She hands two of them to Jade. "Hold my balls," she says with a grin. Then she bends low, bounces the ball once on the ground in front of her, and arches her body toward the basket.

Swish, nothing but net.

Jordy's jaw about hits the concrete. "How did you—"

"Shh." She takes the next ball from Jade. "I'm in the zone." She spins this ball in her fingertips, bends low again, and shoots. This one bounces off the rim and falls in. She cackles, takes aim with the third ball. "She shoots, she scores!" she shouts as the ball swishes through the opening. She turns to Jordy. "That's how it's done."

"You never cease to amaze me, little sis."

"It's all part of my evil plan to become Dad's favorite. You know, since you're Mom's favorite."

"Lucky me," Jordy says. "All that overbearing maternal attention."

Penn furrows her brow as she considers the available prizes. "I think I'll take the dolphin."

"No, not the dolphin!" Jordy cringes. "Maguire hates dolphins."

I bite my lip but a smile escapes anyway. "I do *not* hate dolphins."

Penn accepts a giant stuffed dolphin from the attendant and raps her brother on the head with it.

Jade snatches the dolphin from Penn's arms and presses its pointed snout against my face. "Why you no like me?" she asks in a high-pitched, squealy voice.

"You guys are idiots." I yank the dolphin out of her arms. "Maybe I'll take this on the roller coaster with me. No big deal if it gets mangled, right?"

Penn grins. "Are we ready for that action?"

"I think we should probably save it for last," I say. "Just in case I freak out." Or cause a massive equipment failure that injures nineteen people.

We spend the next hour riding other rides, starting with the bumper cars, an activity that seems safe by amusement park standards. Slowly we make our way through Belmont. I opt out of some of the rides. Fear or not, I've never been big on being spun around in a circle until I'm too dizzy to stand up.

Penn and Jade take a ride on the tilt-a-whirl and Jordy decides to sit it out with me. Turns out he isn't a big fan of spinning either. I do a five-second check as they wait in line and we stand off to the side, leaning on a wooden railing.

"I'm glad I came," he says suddenly.

I turn toward him and the look in his eyes is so intense that for a moment the background fades. The shouts, the smells, the bright colors all seem muted. It reminds me of the day at Joshua Tree, how when we kissed it was like being sucked into a vortex, just the two of us, while the rest of the world carried on oblivious.

If only that feeling didn't scare me so much.

"I'm glad you did too," I say.

The ride starts up and we both turn to watch Penn and Jade get loaded into a car with two other girls who look like eighth or ninth graders. Penn is clutching her stuffed dolphin and each time she and Jade whiz past she holds it out like it wants to kiss me.

Jordy laughs and I realize how much I've missed that sound. I look from him to Penn and Jade as they fly by again and it hits me that even if he and I are never more than friends, making three new friends in a semester is pretty amazing. I've gained so much over the past couple of months, and it all started with my therapy challenges. Sure, I'm able to do things now like ride in cars with other people and hopefully I'll make it on that plane next month, but no matter what happens, working with Daniel has made my life profoundly better.

The ride slows to a stop. A few minutes later, Penn and Jade wander up to us looking windblown and slightly dizzy. Jade has one arm out for balance. We turn as a group and follow the park's main path.

"What's next?" Penn chirps.

"Giant Dipper," I say.

Jade squeezes my arm. "You sure? We won't care if you change your mind."

Did I mention how awesome my new friends are? "It feels like the thing to do," I say. "And look, the entrance is right around the corner."

Sure enough, the path we've taken through the park has

led us to the end of the roller coaster's line.

The Giant Dipper is one of those wooden and metal monstrosities with a lot of steep hills and sharp curves. One of the cars rockets past us high in the air and metal shrieks on metal. The passengers scream. The last car clatters violently on the tracks.

My breath hitches and my chest goes tight. I consider changing my mind, but I know if I walk away that I'll regret it later. *No one is going to die.* This is the right thing to do. I want to face my fears.

"So what do you want us to do again?" Jade asks. "Just be at the ready in case anyone . . . gets hurt? Maybe one of us can hang out near the first hill and one of us closer to the end?"

"I know it sounds a little crazy," I say.

Jade winks. "Normal is boring."

"It sounds thoughtful to me," Penn says, "preparing for an accident that isn't even going to happen, just because you don't want anyone else to get hurt."

Jordy nods slowly. "I agree with both of them. But I still want to ride with you. You made the decision to come here on your own, which is all kinds of brave. But that doesn't mean you should have to sit through the ride alone, or with a stranger next to you."

I pause for a moment before answering, remembering Daniel saying I should have someone with me. "All right, fine. You can come."

Penn and Jade jog off to take their positions. Jordy and I take our place at the end of the line, which seems to have a thousand people in it, almost all of whom appear blissfully relaxed at the idea of putting their lives into the hands of a nameless fun-park architect and a teen ride operator making minimum wage. Okay, sure, there are a smattering of people fidgeting with nerves and the occasional smaller kid gripping a parent's hand. But probably no one believes there's a chance they might die today. And definitely no one is thinking about how their mere presence might kill someone.

I envy them.

I look back at the pathway leading through the park, the warm sun beckoning me to safety. My shoulders turn but my feet stay put. A throng of what look like middle school kids gallop into the chute behind us, breathless and unkempt. For a second I see them as ungainly calves, lining up to go one by one to their slaughter.

"Let's do this like ten times in a row," a boy in a backward baseball cap suggests.

"Ugh," the girl across from him says. "No way, dude. Not unless you want me to puke all over your shoes."

Jordy guides me forward, and now the two of us are essentially trapped in the covered line area. I try not to imagine a fire breaking out, or a masked gunman pulling an assault rifle from a duffel bag and mowing down fifty people. *You can't control the Universe*, I tell myself.

The reality is, all I can control is me.

And sometimes not even that.

I blink back tears, dropping my eyes to the ground and struggling to compose myself. Almost instinctively, my hand reaches out to rap the wooden railing three times.

Jordy rubs my lower back gently, leaning down to rest his chin on my shoulder. "I'm sorry I didn't call you," he says. "It was selfish. I should have accepted that you weren't ready. I should have still been there for you as a friend."

"I'm sorry I left you that night." One of the tears leaks out. "I'm glad we're both here now."

"Me too," he says.

"How are things?" I plaster a smile on my face. "You're back playing international tournaments, and your sister said something about an agent?"

"Things are good. Nothing is definite. I just decided it was time to get all the information. That way my parents and I can have a reasonable discussion."

"Good for you."

He nods as we move forward a few feet. This part of the enclosure is still decorated for Halloween, with tissue paper bats and ghosts hanging from the rafters and a selection of bloody machetes displayed on a pyramid of hay. "Lovely," I mutter. "Shouldn't there be turkeys and stuff instead of murder weapons?"

Jordy cups his hands over my eyes. "I find turkeys almost as creepy. They've got that weird red pouch that hangs off their faces. What is that about?"

"It's called a wattle." I peel his hands away from my face. As much as the Halloween décor is freaking me out, it's worse when I can't see what's happening. I do a five-second check. Everything is fine. We're halfway through the line now. "It's something boy birds use to attract mates."

"Gross. Now I find turkeys even creepier," Jordy says. I smile. "Anyway, I want to give the pro tour a try," he continues. "I feel like so much of my life has been in preparation for this moment. I can't bear the thought of four years of college tacked on to that. I mean, maybe someday I'll want to go to college, but maybe not."

"That makes sense," I say. "But what if you hit the men's tour and don't . . . have success?"

Jordy shrugs. "Then I either keep trying or give up. I can always work for a club or give lessons. I hear I'm pretty good at that."

"You are great at that," I say. And then, "I envy your ability to be so relaxed about everything."

"I love tennis," Jordy says. "Playing makes me happy. To make money doing something I love so much is living the dream. But if I never hit that point where tennis makes me rich, I'm okay with that. I know my parents have sacrificed a lot in order to make that opportunity a real possibility, but if things don't come to that, I hope I don't let them down too badly."

"I'm sure they just want you to be happy."

"Maybe," he says. "Underneath all the superficial worries about me having the best equipment and the best schedule and the best draws in every tournament."

"And the best hair." I reach up and tug on one of the blond pieces.

"Ugh. Sometimes I want to cut it all off just to piss off my mom." He grins. "Would you still be seen with me if I were bald?"

I can't help it. I start giggling at the thought. The harder I try to stop, the more I laugh.

Jordy pokes me in the ribs. "I'm going to assume you're having some sort of nervous laugh attack," he says, "and that the real answer to that question is, 'Of course, Jordy. The combination of your winning personality and hot body renders your hair insignificant in my attraction to you.'"

"Stop it." I blot my eyes on the collar of my shirt. "Okay, you got me. That is *exactly* what I was thinking."

We're about ten people from the front of the line now. A car pulls into the enclosure and stops with a sharp hiss. Exhilarated passengers raise their safety bars with sharp cranking sounds. My smile fades a little.

"Almost there," Jordy says. "How have I been doing with distracting you?"

"Excellent, actually. It helps to focus on other people's problems . . . and potential baldness."

"You should have seen the look on your face back when

those kids got in line behind us. Like a trapped panther. I thought you were going to vault over the railing and make a break for it."

"I almost did," I admit.

Jordy looks down at me. "I will hold your hand the whole time, if you let me."

"Um . . . I plan on holding the lap bar the whole time."

"In that case I will hold your arm."

"Deal."

"And I won't even tell you to put your hands up on the final hill."

"Good, or I will punch you," I say.

"Fair enough."

Another car races into the station, and everyone exits to the right.

"Here we go," Jordy says. He stands behind me as I step down into the car. Then he slides in next to me.

All we have to keep us safe is a lap bar shared between the two of us. Jordy pulls it flush, but there's a bit more of a gap there than I would like. I try to ratchet down the safety bar one more click, but it won't go.

"It's far enough," he assures me.

He's right. Besides, it's not like I'm worried about my own safety. I crane my neck to see into the car in front of us and then glance over my shoulder to make sure everyone behind us has their lap bars fastened. So far, so good.

The ride attendant pulls a big lever, and we start moving.

The first section of the track is in a dark enclosure. Then we shoot out into the sunlight and I can see the parking lot, and beyond it the beach. As we slowly climb the first big hill, my heart descends into my gut, one clickety-clack at a time. Briefly, I close my eyes, but it's even scarier when I can't see what's happening. I fix my gaze on the gentle lapping of the waves. The welcoming, seemingly innocent water.

There's a big sign at the top of the hill that says "DAN-GER" and warns riders to keep their hands and feet inside the car at all times. I try not to think about everyone else on the ride with us. Flesh-and-blood people who can die so easily. I try not to look down either. If I look down, I know I'll see what I saw the day of the accident—wood splinter-ing, metal cars bouncing off the ground, people splayed out amidst the wreckage like broken dolls.

I grip the lap bar until my knuckles blanch white and my joints start to ache.

We hit the top of the hill.

For a moment, everything freezes. The roller coaster comes to a complete stop.

I will not look down.

I will not see broken bodies.

Then, twisting.

Falling.

My heart pulls loose from my gut, clawing at my throat, exploding out through my lips. We hit the bottom of the hill and I gasp, but then the coaster pulls us up and into a turn. I slide left against Jordy. My knees slam into the lap bar and my teeth rattle in my gums. Then another hill, this one gentle enough not to rearrange my insides.

I force myself to focus on a plan, like how I did on the team bus. What would I do if our car derailed? Or if a section of the track collapsed and we crashed to the ground? Yell for everyone to brace themselves and protect their head and chest. Brace myself. Protect my own head and chest.

Another hill.

Call for help. Survey the scene.

Three hills in rapid succession.

Give CPR. Provide pressure to bleeding wounds.

A sharp turn. This time Jordy slides against me.

Keep people with possible back injuries from moving. Enlist the help of bystanders.

I remind myself that I'm not alone. Penn is here. Jade is here. And Jordy, his hand curled around my forearm as promised. I focus on his touch.

Slowly, we climb again. This is it, the grand finale, the final hill, steeper than the first hill.

I am so close. We are all so close. I inch my left hand from my vise grip around the lap bar to Jordy's hand.

"That's my girl," he says.

Freefall.

Weightlessness.

That moment where everything rushes past so quickly that it melds into a blur of nothingness. Then my whole body shudders as we roar toward the station, my bones shaking loose from their joints. I barely hear the screams. I barely hear the hiss of brakes as my body jolts forward and then backward.

We're back at the start. We did it.

I did it.

Jordy nudges me. "You getting out, or do you want to go again?"

"Ha," I say. "Maybe in ten years or so." With trembling muscles, I step from the roller coaster car onto the wooden platform. I pause for a moment, clinging to a metal railing, finding my breath again. I sense Jordy behind me before I feel his hand on my lower back. He shelters me with his arms as people push past us.

"Are you okay?" he asks. "You're really pale."

Instead of answering, I turn into his body, my head coming to rest against his chest, my arms looping around his neck. "Thank you."

"You're the one who did it."

"But you helped."

"But you didn't need my help." He presses his lips to my temple.

He's right. He's so right. For so many years I let fear make me a prisoner. I stood at the edge and looked down. I just needed to find the courage to jump. If I can do this, I can get on a plane. And if I can get on a plane, maybe I'm ready to face some other fears too. Without warning, I turn my head and lift my chin, aligning my lips with Jordy's.

"Maguire," he says.

I kiss him. And then it's my turn to hold him up. I wrap my arms around his waist and crane my neck to look up at him. "I'm not afraid anymore," I say. "Well, I am. But I'm ready. I'm ready to face my fears."

Jordy gives me a long look, one that makes the bottom drop out of my stomach. "What are you saying?"

"I want to be your girlfriend," I tell him. "If you still want that."

And out of all the things I've done since August—making the therapy challenge list, trying out for tennis, kissing Jordy—nothing has been half as scary as saying that out loud.

CHAPTER 34

And now it's Jordy's turn to kiss me. "I would like that very much," he says.

The two of us stand pressed together as another group of riders exits the Giant Dipper and heads back to the main path. Jordy hugs me so hard my insides feel squished. He lifts me a few inches off the ground and spins me around in a circle.

"Careful," I warn. "I'm still a little shaken up. I don't want to throw up on you and wreck the moment."

"Nothing can wreck this moment," he says. But he lowers me back to the ground. "We'd better go find the girls before they start to worry."

We stroll out the exit hand in hand. Penn and Jade are waiting right outside. They both bombard me with hugs.

"I can't believe you did it," Penn says. "You're amazing."

"Bloody brilliant," Jade agrees. "Did you have fun?"

I start to say no, but then think of that final moment

when I held Jordy's hand—that instant of weightlessness when my mind finally let go of the fear. "Maybe a little, in a 'I feel like I just got the crap kicked out of me' way."

"Hey," Penn says abruptly as we all head for the parking lot. "Were you guys holding hands a second ago?"

"Maybe," I say.

She turns to Jade with a grin. "Pay up."

Jade narrows her eyes at Jordy and me. She pulls a ten-dollar bill from her purse and hands it to Penn. "I should've known better than to bet against the awesome romantic power of a roller coaster." She coughs. "I can drive home if you two want to sit in the back together."

"I don't think that'll be necessary," I say wryly.

"So was this your last challenge for Daniel?" Jordy asks. "In preparation for your plane trip?"

"Technically I have one more." I think about the discussion Daniel and I had in his office, about how I need to relinquish control to someone else. "Lucky number seven."

Jordy slings an arm around my shoulder. "I don't think you're going to need it."

"Maybe not," I say. "But my gut says I should finish."

I drop Jade off first and then park my car across the street from Jordy's house. I turn off the ignition, and everyone gets out. Penn gives me a quick hug. "Thanks for driving. I'll see you at practice."

"Thanks for inviting me," I tell her. "You have no idea

how much this day meant."

She glances over at her brother, who is messing with his phone and doing a crappy job of pretending not to eavesdrop on us. "Pretty sure I do."

"Not just about that," I say. "You guys helped me do something I never even imagined was possible." I hug her again. "Right now almost everything seems possible."

"Good." Penn tugs on the end of her braid. "Okay. I'll let you two . . . talk."

Jordy gives her a murderous look and she giggles before turning away and heading up the driveway to the Wheeler house.

After she's gone, Jordy and I stand next to my car for a few minutes. "Do you want to come in?" he asks.

I imagine the look on his mom's face when she sees us together. I shake my head. "One scary thing per day."

"Okay. Just know I'll be next to you for that one too, when you're ready. And you kicked ass today. I'm proud of you."

"Thanks," I say. "Speaking of kicking ass, now that you're talking to me again, how was Brazil really?"

"Brazil was stellar." Jordy tosses his hair back from his face. "Amazing people. Amazing food. I wish I had made it to the finals. I still feel kind of sluggish, like I'm not quite myself. But just getting back out there on the circuit helped a ton."

"I'm feeling better too. Like the challenges are more than

just therapy. Like they're . . . a ceremony—a way to tell the Universe that I'm done letting it scare me."

Jordy smiles. "Substitute in 'my mother' for 'the Universe' and I'm right there with you."

"Well, it sounded to me like you were making progress with her," I say.

"That's because I finally have something I'm not willing to let go of."

I blush. "I wanted to ask you something. Daniel said part of my problem is that I'm a control freak. He said I should have someone else set up my last challenge for me. That I should relinquish control completely."

Jordy steps in close, one hand coming up to touch my face. "You want that someone to be me?"

I nod. "I trust you."

His smile is positively radiant. He's looking at me like I just asked him to prom or something instead of asking him to set up a therapy challenge. "The Giant Dipper is going to be tough to beat," he says. "Let me think about it."

Jordy calls me later that night. "I got it. I came up with something to do for your last therapy assignment. I also told my mom we're hanging out again, but we can wait until afterward to make things with us official if you want. Hell, we can wait until you get back from Ireland if you want."

"Official . . . Is there some sort of Wheeler girlfriend ceremony I don't know about?" I ask, only half joking. I imagine his mother producing a stack of release forms for me to sign okaying a criminal background check and review of my report cards.

"No, but it'll be harder to shield you from my parents if Penn and I are using the G-word. They'll probably want to invite you over for a nice dinner and interrogation."

"Yeah, like I said earlier, I'm not quite ready to meet your mom in the daylight."

"Okay, there's no rush. She'll come around. She doesn't think you're some scandalous groupie who's after me for my fame or anything."

"Ha. Kimber seemed to think that." I tell him about my bathroom conversation.

He chuckles. "Wait. You thought the two of us hooked up?"

"Everybody thinks that, Jordy. Because of how possessive she is around you. Besides, you told me you guys kissed. I just assumed you used to be together."

"Well, instead of assuming, maybe ask me next time," he says. "That was my first kiss. It happened at tennis camp when I was thirteen—more because both of us were curious about kissing than because we wanted to kiss each other. Now she's almost like a sister looking out for me. That's how we are."

"Yeah, she told me," I say.

"Is there anything else people are saying about me that has you concerned? Rumors I should know about?"

I want to say no, but maybe this is the perfect moment to get rid of all my doubts. So I tell him what I've heard about him hooking up with girls at parties and then ignoring them.

Jordy sighs deeply. "Okay, here's the real story. I've been doing the online-classes thing since eighth grade. It's been great for my game, but I missed out on a lot of social stuff early on. When I started playing in bigger events, the local players always seemed to be having after-parties. My parents let me go so I could get to know the other guys on the tour. There were girls at these parties. I was an idiot. Shit happened."

"So it's true then," I say softly.

"I hooked up with girls, but I never took advantage of anyone, if that's what you're asking. And I never lied about my intentions. There was one girl from around here who really seemed to like me, and I liked her too. We dated for a while, but my mom caught me skipping out on a practice session to meet up with her. Then I lost a couple of important matches, and someone posted a photo of us kissing online. My parents found it and told me I had to choose. I could be a normal teen with a normal social life, or I could keep training to hopefully turn pro. But they weren't going to spend thousands of dollars a month on my coaching and tournament fees if I was going to blow matches because of a girl."

"Ah," I say.

"Plus I was sixteen and the girl was eighteen, and I knew she was going off to college in Florida, so the decision seemed obvious. I texted her and said I wasn't allowed to date anymore and then avoided her at a few events. Pretty lame, I know." He sighs. "I tried to apologize after she left for college, but she didn't want to hear it, and I don't blame her."

"Alyssa?" I ask.

The silence at the other end of the line is deafening. Then Jordy says, "Did Kimber tell you about her too?"

"No." I sigh. "I looked you up online."

"Oh," he says. "Sometimes I forget that I'm not allowed to have any secrets."

"I'm sorry," I say. "I guess I got scared. I didn't dig very deep." My excuses sound lame, even to me. "I won't do it again."

"I'd appreciate that. If there's something you want to know, just ask me." He pauses. "Things are different now, okay? I'm not the same person I was back then. I know what I want. I can balance a personal and professional life. And if my parents refuse to accept that, then I guess I can go pro on my own."

"But you told me you needed your parents."

"Yeah, well, I'm hoping it won't come to that," Jordy says. "My parents and I need each other. I just have to make them understand that I'm not a little kid anymore." He clears his throat. "Anyway, I'm running a youth workshop next Saturday, and what I have planned for your last assignment is kind of an all-day thing. Maybe we can do it next Sunday?"

"Sounds good to me." Anticipation courses through my blood. I try to imagine what it's going to feel like to be finished.

"Next Sunday it is then," Jordy says. "Your final challenge."

CHAPTER 35

The week flies by. I wake up on Sunday shaking with anxiety. I tell Mom and Tom that I'm going to hang out with Jordy, and luckily they don't press for details once I promise to text them if we're going to be out of cell-service range. On the way to Jordy's house, I struggle to focus on my driving. I keep thinking about what it all means—that I have a boyfriend. That we'll go on dates, maybe to prom. My life is totally about to change, and I should be excited, but I can't shake off this nagging sense of dread. Like none of this is actually happening.

Like the past couple of months have been a dream and I'm about to wake up.

When I pull up and park in front of Jordy's house, he's sitting on the porch, his long legs stretched out in front of him. He watches me walk up the driveway.

I sit next to him, gently bumping my knee with his knee. "So are you going to tell me where we're going?"

"Nope." He runs his hand along the scar on my thigh, the only evidence remaining of my ill-advised jump from my bedroom window.

His touch warms me from the inside out. I purse my lips into a fake pout. "Come on. What is it? Bungee jumping? Skydiving?"

He gives me a cryptic smile. "It's weird to think about being done, isn't it? Are you going to keep seeing Daniel? Maybe add to your list of challenges?"

"I think my mom said my treatment package is twenty sessions, so I'll still have a few left. I don't know. I'm less nervous and I'm doing fewer checks, but I wouldn't say I'm ready to go it alone. I guess we'll see how I feel when I get back from Ireland."

"Cool." Jordy stands up and stretches his long arms over his head. As we walk down the driveway, he wraps an arm around me. "How are you feeling about your trip?"

"Better. Still scared, but I have a whole month to keep riding the team bus and some local buses. And then my step-dad is going to take me to San Jose with him for a work thing." I smile as I think about my conversation with Tom. "We're going to ride the bus up there and maybe take a plane home."

"That's perfect!" Jordy opens the door for me and then jogs around to slide behind the wheel. "And remember, you don't ever have to go it alone. If you want me to ride a city bus with you or something, just say the word." He squeezes my hand and then clicks his seat belt and checks all his mirrors. He signals before pulling away from the curb.

We wind through his subdivision, taking the back exit. He makes a left and a right and merges seamlessly onto a highway that leads to downtown San Diego. I start guessing things to do that are close to the city. "Gaslamp Quarter? Maritime Museum? SeaWorld?"

He shakes his head to all of them. We pass straight through the city and head toward the coast.

"Ooh, surfing?" I ask. "Snorkeling?"

"No."

"Shark diving?" Man, I hope it's not shark diving.

"I'm not going to tell you, Maguire."

"Why not?"

"Because that's the idea, right? If you don't know where you're going, then you can't try to control things." He peeks at me out of the corner of his eye. "I'm hoping you won't be mad at me when you see what it is."

"Why would I be mad at you?"

Instead of answering, Jordy flicks on the radio.

I reach out and turn it off. "Sorry," I say. "I'm not ready to drive with distractions yet."

"No worries." He smiles without taking his eyes off the road.

I try to think of all of the possible things we might do involving the ocean. Surfing, snorkeling, shark diving, sailing—all risky activities. But none of them seem like they would make me angry at Jordy.

But if we were going to get wet, he would have told me to bring dry clothes. Unless of course he didn't want to tip me off about where we were going. Or maybe he has dry clothes in the trunk.

I watch the miles of highway fly by. We slow to a snail's pace outside of Los Angeles, but Jordy only shakes his head when I look at him expectantly. We sit mired in traffic for the better part of an hour, but eventually it thins out and we leave the glitzy skyline painted with smog behind. I sit back and try to relax as we continue along the Pacific Coast Highway. But then a terrible thought flickers through my mind.

"How far is this place?" I ask, my throat going dry.

"Not much farther now," Jordy says, his voice also uneven.

I turn in my seat to face him. He's staring straight ahead, both hands tightly gripping the wheel. "We've been driving for over three hours. Where exactly are we going?"

No answer.

"Are we going where I think we're going?" This highway is good for only two things—travel to the ocean and travel to the cities along the coast. Another hundred miles north of us is San Luis Obispo, the city where I was born.

The city where my father, brother, and uncle are buried.

And outside the city, the place where the three of them died.

Jordy mutters something about a faster route. We leave

the coastline, turning north into a wooded area. I pull out my phone and Google a map of California. This road will take us to SLO. The car starts to feel like a trash compactor, like the walls are closing in on me. I should have known—the party at Kimber's, the roller coaster. History repeats itself. Of course the Universe was leading me back to what started it all. "Sometimes forgetting is more therapeutic than remembering, don't you think?" I ask through clenched teeth.

"But you *haven't* forgotten."

He's got a point. I can't forget. I will never forget. I think of that day every day when I do my morning rituals. "How do you even know where it happened?"

"You're not the only one who's been doing internet research."

"You spied on me?"

"It's okay for you to look me up, but not the reverse?" he asks. "How is that fair?"

I don't answer, because it's not fair. "I'm scared," I say. "I don't know if I should go back there." The warm day suddenly feels chilly. I hug my arms around my chest.

"What about last week? You said your gut wanted to finish."

"My gut would like to change its answer."

Jordy glances over at me. "Do you really want to turn around?"

"I don't know." Trees fly by on either side. The road narrows. I haven't seen another car in a while. We're all alone—me, Jordy, and my memories. "No. I guess not, but please realize things aren't as easy for me as they are for you."

"Things aren't easy for me either," Jordy says. "I know my issues seem silly and weak compared to yours, but it was hard for me to stand up to my parents, to tell them I was going to make time for a life beyond tennis and studying."

I fiddle with the strap of my seat belt. "What did they say?"

"They were pissed. They accused me of trying to sabotage my future, said that I was just setting myself up for failure."

"What did you tell them?"

"That they were wrong. I don't have to cut back on tennis to care about other stuff. It's not like I practice ten hours a day every day. I can be with you and play on the tour. I just might have to organize my time a little differently."

"You really believe that, don't you?"

"I have to believe it. There are pro tennis players who are married with kids. There are guys doing the tour who work other jobs. I should be able to have a girlfriend if I want. Playing tennis is not worth giving up everything."

I turn and study the landscape outside of my window—the trees in the foreground, the ridge of mountains way off in the distance. Everything is green and gray.

Everything is gray.

"What about you?" he continues. "Would you give up *everything* to stay in your safe little bubble if it meant not feeling responsible for anyone being hurt?"

I pick at a ragged cuticle. I feel like the answer should be yes; two months ago it would have been yes. But now I don't know. How do I weigh the presence of joy against the absence of guilt?

Jordy lets out a deep breath. "Dammit, Maguire. Your answer should be no." He turns to me. "You deserve a chance to be happy. You can't live your life for everybody else."

I don't respond. Something moves at the side of the road. A bit of brown amidst the green and gray. A deer. She leaps out of the woods and onto the pavement, but Jordy's still looking at me. "Watch out!" I gasp. I brace myself by grabbing for the door handle.

Jordy's head snaps around. He swears loudly as he hits the brakes. I pitch sideways in my seat, my head slamming against the window. Rubber burns, rank and hot. Jordy swings the steering wheel to the right. We skid. I try to scream but nothing comes out. The car tilts wildly. I catch a glimpse of the deer's slender legs moving out of the roadway as Jordy's car careens off the pavement.

My head hits the window again and I see stars.

I see glass.

I see blood.

And then I don't see anything at all.

CHAPTER 36

The pain awakens me, sharp and shredding, like someone is putting my left arm through a meat grinder. My eyes are caked with dirt and blood. The air is full of haze. My first thought is that I'm dying. If you've never been close to death, life probably seems pretty solid. The truth is, it can be destroyed in an instant, like a photograph. One moment your world is slick and shiny. But then the Universe crumples everything into a ball. And even if you don't get crushed, if you fight to straighten things out, your life will never be the same again.

The world is full of holes and uneven seams, wrinkled places that you can't make smooth, no matter how hard you try.

I have to try.

I lie smashed against what I think is the floor but turns out to be the passenger door. The car must have flipped onto its side when we went into the ditch. Bits of broken glass cut straight through my shirt and into my skin. My black curls snake out from my face like they're trying to slither away from the wreckage.

I try to sit up, but can't. I'm not even sure which way is up. It takes a fair amount of effort just to turn my head. Jordy is still strapped into his seat. Blood drips from a cut above his eye. He's pale. Too pale. Reaching over, I shake his shoulder gently. His arm flops back and forth like he doesn't have any bones.

No. He's not dead. He can't be.

This is my fault, I think. I should've stayed in my room, in my bed, reading under the covers where it was safe. Why did I leave? Why did I risk everything?

I did it for a lot of reasons.

I wanted to go to Ireland with my mom, to honor my family.

I wanted to be good at something for once.

I wanted things to be different.

I wanted Jordy's attention, as much as I hate to admit it.

Mostly I did it because I wanted to believe. That I wasn't cursed. That the past wasn't my fault. That the future still held possibilities.

But maybe the only possibilities for me are ones that involve hurting the people I love.

The inside of the car begins to blur, darkness sneaking up on me slowly, gently, like a blanket unfolding.

You did this.

Maybe I did.

Bad Luck Maguire.

Maybe that's who I am.

But maybe I can choose to be someone else.

"Jordy." The word falls from my lips in pieces. I reach out for him again. There are two ways this can end. *Fight or give up*, I tell myself. *But choose. For once in your life, don't let the Universe choose for you.*

"Jordy, wake up." I nudge his shoulder again. No response. Lifting my hand to his neck, I search for a pulse. I think I feel one, but I'm not sure.

A drop of blood runs across his forehead and drips onto my injured arm. A wave of dizziness washes over me. I bite my lip, embrace the pain, fight to stay conscious. Wriggling out of my seat belt, I scan the wreckage for anything useful. Everything fell out of the center console when we flipped. Everything including pens, napkins, insurance cards, and Jordy's cell phone.

I grab the phone with my right hand. The screen is shattered. It won't turn on. "Shit." I look around for my purse, but it's nowhere to be found. I refuse to panic. There has to be something. A black strap in the periphery of my vision catches my eye. Of course. Jordy's emergency kit. I can't reach it with my right hand, and my left arm refuses to bend like it should. I end up craning my neck and grabbing the strap with my teeth. Gagging, I pull the black bag into the front seat.

With shaking fingers, I unzip it and find the emergency phone. I flip open the cover with my thumb. The screen comes to life. "Oh thank God." With my left arm braced against my body for support, I call 911 and say we've been in an accident.

"What is your location?" the dispatcher asks.

"I—I'm not sure. I can't think of the name of the highway." I'm not sure whether it's panic or if I have a head injury, but the number refuses to come to me. "North of San Diego, heading toward San Luis Obispo."

"It's all right. We can GPS you," she assures me.

"Should I try to get out of the car?"

"Stay put unless you smell gasoline or there's a fire," she advises. "Try not to move at all. I'm going to stay on the line with you until help arrives."

"My friend was driving," I rasp. "He won't wake up. I'm not sure if he's okay."

"Help is coming," the dispatcher says. "What's your name?"

"Maguire."

"Maguire. Is your friend still in the car with you?"

"Yeah, he's still in his seat belt, but his head is bleeding."

"Can you tell if he's breathing? Maybe put a hand on his chest?"

I reach across my body and press my right hand against Jordy's chest. I'm relieved to feel movement.

"He is."

"Okay, Maguire. Then put gentle pressure on his head wound if it's bleeding a lot. But don't try to move him, okay? And try to keep his neck stable."

"Okay." I put the phone on speaker and set it next to me. Then I press my right hand gently to Jordy's forehead.

His eyes flick open for a moment. "What. Happened," he chokes out.

"There was a deer. We went off the road. Help is on the way."

Jordy lifts a hand to his ribcage. "It hurts to breathe."

"Just hang on," I say.

"You know . . . this . . . not your fault . . . right?" Each bit takes him an entire breath to expel.

Tears flood my eyes, hot, desperate to fall. I'm not sure whether it's relief that Jordy is awake or the fact that he's injured and bleeding and the first words out of his mouth are meant to comfort *me*. "Yeah," I tell him, not because I believe him but because it's what he needs to hear. "I blame the deer."

A sharp laugh erupts from his lips, followed by a grunt of pain. "You . . . okay?"

"Yes. Now stop trying to talk."

Jordy makes a movement with his head that I think is supposed to be a nod. Then he swears under his breath. "My side . . . it hurts so bad."

"Maguire?" The tinny voice of the dispatcher is barely audible through the phone's speaker.

"Yes?"

"Help should be arriving momentarily," she says.

"Okay." Sirens sing in the distance. "I hear them coming. And my friend woke up."

"Good. I'm going to disconnect then. Just sit tight. The first responders will get you out of the car safely."

"Okay," I say again. After a couple of seconds I add, "Thank you."

"You're welcome," the dispatcher says. The screen goes dark as she ends the call.

The sirens grow louder. An ambulance bleats a shrill horn as it screeches to a stop. Blue-and-red lights reflect off the inside of the car. Jordy seems to have lost consciousness again. A door slams. There are shouts. Then a medic bends down to look through the windshield. "Miss," he says. "We're going to get you out, okay?"

"Him first." I gesture at Jordy. The medic looks ready to argue, so I quickly add, "He's bleeding. He said it hurts to breathe."

"Okay. Hang tight."

A group of firefighters approach the car dressed in their hats and heavy coats. They break the windshield glass and secure a big plastic collar around Jordy's neck. Then they stabilize his body and cut him free of his seat belt, working as a team to move him from the car to a stretcher.

All I can do is watch. Helpless. No control.

No one is going to die.

I hope.

Paramedics load the stretcher into the back of an ambulance.

I'm next. Everything starts to fade out as my body is quickly and safely removed from the car and placed onto a stretcher. As the medics wheel me toward a second ambulance, my eyes skim over the carnage, the streaks of black rubber on the road, and the dense foliage that lines it. Somewhere back in the trees, I swear I see the soft dark eyes of a deer looking out at me.

CHAPTER 37

I end up in a hospital in Santa Barbara where a doctor tells me it looks like I have a broken arm but he can't treat me without permission from my mother. It takes me a couple of minutes to calm down enough to remember her phone number.

My arm is throbbing by the time a nurse pops in my room to tell me my mom is on the way. She has a soft Spanish accent, and her hair is dark and curly like mine—just not quite as long, or as "big," as Jordy would say. My eyes water when I think of him. I lean over. The nurse's name tag blurs as I blink back tears. "Pilar?" I say.

"Yes." She corrects my pronunciation with a grin, rolling the R-sound at the end. "But you can call me Pili if you like."

"Do you know if my friend is okay? The guy I came in with?"

"I'm not sure. But I'll see what I can find out." She inserts an IV, injects me with pain medicine, and takes me to radiology for an X-ray.

After the X-ray, Nurse Pili brings me back to my room in the ER, where I'm left alone for about an hour. At some point during that time, the shock of everything starts to wear off, and the horrible reality comes crashing down on me. I might have saved Jordy and myself by finding the phone and calling 911, but I failed my therapy challenge massively.

I was so close to feeling normal again. I think about how far I came—the driving, the team bus, the party, even the roller coaster. And now what? How can I do anything but go back to my old life after this? I don't want to hurt Jordy again. I don't want to hurt Jade, or anyone from the team. I don't want to risk the lives of a bunch of strangers on an international flight.

All Jordy wanted to do was turn pro, and who knows if his injuries will keep him from doing that? Who knows if he's even okay? *Well, that's not all he wanted to do* . . . Fine, whatever. He wanted to be my boyfriend, too. And now I've screwed up both of those things.

Nurse Pili pops her head in the room. "Hey, sweetie, it looks like you have an ulnar fracture—that's the smaller bone in your forearm. An ortho doc is looking at your films, and your mom said she's about twenty minutes away . . ." She trails off, approaching the bed with a concerned look. "What is it? What's wrong?" She touches the fabric of my pillow.

It's wet. I didn't even know I was crying. "I've ruined

everything," I say. "This is all my fault."

She bends down so we're at the same level. Her brown eyes are full of concern. "What is all your fault?"

"The accident," I whisper. "Can you please, please find out if Jordy is okay? What if I killed him?"

"What?" She blinks rapidly and then leans in closer like she thinks maybe she heard me wrong. "Were you the one driving?"

I shake my head. I hold my breath to keep from sobbing.

"Then how could you have killed him?"

My only answer is a steady stream of quietly dripping tears. I imagine explaining it all to her, the person I've been for the past few years, what it feels like to hurt anyone you get close to. Exhaling deeply, I collapse back on my pillow. "Can I have more pain medicine?" My arm feels like it's on fire, but that's nothing compared to the crushing sadness in my chest.

She grabs a box of tissues from the counter and sets it on the bedside table. "How would you rate your pain on a scale of zero to ten?"

"Seven?" I choke out. "A million? I don't know."

"Sorry. Everyone hates that question, but we need it for our charting. Let me check with the doctor." Nurse Pili leaves the room and returns a few minutes later with a small syringe. "He said another half dose would be okay. He also said your friend got transferred to a hospital in San Diego. I can't give you details, but we don't transfer patients unless they're stable, so try not to worry too much."

I nod. "Thank you for checking."

She smiles. "Clearly he means a great deal to you. I'm sure the doctors are taking excellent care of him." She wipes the valve of my IV with an alcohol swab and flushes the medicine into my system. Warmth rushes up my arm, followed by a dullness that spreads throughout my body. Another half-dose is more than okay—it's perfect. A dark, dreamless sleep steals me away.

When I wake up, my mother is sitting in a chair next to my bed, my luck notebook balanced on her lap. *Uh-oh.* I roll over to face her and a dull ache spreads throughout my arm. A blue and gray fiberglass cast runs from my hand to just below my elbow. I peer down at the cast suspiciously.

"Maguire!" My mom pulls her chair close to the bed. "Oh thank goodness you're okay." I'm still staring at the cast, so she adds, "They did some sort of external fix where they reset your bones without having to do surgery. Cool, huh? I asked for your school colors. You slept through the whole thing."

I lick my lips. "I don't even remember a doctor coming in."

"The nurse said you had extra morphine, and then you got a sedative for the procedure. I guess it kept you pretty knocked out."

Without lifting my head from the pillow, I nod. "Jordy?" I ask. "Do you know if he's okay?"

"His sister called your phone about twenty minutes ago." She holds up my purse. It's battered and the strap is bloody, but otherwise it's mostly whole. "They stabilized him here, and then his parents had him airlifted back to San Diego. Apparently he has a collapsed lung and a lot of minor cuts and scrapes, but Penn says he's going to be fine."

I weep with relief. I curl onto my side and pull my legs up to my chest.

Mom bends low and strokes my hair. "Are you hurting? Do you need more morphine?"

I cry even harder. If only medicine could fix this. Mom doesn't say anything else. She just rubs my back repeatedly until I calm down. Then I roll over, wipe my eyes with my good hand, and take three deep breaths. "He asked me to be his girlfriend. We were going to make things official after we got home tonight."

"Home from?"

"SLO. The accident site."

"Ah," my mom says. "Another one of your therapy challenges?"

"I should've told you," I say. I don't know if it's the pain medicine or if the secrets have just grown too big for me to hold inside, but I tell her everything—my curse, my rituals, my five-second checks. I'm expecting her to be surprised, but then I remember my luck notebook perched on her lap. She must have found it in my purse when she went to answer my phone.

"Did you read it?" I ask.

She looks down at the floor, lets out a big breath of air. "I skimmed it. So this whole notebook—it's full of things that have happened since Kieran, your father, and your brother died?"

"Mostly."

My mom flips through the pages of my notebook. "And you . . . blame yourself for these things?"

"Kind of," I whisper.

"You really spent years thinking you were *cursed*?" Tears fill her eyes, and then we're both crying. "I knew you worried about bad things happening. I didn't realize you felt responsible for them." She pulls a tissue from the box on my bedside table and blots her eyes. "I recognized you needed help when you got so upset about the fire, but I had no idea it all went back to the accident. Or maybe I did and just didn't want to connect it all. What kind of a mother does that make me?"

"You didn't do anything wrong, Mom. It's not your fault if I'm—"

"Maguire," my mom says firmly. "You are *not* cursed. You are not bad luck. You are not to blame for any of these things."

I pick at a ball of lint on my thin hospital blanket. "Then how do you explain it all?"

"Sometimes terrible things happen and it's no one's fault. Sometimes we do the best we can and still have bad outcomes."

"I still want to be with him," I whisper. "How selfish does that make me?"

"It doesn't make you selfish. Luck isn't a zero-sum game where you being lucky means someone else has to be unlucky. If you want to be with him, then be with him," my mom says.

It seemed so easy when we were broken and bleeding. Choose to live. Choose to fight. But I can do both of those things without becoming Jordy's girlfriend and potentially putting him at risk. Maybe we're both better off if I love him from a distance.

"How can I do that, Mom, knowing that bad things might happen?"

My mom scoots her chair closer to the bed and squeezes my good hand. "There is always the chance someone might get hurt. You can try to control the situation with rituals or staying home or locking yourself away from the world, but in the end it's not up to you."

"But how can I live like that?" My voice rises in pitch.

"Because there's no other choice," my mom says. "And because you're brave."

My IV pump chimes sharply, and my mom and I both turn to look at it. A tiny red light flashes. The bag of saline the nurse gave me is almost empty. About ten chimes later Nurse Pili bustles back into the room. She shuts off the IV and takes a set of vitals.

"How's your pain?" she asks.

"It's fine," I say. "Maybe two out of ten."

"Are you feeling confused at all?"

"No, I feel okay."

She rests a hand on my arm. "Your vitals are all within normal limits. I'm going to check with the doctor to see if we can get your discharge paperwork processed. I'll be back to update you."

"Thank you," my mom says. When the nurse is gone, she bends over and wraps her arms around me, her lips pressing against my forehead. "I feel so bad that you've been struggling for so long." Her eyes water. "Maybe Tom and the kids seemed like they needed more from me, so I left you floundering." A tear streaks down her cheek, and she swipes at it.

"I should've told you how I felt. I guess it just seemed like there was nothing you could do to help. And you had your hands full with Erin, and then Jake too. They do need you more." I swallow hard. "I didn't want to take you away from them."

"Well, I need all of my children exactly the same." My mom sniffles. "Please don't ever feel like you can't ask me for anything, Maguire. I will never be too busy for you. I will never not make time."

"Really?" I ask.

"Really." Mom blots at her eyes again.

"In that case, there is one thing I would like to do."

CHAPTER 38

My mom signs my discharge paperwork, and we head out to her car.

"If we're doing this, I'm driving," she says. "You're all zonked out on pain meds."

I slide into the passenger seat and buckle my seat belt. Mom buckles up and then looks both ways as she pulls out of the hospital parking lot. My phone rings. It's Penn again. I slip it back into my purse unanswered. I can't talk to her. Not yet, not until I'm finished. I can't let anything distract me.

Two hours later, Mom and I reach the site outside of San Luis Obispo where Dad, Uncle Kieran, and Connor died. The place where I inexplicably lived. I recognize the road before she even says anything, as if its particular collection of curves imprinted itself on my memory all those years ago. There's a tiny white cross peeping out of the steep hillside at the scene of the accident. A tiny white cross with fresh flowers.

"Who?" I ask.

Mom slows the car as we pass the site. "The firehouse, probably," she says. "I think they come out every month. We can go there, if you'd like to speak to some of them."

I shake my head. I already know what they'll say. My dad and uncle were heroes. They died too young. Everyone loved them. Everyone misses them.

I turn around in my seat and watch the cross disappear through the back window. "I need to get out of the car for a moment. Is that okay?"

"Sure, but I'm coming with you." Mom finds a place to park about a half mile down the road at the turnoff for a trail-head. We get out of the car, cross the street, and start walking back toward the scene of the accident.

As we draw close, it all rushes back to me. The warm day, the sunshine, the car radio cranking, my brother teasing me. Part of me wants to turn around, go back to Mom's car, forget I ever had the idea to come here. But I can't, because Jordy was right. I do need to see this.

I need to face this place.

Just beyond the cross, a curved metal guardrail skirts the edge of the narrow shoulder. I study the road and then look down the hill, at the clusters of rocks peppering the side of the grassy incline. I remember seeing the truck veer into our lane and then the sickening feel of dropping off the pavement, the impact of each jolt as the car bounced end over end. But my memory doesn't give up anything else. No clue as to why the driver lost control of his truck. No long-kept secret about how I survived.

"You all right?" my mom asks.

"Yeah," I say. "I guess I was just hoping I'd find answers. How it happened. Why it happened. How I . . ."

"How you lived?"

"Yeah."

"The fire chief said it happens more than you'd think. One movement this way or that way, one second sooner or later, and someone lives or dies. He said maybe the car twisted in such a way that one of the guys broke your fall. Or perhaps that you ended up on the floorboards and fit just right so the front and back seats cushioned you from the impacts." She puts an arm around me. "But I'm afraid we'll never know for sure, honey." She stares out, past the guardrail and the steep embankment. A single tear streaks down her pale cheek. "I just know I'm awfully glad that you did."

"Me too." I lean into my mom's body, and she wraps me in a hug. "Thank you for bringing me here."

She pulls back a little to look me in the eye. "Thank *you* for bringing *me* here."

I turn in a slow half circle, taking in the road, the trees, the incline, the wooden cross. I know my dad, uncle, and brother aren't with us, that they're long gone to wherever people go when they die, but somehow I feel connected to them. "I just need another minute."

"Take all the time you want," Mom says. "I could use another minute myself."

We stand there, together but separate, both of us thinking about the past in our own ways. "I miss you guys," I say. "I'm sorry you're gone. Connor, I'm sorry I was mean to you." I pause, take in a deep breath. "You were the best brother a girl could ask for."

Mom rests a hand on my lower back but doesn't speak. I glance around for any kind of sign that my family has heard me. But there's no sudden rush of wind, no strange beams of light in the darkening sky. There are no signs, just like there are no answers. And I can either accept that or not accept it, but neither choice will change what is. I'll never know for sure what caused the crash or why I survived. I'll never know for sure whether I'm lucky, unlucky, being tested, or merely a victim of probability. I'll never know which of the bad things led to good things, or which were actually good things in disguise. Any control I thought I gained by doing my checks and rituals and shutting out the world was an illusion.

The time for illusions is over.

Reaching up, I remove the mystic knot necklace from around my neck and drape it over the top of the cross. "Now we'll always be together," I say.

My mom smiles and then removes her own necklace, a tiny gold heart. "Now we'll always be together," she echoes, looping her chain over mine.

The sun falls below the horizon as we turn away from the site.

By the time we get back to the car, there are three more messages from Penn. They all say basically the same thing. "Jordy is doing okay. He's awake and wants to see you. His phone was destroyed in the accident, so please call me on my phone." The third one is slightly more frantic, as if she thinks I'm not going to call her back.

"Are you ready to head home?" my mom asks.

I nod. "Thanks for doing this. Did you have to trust Tom with Erin and Jake?"

"It was about time I gave him a shot." She smiles. "How's Jordy?"

"Doing okay, according to his sister."

"Do you need me to drop you at the hospital?"

"It's going to be past visiting hours by the time we get back to San Diego," I say. "I'll go by after school tomorrow."

My mom pats my hand. "You were in a serious car accident and broke your arm. You can take a day or two off school."

"Thanks, Mom."

I call Penn and let her know I'll be coming by in the morning.

"Thank God," she says. "Jordy keeps rambling about how he thinks you're going to break up with him because of the accident. We all figured it was the pain medicine talking, but he seems to think he might never see you again. Hang on. I'll wake him up so he can talk to you."

"No," I say quickly. "I mean, don't disturb him. I'm all achy and dirty. I'm just going to take a bath and go to bed. My mom is letting me skip school, so I'll see him early tomorrow morning. I promise."

"Okay," she says, but there's a note of fear in her voice. "You're not going to hurt him again, are you?"

"Believe me," I say. "That's the last thing I want to do."

CHAPTER 39

To say I'm nervous about going to see Jordy is an understatement, especially since Penn is at school and it'll be just his parents and me.

I still do all my rituals in the morning, but there's a different feel to them today. It's less like "I need these to survive" and more like "These remind me of everything good in my life, the things I love and want to protect." I go to twist my hair into a bun, but I change my mind at the last minute and leave it down. It'll cover some of the scratches and bruises on my face.

I pull into the hospital parking lot about fifteen minutes later. When I find Jordy's room, the door is propped halfway open. He's in bed, covered in white hospital blankets and picking at a tray of breakfast food. The rest of the room is empty, but it still takes me a few seconds to work up my nerve to knock gently on the doorframe.

His face goes through a whole range of emotions when

he sees me—relief, happiness, anxiety, fear. I know what it's like to feel so many different things at once.

"Can I come in?" I ask softly.

"Of course." He makes an attempt to finger-comb his hair, which I find kind of adorable given the circumstances. There's a bandage above his left eye with a purpling bruise peeking out the side.

"Nice dress." I gesture at his hospital gown.

He perks up slightly. "You should see the back."

I smile as I drag one of the chairs to the side of the bed and sit in it.

"So you're okay?" he asks.

"Just this." I hold up my broken arm.

Jordy rubs at the stubble on his chin. "Doesn't really count as unscathed." He gestures at his blanket-covered body. "I didn't even break anything. I win."

"You're so competitive."

"It's true." He takes my casted arm in his hands and studies the blue and gray fiberglass wrap. "Looks like we're going to have to work on your one-handed backhand."

"You're right." I haven't even thought about tennis since the accident. But there's probably no reason I can't play with my cast.

We both fall silent. The red hand on the wall clock ticks off about fifteen seconds. Then Jordy says, "You're going to break up with me, aren't you? For my own good?"

"I thought about it," I admit.

He sinks back against the pillows. "Just because you failed a stupid therapy challenge?"

"Actually, I finished it with my mom yesterday."

"Really?" Hope flickers in his eyes.

"Yep. We went to the crash site."

"How was it?"

I pull my legs up onto the chair and wrap my arms around my shins. "It's hard to explain. I guess I was hoping for something more, maybe a memory of why it happened or the answer to why I lived. For some sort of closure, you know?"

"And?"

"None of that was there, but I still felt . . . better about things."

"So where does that leave us?" Jordy asks.

I rest my chin on my knees. "I wish I knew why bad things happen. I wish someone could tell me definitively if our accident was my fault."

"Our accident was because I'm a crappy driver," Jordy says. "Or maybe the Universe just really needed that deer."

I laugh softly. "I swear I saw it watching us after the crash, like it felt guilty."

"Poor Mitzi! I was going to give that car to my sister for Christmas. That deer *should* feel guilty. Maybe it's the one who called 911."

"Nope, that was me."

"Oh," Jordy says. "So basically I wreck the car, you save my life, and now you're here trying to tell me you think the accident was your fault."

"I'm trying to tell you I don't know. I'll never know for sure if someone or something is pulling the strings or if it's all like you said—totally random, and I've just had a few epically bad rolls of the dice. It's hard to imagine being with someone when I'm feeling like that."

"What about the roll of the dice where you met me?" Jordy asks. "Your life is more than just a bunch of unfortunate events jotted down in a notebook, Maguire." His words are coming out faster now, amplified by pain and frustration.

"You're right," I say.

He keeps going like he didn't hear me. "I mean what makes you think you can decide what's best—" He stops. "Did you just say I was right?"

"Yes."

"I'm not sure a girl has ever said that to me before."

"Well, I wouldn't get used to it or anything." My lips curl into a grin. "But no, after the accident I kept flipping back and forth—trying to choose between the presence of happiness and the absence of guilt. Between going back to the Maguire I used to be and taking a risk. And here's what I figured out: the only thing scarier than blaming myself for bad outcomes is accepting the fact that sometimes *no one* is to blame—that horrible stuff might happen to the people I care about, and no amount of five-second checks or knocking on wood will prevent it."

Jordy nods. "It's easier to blame someone than to accept

that sometimes we're all powerless. Of course, most of us blame *other* people."

"I can't control other people," I say. "I can only control me. But I can't control the Universe that way. The whole time I was just fooling myself."

"So what now?"

I look over at him, at his bruised and bandaged face. All I want to do is touch my lips to every tiny wound. "Now I choose happiness, even if the whole idea scares the crap out of me."

"Good choice." Jordy's smile lights up my insides. Any lingering reservations I had about my decision flicker out. He reaches for my hand. When we touch, I swear I can feel the tension ebbing out of his body. He pats the bed with his other hand. "Sit with me."

I blush. "Why?"

"Because I want to kiss my girlfriend, that's why."

I move from the chair to the edge of the bed. Jordy pulls me down so that I'm half on top of him.

"I don't think your nurse—"

"Is going to stop by in the next two minutes." He presses his lips to mine.

I pluck the TV remote out from under my hip and adjust myself so that Jordy and I are lying side by side. I cradle his face with my good hand, mindful of his injuries and bandages as our mouths connect, gentle, and then harder.

There's a cough from behind me. I pull away from Jordy

so fast I nearly tumble off the side of the bed. A gray-haired man in a white coat is standing in the doorway. He's holding a tablet in his hand. "You might want to be careful of the chest tube." He goes to the other side of Jordy's bed and lifts up a clear canister that's partially full of blood. Flexible plastic tubes travel from the container to beneath the thin hospital blanket.

"Hey, dude. What's up?" Jordy asks.

"I'm Dr. Cantor. I'm a vascular surgeon," he says. "Are your parents around?"

"My mom's here. She went to get breakfast but should be right back." Jordy frowns. "Vascular surgeon. What's wrong with me?"

Dr. Cantor smiles. "Nothing we can't fix."

"Your mom is here?" I hiss. I scoot from the bed back to the chair just in time.

Jordy's mom strides into the room holding a cup of coffee in one hand and a small container of fruit in the other. She looks back and forth from me to the vascular surgeon, her thin lips pinching together in the center.

Jordy beats Dr. Cantor to the punch. "Mom, you remember Maguire, right? She's my girlfriend now."

"Um, hi," I say. "Nice to see you again."

She forces a smile. "You too, dear. I'm glad you're all right." She turns to Dr. Cantor, who is tapping away on his electronic tablet. "Can we help you?"

"You're Stanford's mother?"

"I am."

"When the ER physician was checking the placement of the chest tube yesterday, he noticed an anomaly on the chest film."

"An anomaly?" Jordy's mom asks.

"Yes, on the X-ray," Dr. Cantor says. "We did a CT scan to get a closer look." The doctor looks questioningly at me.

Jordy rests his hand on my casted arm. "She stays."

"All right." Dr. Cantor turns his tablet toward Jordy's mom. "Stanford has what appears to be an aortic aneurysm." He highlights an area on his screen, but it all just looks like random shapes to me. "Sometimes we just monitor them, but this one is large enough to require surgical repair."

"The accident gave him an aneurysm?" I shrill. I know it's not my place to be asking questions, but I can't keep the words from spilling from my lips. People *die* from aneurysms. All of my resolutions about choosing happiness and relinquishing the illusion of control start to crumble.

"What does that mean, exactly?" his mother asks.

"An aneurysm is a weakening in the wall of a blood vessel. They can become life-threatening if left untreated, but the accident didn't cause it. I believe it's been growing inside of Stanford for a while." He pauses. "Are you familiar with Marfan syndrome?"

Jordy's mom purses her lips. "It's some sort of genetic thing, right? Seen in taller people? There's no one in our family who has that."

"In about twenty-five percent of cases, it appears spontaneously," Dr. Cantor says. "With no family history whatsoever." He clicks through a few pages on his tablet. "I notice you told the ER doc that you've been having some issues with fatigue during your matches."

"That's right," Jordy says. "And I'm taller than anyone else in my family, too."

"Many Marfan patients have heart valve issues that can cause fatigue or shortness of breath."

"So if I have this, this thing, it would explain why I've been getting tired?"

"Yes, there's a good chance it might."

"Can you fix it?" Jordy asks.

Dr. Cantor steps close to the bed. He studies Jordy for a moment and then takes his hand and does something with his thumb. "We'll need to run some additional tests so we know more about what we're dealing with. But yes, theoretically, we should be able to fix whatever is causing your fatigue."

"So then I can still play tennis?"

Dr. Cantor looks back and forth from Jordy to his mom. "You should be able to get back on the court after you recover from your surgery, and then we'll see how things progress. Marfan patients are at a higher risk to develop additional aneurysms, but we could monitor you with regular CT scans." He clears his throat. "We'll talk about the potential risks involved with competing professionally after I get your test results."

Jordy looks down at his hands and I want to reach out for him. I can't even imagine everything that's going through his head right now. So much scary information to receive all at once.

"So we just need to take things day by day?" his mom asks. She grips her coffee cup with both hands.

"Well, like I said. This is all academic until we have more information. The important thing right now is to repair the aneurysm." Dr. Cantor pulls a pager from the pocket of his lab coat and frowns at it. "I'll have one of my residents schedule you for additional testing later today, and I can fit you into my surgical schedule tomorrow."

Jordy's mom pales slightly. "So soon? I need to call my husband."

Dr. Cantor nods. "We really shouldn't wait."

"Mom. Tomorrow is fine," Jordy says. "I'm eighteen. I can make decisions for myself, remember?"

"All right, but let me just update your father." Pulling a cell phone from her purse, she ducks out into the hallway.

The doctor turns back to Jordy. "Do you have any questions?"

"Just one right now. If this accident hadn't happened and I didn't get that chest X-ray, could I have died before anyone diagnosed this?"

The doctor nods. "The aneurysm would have continued to grow until it eventually burst, unless it caused you pain prior to that point. A lot of aneurysms are asymptomatic.

Your accident could have very well saved your life."

Jordy looks over at me, and I know what he's thinking. I drop my eyes to his hospital blanket and study the woven pattern as I blink back tears.

Dr. Cantor clears his throat. "I'm going to leave you alone to discuss things. I'll have one of my residents bring the consent paperwork by later. But no . . . strenuous activity until after the surgery, all right?"

I blush. "We're not. I mean—"

"We hear you loud and clear, Doc." Jordy says.

He turns to me once we're alone. "You hear that? Your bad luck saved my life."

"Well, it was either me or that deer," I say jokingly. But inside I'm thinking about how every single thing that happened to me in the past few years played into this moment. If my life hadn't unspooled exactly the way that it did, I wouldn't have ended up in Pacific Point, on the tennis team, with Jordy. Not that someone or something took away three members of my family and replaced them with a boyfriend. People aren't replaceable—it doesn't work like that. Just that the Universe had taken them for its own reasons, and like my mom, I had created something good in the aftermath of tragedy. Maybe I was wrong about the never knowing. Maybe you do get your answers, at least some of them, if you're patient.

"Are you scared," I ask.

"Yes," Jordy says. "But for once I think my mom is right.

One day at a time." He pauses. "Do you think your mom will let you be here for my surgery tomorrow?"

"I think she will." I reach out for Jordy's hand and embrace his warmth.

"Awesome. I'll feel better knowing my good luck charm is close by." His lips curl upward into his perfectly perfect smile.

I grin right back at him. "Good luck charm, huh? I like the sound of that."

DECEMBER

CHALLENGES

1. ~~Make the tennis team.~~
2. ~~Ride in a car with someone besides Mom. Jordy.~~
3. ~~Spend a day in a crowded place. Tennis tournament.~~
4. ~~Take something back from the Universe. Rock climbing.~~
5. ~~Ride public transportation. Team bus.~~
6. ~~Face a specific past fear. Roller coaster.~~
7. ~~Relinquish control to someone else. Jordy, scene of accident.~~

GOAL

Plane ride to Ireland for memorial service.

CHAPTER 40
Session #20

I'm back in Daniel's office the Monday after Christmas. He fit me in near the end of the day since I missed two appointments due to Ireland and the holidays. Turns out Jordy switched his appointment too, so he'll be right after me as usual.

"So how was it?" Daniel asks.

"Ireland? It was good."

I smile as I think about the past week, Mom and me riding horses with my grandma, the road trip we took all around the countryside so Siobhan could point out where her sons got into trouble doing this or that. And then the memorial ceremony. I'd expected it to be this somber affair, but it wasn't. My aunt started things off with a slideshow of Dad, Connor, and Uncle Kieran set to music that did make me cry a little. But after that my relatives all got up and told stories, each one funnier than the last. Then my cousins and their friends did a performance of traditional Irish dancing, after which it was time to eat. I think everyone who lived within fifty miles dropped by Siobhan's farmhouse with some sort of baked good and/or alcoholic beverage.

I went thinking it would be a good way to finally put the tragedy behind me, but I ended up celebrating everything that came before instead.

Daniel cocks his head to the side and studies me for a moment. "Good? That's it? That's all I get?"

"It was . . . therapeutic. Seeing my grandma, meeting some cousins for the first time, sharing stories about Dad and my uncle. I'm glad I went."

"How was the plane ride?"

"Horrible!" I shudder. "Luckily my mom made this playlist of music she and my dad used to listen to, and then we watched some of his favorite movies on my laptop, and even though I could tell she was about to fall asleep, she stayed awake with me the whole flight."

"You didn't sleep?"

"No. No chance." I suck in a sharp breath. "Oh, and there was all this turbulence as we approached Dublin, and I was pretty sure everyone was going to die. I kept thinking I'd have to make my way back here so I could haunt you from beyond the grave."

Daniel laughs. "You're not the first client to threaten me with that." He leans back in his chair. "But you survived."

I look down at myself. "Apparently I did."

"And so did everyone else?"

"Yep."

"So then did you celebrate Christmas with your family here when you got back?"

"We did. Our flight landed on Christmas afternoon, so we celebrated that night, exchanging presents and taking my little sister out to see some lights. And then Mom and I slept for about two days."

Daniel smiles. "Did you get anything good?"

"Mom and Tom wanted to talk about getting me my own car, but honestly the trip to Ireland was more than enough. Maybe next year if I get a job or something."

"A job." Daniel whistles under his breath. "I like the sound of that. Anything else new?"

I scrape the toe of my flip-flop back and forth across the carpet. "My mom and I joined a survivor's guilt group that meets every week at the community center. It's mostly military people, but I think it'll be helpful. Tom might even come too. He and I have been talking more. He's pretty cool. I think he got bored while Mom and I were gone, so he started reading my books. He wants me to join a book club with him."

"Sounds fun," Daniel says. "How are you feeling about everything you've accomplished?"

"I feel like you're a miracle worker. I'm practically a new toaster." I grin. "Okay, maybe not quite like that, but I feel a lot stronger."

"Good. But most of the credit belongs to you. You're

the one who came up with and then completed all of those challenges."

"Right. I guess I should keep trying to repeat them? Reinforce things, like you said?"

"You can make up more challenges, too, if you want," Daniel says. "Though you should probably come up with a new goal first."

I smile. "I'll work on that."

"How is your boyfriend doing?"

I blush. "I thought you weren't allowed to talk about him."

"Well, I can't talk about him as a client. But I know how shaken up you were after the accident and then his surgery."

"He's good," I say. "So far the doctors have cleared him to play tennis. He's taking it slow, but he's hoping to be competing in tournaments again by next summer. He knows a lot is going to depend on what happens with his condition, but right now he's just happy to get back out on the court. But you know all that, don't you?"

Daniel nods. "How is it for you, being in a relationship, caring about another person like that? Does it make everything more scary?"

"Yeah, but that's how it is, right? The more good things you have, the more there is to lose."

"Well said." Daniel's eyes crinkle at the corners as he smiles again.

"Since we're getting all personal, how's your girlfriend?

Still with the sad guitar solos?"

His expression goes flat. "I don't have a girlfriend any-more," he says somberly. Then when my face falls, he adds, "She's my fiancée now."

"High five." I hold up my hand. "Congrats, Doc!"

"Thanks." He slaps my palm. "I'm impressed with every-thing you've accomplished, Maguire. Including the sneaky way you even get me to talk about myself sometimes. Your mom added on a couple of sessions, so maybe we can do every other week in January and then re-evaluate how things are going."

"Sounds good." I've come a long way in the past few months, but that doesn't mean I'm all better. I know there will be good times and bad times, but I'm ready to face them.

Jordy hops up from his seat and pulls me into a kiss the sec-ond I leave the office. "Hi," he says, after we finally break apart.

"Hi." I reach out and steady myself against the back of the nearest chair. His kisses have a way of making the whole world wobbly.

"Are you headed home?"

"I was. Why?"

"You should hang out and wait for me. I could use your help later with another homework challenge."

"What is it?" I ask.

"It's a secret."

I give him a sideways glance. "Does it involve dolphins?"

He scoffs. "Something way better."

"What's better than dolphins?" I ask incredulously. "They've got those big brains and they're always saving drowning fishermen." I run my fingertip across his lower lip. "They've got those perfect smiles."

We kiss again, and then Jordy says, "Whales, of course."

"Do you have a secret whale island too?"

"Nope, but it's peak season. Have you ever seen whales in the wild?"

I shake my head. "I haven't been to the beach in years."

"I think we need to fix that. Do you have a book to read or something?"

"I didn't bring one, but I can just mess around on my phone."

"I have something you can read." Jordy pulls out a small, flat package. It's not nearly big enough to be a book.

"Jordy. You already gave me a present." I hold up my wrist to show him that I'm wearing the charm bracelet he gave me for Christmas. So far it has exactly seven charms on it: a tiny likeness of Ireland, a tennis ball, a heart, a book, a rock-climbing shoe, a four-leaf clover, and a dolphin.

"I know. But this is more something I *made* you. Girls like that, right?" He presses the wrapped square into my hands and then heads for Daniel's office. He turns back at the last second. "If you don't like it, I might actually go for option A this time and pretend I didn't give it to you."

"Whatever." I smile. I sit down in a chair and turn the package over in my hand. Using one finger, I break the tape. It's just a folded piece of notebook paper. When I unfold it, I realize it's Jordy's challenge list.

Jordy Wheeler's super-awesome shrink homework

GOALS:
Make Real Jordy and Tennis Jordy into one person.
Stand up to my parents; decide my future and do it on my own terms.

CHALLENGES:
1. ~~Make a list of how Real Jordy and Tennis Jordy are different.~~
2. ~~Hang out with someone who doesn't know Tennis Jordy: girl from Daniel's office~~
3. ~~Do something both Real Jordy and Tennis Jordy want to do: work with the girls' team~~
4. ~~Do something just for Real Jordy: help Maguire with her serve~~
5. ~~Do something parents wouldn't approve of: sneak out to help Maguire~~
6. ~~Pick Real Jordy over Tennis Jordy: forfeited match when Penn got hurt~~
7. ~~Hang out with someone who prefers Real~~

~~Jordy: Kimber, Penn, Maguire~~

~~8. Do something for Real Jordy and not lie about it: Climbing with Maguire~~

~~9. Stand up to parents: That one night with Mom, and every day since then~~

~~10. Acquire all the info I need to make future decisions: coach, agent, etc.~~

~~11. Make a list of pros and cons for going pro vs. playing in college.~~

~~12. Make a decision based on what's best for Real Jordy, not Tennis Jordy.~~

Bonus lucky 13: Tell Maguire that I love her.

The paper trembles in my fingertips. I read his list again, blinking back tears.

"I love you too," I say quietly, but the words feel awkward. Foreign. I try it again. And again. I want to be ready when he is.

Then I decide to try something different. Jordy has always been ahead of me, in therapy, on the tennis court, in admitting his feelings. I tilt my head upward. "I love you," I whisper into the face of an imaginary Jordy. I giggle slightly. My heart starts racing in my chest, but it's a good kind of fear. I practice once more. "I love you, Jordy Wheeler."

Maybe this time I'll take the lead.

AUTHOR'S NOTE

Like most people with mental illness, Maguire is afflicted by multiple disorders, the severity of which can change from day to day based on internal and external factors. A lot of people think that therapy is only for those who are unstable, suicidal, or impaired to the point of being unable to function at school or work. This is simply not true. If you are experiencing emotions that are affecting your quality of life, please consider seeking help. If you are uninsured or think you cannot afford therapy, speak to a teacher, counselor, school nurse, clergyman, social worker, or general medical doctor about your concerns. Schools and colleges often provide free services, and community leaders can frequently help people find online or local low-cost support groups.

The National Alliance on Mental Illness (NAMI) estimates that in the United States, one in four adults and one in five teens experiences mental illness in any given year. Fifty percent of chronic mental conditions begin by age fourteen, yet despite the effective treatments available, it is often decades before people seek help. Failure to seek help can be devastating not just to the afflicted, but also to family and friends. For more info, or to find support, please visit NAMI at www.nami.org.

I have taken some minor liberties with the portrayal of the cognitive behavioral therapy (CBT) that Maguire undergoes during her sessions with Dr. Leed. Parts of her initial assessment and self-monitoring have been omitted for the sake of length. CBT is actually an umbrella term for styles of therapy that combine strategies from Beck's school of cognitive therapy with the behaviorist principles made famous by Watson and Skinner.

What is important to know is that there are many different types of CBT, as well as other types of therapy like psychoanalysis. If you try one and find it unhelpful, please don't give up on your treatment. Just like with medication regimens (of which there are also many options), it often takes a few tries for a healthcare provider to figure out what works best for an individual client. Communication is key. If your treatment isn't working, please let your doctor or therapist know so they can help you.

If you're currently struggling, please remember there

are a lot of people in the Universe who understand what you're going through. And there are people in your own Universe who want to help you—who will help you—if you just reach out.

ACKNOWLEDGMENTS

As always, I am extremely grateful to my family and friends, and to my agent Jennifer Laughran, aka my publishing good luck charm. Thanks, all of you, for continuing to make everything seem possible.

Extra-special thanks to my editor, Karen Chaplin, whose feedback guided this book into an entirely new realm. I've never revised as deeply as I did with this novel—and the process was brutal!—but the end result was so worth it. Thank you for helping me find the true meaning of Maguire's story.

More thank yous:

To Rosemary Brosnan and everyone else at HarperTeen who had a part in turning Maguire's story into this gorgeous book that I love from cover to cover. Also to the people who work hard to promote and sell the books. You guys are all geniuses!

To booksellers, librarians, and teachers everywhere, aka my superheroes. Thank you for being tireless advocates for books and authors.

To my beta readers and publishing forever-friends, including the YA Valentines; the Apocalypsies; Marcy Beller Paul; Jessica Fonseca; Cathy Castelli; Heather Anastasiu; Elizabeth Richards; Jessica Spotswood; Christina Ahn Hickey, MD; Crystal Leach; Jennifer Gaska; Stacee Evans; Sara Slattery; and María Pilar Albarrán Ruiz. Sara won a contest where she got to name a character (or two or three) and Pili found her way into these pages by being so kind and enthusiastic that when I needed a nurse character I could think of no one but her. Additional thanks to those people who candidly shared their own experiences with therapy in general and CBT in specific.

To several of my street teamers and Twitter friends who were incredibly supportive while I attempted to rewrite this book and revise another book for deadline at the same time: I really want to name all of you here, but this is where I fear I would forget someone. Just know that if you sent me tweets, emails, cards, stroopwafels (okay, Debby Kasbergen totally deserves mention for sending the most amazing treats—internationally. Love you, Debby!), etc., telling me you believed in me and my work, that those words made all the difference.

And last, but never least, to you, just for being a reader, and also for giving my book a chance when there are so many others to choose from. I struggled trying to decide who I should dedicate this story to, but the answer turned out to be obvious. All the hearts for you.